My Life

Giuseppe Garibaldi

Translated by Stephen Parkin

ET REMOTISSIMA PROPE

Hesperus Classics

Hesperus Classics
Published by Hesperus Press Limited
4 Rickett Street, London sw6 1ru
www.hesperuspress.com

Garibaldi's complete memoirs first published in Italian as part of the *Edizione nazionale degli scritti di Giuseppe Garibaldi* in 1932
This translation first published by Hesperus Press Limited, 2004
Introduction and English language translation © Stephen Parkin, 2004
Foreword © Tim Parks, 2004
Maps by Sir Emery Walker

Designed and typeset by Fraser Muggeridge
Printed in Italy by Graphic Studio Srl

ISBN: 1-84391-093-4

CONTENTS

Giuseppe Garibaldi is the most colourful and immediately attractive figure of the Italian Risorgimento, and indeed of modern Italian history in general. Yet his memoirs are rarely read in Italy and certainly never recommended to the schoolchildren who are taught to revere his patriotism. So I had long assumed they must be dull. Nothing could be further from the truth. About halfway through this book you realise that Garibaldi is not read in the country whose cause he served because so much of what he says would make unwelcome reading to many sections of contemporary society. Italy has an uneasy relationship with its recent past.

One need only reflect on the four major players of the last phase of Italian unification – Mazzini, Cavour, Victor Emmanuel II, Garibaldi – and the idea of national stereotype has to be dropped at once. The revolutionary ideologue, the cautious parliamentarian, the capricious monarch and the fearless soldier are as different as men can be. Yet looking at the whole process of Italian unification, from the end of the Napoleonic wars in 1815 to the annexation of Rome in 1870, it is equally clear that certain patterns of behaviour and interaction do repeat themselves: if there is no one national type, there is nevertheless a recognisable constellation of Italian figures who become themselves in relation and opposition to each other, in the creation of an Italian dynamic. So, in a sense, Mazzini can only play the revolutionary in so far as Victor Emmanuel resists him. Caught between the two, Cavour is obliged to outwit both. In particular, there is a tendency for everybody to imagine they can exploit the energies of the others while in fact promoting a secret agenda. Everybody except Garibaldi, that is. For of all these figures, it is he, with his extraordinary determination to push things to the limit, to risk the impossible, who forces the other players to come out into the open and declare themselves.

This abridged edition of his memoirs picks up Garibaldi's story shortly after his fortieth birthday. Born to a family of fishermen in Nice in 1807, he had become a ship's captain in his mid-twenties, been sentenced to death *in absentia* for his part in a failed revolution in Genoa in 1834 and, as a consequence, escaped to South America where for twelve years he had mixed seafaring with guerrilla warfare, discovering in the process an extraordinary vocation for military leadership. His great frustration, however, as the years passed, was the growing awareness that the supposedly revolutionary causes he was fighting for were less noble than he would have liked. For if the first major surprise of Garibaldi's life was that men would willingly follow him to their deaths, the second was the discovery that his talents were the object of much manipulation by the politicians he was involved with. It was the determination to fight exclusively for a cause he knew was right – Italian unification – that eventually prompted Garibaldi to return to Italy in 1848, just as a series of liberal revolutions were breaking out in Milan, Venice, Rome and elsewhere.

Recent histories of the Risorgimento find it difficult to present Garibaldi without a patina of irony and condescension. The modern intellectual's suspicion of the folk hero – pursued by drooling ladies of the British aristocracy, believed by Sicilian peasants to have been sent by God – is everywhere evident. In an otherwise excellent biography, the English historian, Denis Mack Smith, frequently refers to Garibaldi as 'simplistic' and 'ingenuous', makes fun of his habit of wearing a South American poncho, and sees his decision to set up home on the barren island of Caprera (between Sardinia and Corsica) as merely idiosyncratic. To Mack Smith, the learned statesman Cavour, consummate practitioner of realpolitik, is clearly the more appropriate object of study. Yet to read these memoirs is to understand how absolutely necessary, how *intelligent* those idiosyncrasies were. Without Garibaldi's poncho, we might say, northern and southern Italy would not have been united, or not in 1860.

This book does not substitute for a biography, if only because Garibaldi is not interested in telling us about his private life. There is very little about his marriages and love affairs. Even the dramatic death of his pregnant wife, Anita, as the couple escaped from Austrian troops, is passed over fairly rapidly. Nor does Garibaldi go into detail on his dealings with politicians. What comes across instead is the immensity of the obstacles that lay in the way of Italian unification and the astonishing energy and confidence with which these were faced. In two years alone, for example, between 1848 and 1850, in a series of hopeless battles, always ill-supplied, and half-heartedly supported, Garibaldi moved from Nice to Genoa, to revolutionary Milan, to Como, escaped the Austrians to retreat into Switzerland, went home to Nice, returned to Genoa, formed an army of volunteers in Florence, marched back and forth three times (mainly at night, often pursued) across the freezing Apennines, advanced into the Papal States, joined in the defence of revolutionary Rome, won various battles against a huge French army, escaped capture in a grim retreat to San Marino, again evaded the Austrians in a bid to sail up the Adriatic to Venice, was almost captured on the coast near Ravenna, walked across the Apennines (again!) to Genoa where he was (again!) obliged to go into exile, this time for four years.

Obviously, this kind of hectic life, shared with a riff-raff of adolescent idealists, hardened adventurers and criminal ne'er-do-wells, did not give him time to develop the cultivated tastes of a Cavour, but it did alter the reality the politicians were obliged to deal with. Someone was ready to fight and die for Italy.

The characteristic condition of Italian political life is the complex stalemate. *Veti incrociati* is the expression the newspapers like to use, 'cross-vetoes': i.e. this party rejects that proposition, that party rejects the other and yet another party rejects the only thing the previous two have agreed on. The situation in the early 1850s was no exception. Mazzini and his followers wanted Italian unity, but favoured a republican government. Victor Emmanuel, King of Piedmont, would support the nationalist cause, but only in so far as it meant an expansion of his territories and excluded a republican government; his Prime Minister Cavour persuaded the French to help Piedmont attack the Austrians in north-eastern Italy, but only on the understanding that there would be no attempt to take over the papal territories around Rome. Having no ambition to add the South to his worries, Cavour didn't mind. The Austrians, meanwhile, were determined to resist the principle of national determination, since once accepted it could only lead to the collapse of their empire. Central Italy was split into various duchies. The Pope, whose backward and ill-governed state divided north from south, was reactionary and anti-nationalist to a degree and exploited Catholicism's grip on minds throughout the country to prevent any progress from being made. Naples, at the time the third largest city in Europe, was run by a Bourbon dynasty that very much agreed with the Pope over these and other matters. How could such divisions, such opposition be overcome?

More than anyone else, Garibaldi appreciated that only complete singleness of mind could make anything happen. Unlike Mazzini, Cavour or Victor Emmanuel, he sacrificed every other consideration for Italian unity. He was willing to forgo his republicanism, he was willing to be exploited and then disowned, to conquer and then forgo the conquest, in short, to give everything for nothing, so long as the cause was Italian unity. In this sense his wild dress habits were essential. They declared that he stood outside all other schemes and conventions. At a minor but very visible level, they demonstrated the possibility of difference and change. Likewise, his repeatedly expressed contempt for the Mazzinians, for the Piedmontese parliamentarians, and above all, most repeatedly and violently (and this perhaps is the most important reason why the book is not widely read in Italy today), for the church and its clerics, were an absolutely necessary instrument for communicating this singleness of purpose. He who must steel himself for action will not gratify us with his intellectual subtlety. But this doesn't mean he is unintelligent.

Time and again, from the utter isolation of Caprera, where he could live uncontaminated by other agendas, Garibaldi plunged into the paralysis of Italian politics. His integrity, his determination and his astonishing military charisma, all of which grew with age, immediately focused everyone's attention. The peninsula was galvanised by a feeling of danger and possibility. More often than not, after a series of minor victories, the visionary warrior would be obliged to retreat wounded and overwhelmed to Caprera. He was crippled by arthritis, exhausted with malaria, but never dismayed. And then, in 1860, to everyone's surprise, something gave. With just a thousand volunteers Garibaldi sailed to Sicily and in a series of battles that must count among the most extraordinary of the nineteenth century, captured half of Italy.

The memoirs tell the tale with a mix of propagandist rhetoric and unambitious chronicle. What counts is the accumulation of remarkable detail: the number of times the politicians try to thwart him; their interminable ambiguity and guile; the implacable resistance of the

Church; the number of battles won by men with no military training and hardly any equipment; the endless forced marches through mountainous territory; the rain, the sun, the privations. Extraordinary images are conjured up with almost no comment: the women of Palermo tossing mattresses out of their windows to be piled up against the enemy; a sinking ship caulked with animal dung; a girl rushing out of a village to warn of an ambush. One of the words Mack Smith most frequently uses in relation to Garibaldi is 'absurd': his absurd belief in himself; his absurd confidence that Austria was about to collapse. But while many would have found it absurd to fight and die for a self-regarding Victor Emmanuel II, Garibaldi's absurdity (and it is the absurdity of all religious belief) was able to give his volunteers a sense that their struggle had meaning. Reading the memoirs you are struck by the idea that, despite all our contemporary scepticism, there is indeed such a thing as a glorious death.

On the second of July 1881, about a year before his death, Garibaldi wrote out an appendix to his will. He wanted his body to be cremated in a red shirt. 'Plenty of wood for the pyre', is his last exhortation. The remark is emblematic of his personality. He consumed his whole life and the lives of thousands upon thousands of others in a conflagration that is still the most illuminating moment in modern Italian history. Very few of those warming their hands at the bonfire look well in the weird light it casts. This is incendiary material.

– *Tim Parks, 2004*

INTRODUCTION

The history of the composition and publication of Giuseppe
Garibaldi's memoirs mirrors their author's complex and peripatetic
life. Garibaldi wrote, rewrote, supplemented, updated and revised his
text over a period of twenty-three years, from 1849 to 1872, a period
which saw his most important engagements and his greatest
achievements in the Risorgimento struggle for the unification of Italy.
When he completed the first version of the work he entrusted the
manuscript, now lost, to foreign friends and supporters to edit and
prepare for publication, either because, as Giuseppe Armani suggests,
he thought his work needed revision, or because he was reluctant to
publish under his own name. This original text was first published not
in Italian but in English translation in New York in 1860, followed by
a London edition in the same year: *The Life of General Garibaldi*; the
American editor added an account of the siege of Rome and the fall of
the Roman Republic in 1849. As the course of events developed over
the next twenty years and as Garibaldi added to his account of them,
new versions, translations and abridgements followed all over Europe, a
testimony to the European and international reputation Garibaldi
quickly acquired after 1859. The first part of the text to appear in Italian
was Garibaldi's account of his South American years which appeared
in Francesco Carrano's book on the 1859 campaign, published in Turin
in 1860. Following his final military campaign on the side of the French
Republican Government in the continuation of the Franco-Prussian
War of 1870–1, Garibaldi returned to his home on the island of Caprera
and began a revision of the whole text; although one of his stated
reasons for undertaking the revision was to prepare the text for
publication and earn money, he in fact never sent the manuscript to a
publisher and this final version only appeared after his death in 1882.
An edition based on the two surviving autograph manuscripts of
Garibaldi's text – an earlier version dating from 1859 and the final
revision from 1871–2 – was published under the auspices of the Italian
state in 1932, to mark the fiftieth anniversary of his death. The present
translation uses Giuseppe Armani's 1982 edition of the 1872 version
which is itself based on the text as found in the so-called *Edizione*

nazionale. It is an abridgement of the original work, concentrating on Garibaldi in Italy from the date of his return from South America in 1848 to his final campaign on the Italian mainland in 1867. These were the years in which Italy was made – as described by the English historian G.M. Trevelyan, who wrote what is still after nearly a century one of the best and most readable accounts of Garibaldi's campaigns – principally by Garibaldi and his volunteer forces.

The circumstances of its composition help to explain some of the idiosyncrasies of the text. Written and revised so extensively over so long a period, with lengthy intervals when Garibaldi was campaigning and the work was left untouched, repetitions, sudden abbreviations in narrative and inconsistencies of detail are inevitable. Moreover, whenever he took up his memoirs again at each voluntary or enforced interval of leisure, he often interpolated comments on the current state of the country, which were, presumably during the final revision and for purposes of clarity, occasionally but not consistently dated in parenthesis.

More generally, it is a useful and instructive exercise to read his memoirs in parallel with a standard modern biography of the man or a standard historical account of the events he relates, for such a comparison reveals the striking extent and nature of what Garibaldi omits or chooses to emphasise. All memoirs by their nature are partial accounts of experience, and some of these omissions and emphases can be explained by the fact that Garibaldi was describing events from his own perspective. It is also the case that some of what he left out he must have assumed his intended readers would already have known: the succinctness of his narrative account, which forms such a striking contrast with the often passionate and rhetorically high-flown denunciations and encomiums with which he intersperses it, depends partly on the fact that he was writing about comparatively recent events which would have been familiar to all Italians as well as many people around the world, which were indeed already entering the realm of legend. But it is also true that other omissions and emphases, seen cumulatively, testify to a controlling design which guided his work and reveal the didactic purpose behind it. Garibaldi's memoirs are not only – or even primarily – a record, drawn up with the benefit and calm of hindsight, of his life and experiences, but work in progress, a further action undertaken by this supreme man of action, an account of what he sees as the unfinished project of the Risorgimento and of the lessons which can be learnt from its better aspects if the ultimate goals it set itself are to be achieved. His passionate anti-clericalism is one indication of this continuing political commitment (and it is in fact the case that relations between the new Italian state and the Catholic Church were to remain strained and unsettled for many decades). But we see Garibaldi's intention most clearly in the space he devotes to the political and military aspects of the Risorgimento, in both of which he was deeply involved, and where there is an evident wish to exalt the importance of the latter over the former. The enthusiasm for military action shown by the volunteers who flocked to join him and their extraordinary achievements in the field, often against all odds (many other contemporary accounts attribute these successes to Garibaldi's intense charisma and unusual ability to inspire, almost bewitch, his men, a fact to which, with characteristic modesty, he makes no reference), he saw as the Risorgimento's greatest asset and its enduring legacy for the future life of the unified nation. This heroic commitment is contrasted to the world of calculation, negotiation and compromise (all negative words in Garibaldi's lexicon) which are typical of the political process: a world which in his view only served to thwart his campaigns up to 1867 and which continued to characterise democratic parliamentary life in the new state after unification, much to his disgust. Such patriotic heroism for Garibaldi is an eternal value and cancels out the compromises he himself had to make to achieve his goals, most notably his acceptance of serving under the Savoy monarchy, despite his profound republican beliefs.

Even an element which at first sight appears to be purely retrospective and memorial – the roll-call of names of the valiant men who fought and often fell alongside him, as well as of the Italians (they are first and foremost Italians, whatever their regional origin) who welcome him into their homes, help him escape when in trouble, give him food and money (when he cannot remember their names he always mentions the omission with regret) – even those memorialised and thanked in this way also serve as examples which coming generations should remember and imitate.

Other aspects of the memoirs, which do not conform to some of our stereotypes of the genre, follow from their didactic and committed purpose. There is no tone of mellow reflection: Garibaldi makes no attempt to step back from the events he recounts in order to try and see the full context which was not apparent at the time: he remains, for example, embittered and antagonistic towards the other two leading architects of Italian unification, Cavour and Mazzini, both of whom were dead by the time he was working on his final revision. These were highly complex men whose attitudes towards Garibaldi and relations with him were correspondingly complicated, but his portraits of them remain polemically one-dimensional, unmodified by the passage of time. His memoirs are not about the private man: there is almost nothing about the events in Garibaldi's personal life, his home on Caprera, his relationships with women, or with his children (his son Menotti is mentioned only when he participates in the 1867 campaign to seize Rome, and only as a soldier), or the extraordinary international cult which grew up around him in the 1860s, most notably in England, and the array of social and political contacts it brought him. Thus the work is in no sense a self-portrait, although it still evokes a vivid impression of what Garibaldi was like: his bravery, his military and seafaring skills, his stamina and power of physical endurance, his self-belief, his concern for his fellow-men, his passionate hatreds, his generosity of spirit, his natural simplicity, his ingenuousness and his canniness, his desire for independence and intolerance of authority, his love of country life (though not of Italian peasants, who for the most part did not support his campaigns). Finally, in later life Garibaldi was both a novelist and a poet, but it is clear that he had no literary ambitions in writing his memoirs; there is no desire to embellish the events which he relates with such dry concision and matter-of-factness or to create any stylistic effect in telling them. Nevertheless, in their narrative impetus – at times they read like an adventure story – and the clarity and spareness of the accounts of the repeated battles and trials in which the destiny of the Risorgimento hangs in the balance, they accumulate a kind of epic grandeur, in which, like Ulysses or Aeneas, Garibaldi's wanderings over twenty years through almost every part of the peninsula painfully piece together and pre-enact the unity which was their goal – with Rome as the final elusive fragment.

As the bicentenary of his birth in 1807 approaches, Garibaldi remains an iconic but also a controversial figure, just as many of the most important issues of the Risorgimento which lie behind his concerns in this work – republicanism and constitutional monarchy, centralism and regionalism, the relations of Church and State – have continued to dominate the history of post-Unification Italy until the present day. Yet Garibaldi wrote his memoirs to be read in the present rather than the past tense; and this is still perhaps, 120 years after their first complete publication, the best way to read them.

– Stephen Parkin, 2004

My Life

Sixty-three of us left the River Plate[1] to sail to Italy, there to wage the war for its redemption. We had heard news of uprisings all over the country, but even if this turned out not to be true we had decided to trust to fortune and attempt to instigate them ourselves, after we had landed in the woods along the coast of Tuscany or wherever we would be welcomed and could be of use.

We embarked on the brigantine *Speranza*, which we had been able to hire thanks to our own savings and the patriotic generosity of some of our fellow-countrymen.

We set off to fulfil the desire which had dominated our lives. We had fought gloriously to defend the oppressed in other countries; now we were hastening to take up arms for our own beloved motherland. The very thought of it made up – more than enough – for all the dangers, discomforts and sufferings encountered over the course of lives which had known only tribulation. The fifteenth of April 1848 was the day of departure. We left the port of Montevideo with a favourable wind and by evening, although the weather turned threatening, we found ourselves between the coast of Maldonado and the Lobos Island. On the following morning we could just make out the summits of the *Sierra de las animas*; then they sank below the horizon. Only the empty spaces of the Atlantic lay before us – and the most beautiful and sublime of aspirations, the liberation of our homeland.

Sixty-three men, all young and all formed on the battlefield, except for two who were ill: Anzani was weak with consumption, having overtaxed his health in fighting holy crusades on behalf of oppressed peoples, while Sacchi had received a bad wound in the knee which had left his leg in a terrible condition. His own faith and the attentions of his fellow-crew members succeeded in returning him safe if not sound to Italian shores. As for Anzani, only a grave awaited him in Italy, next to his parents' tomb.

Our progress was rapid and joyful. Empty periods on board were filled for the most part with edifying pastimes. Those who could read and write instructed the illiterate and there were frequent gymnastic exercises. A patriotic anthem was written and set to music by Luigi

Coccelli, one of our number, and it became our evening prayer. We would sing it gathered together on the deck; Coccelli gave the lead, with a repeat of the chorus, enthusiastically accompanied by sixty voices.

In this manner we crossed the Atlantic, all the while uncertain of Italy's fate, although we knew of the reforms which Pius IX had promised to introduce. We had chosen the Tuscan coast as our destination; we planned to land there whatever the political situation and whether we found ourselves among friends or forced to fight with foes. But when we arrived in Santa Pola on the Spanish coast, we changed our plans and directed the ship towards Nice. Anzani was getting worse. Our limited supplies, enough for the voyage across, had almost run out: we needed to land in order to reprovision. So we arrived in Santa Pola: the captain, Gazzolo, went on shore and swiftly returned with news which would have driven men less exalted than we already were crazy with joy. Palermo, Milan, Venice and a hundred other cities had revolted; the Piedmontese army was in pursuit of the routed Austrian troops; the whole of Italy had responded to the call to take up arms and sent its noble fighters off to wage the holy war.

The reader can imagine the effect this news had on us. We ran about the deck of the *Speranza* in wild excitement, embracing each other and weeping for joy. Anzani forgot how weak he was and leapt to his feet. Sacchi demanded to be lifted from his sickbed and taken up on deck.

'Hoist the sails!' all cried – and if we hadn't set off that very instant a riot would have broken out. We raised the anchor and set sail. The wind seemed to second our desire, our impatience. We sailed up the coasts of Spain and France in a few days and arrived within sight of the promised land, Italy – no longer as outlaws, no longer forced to fight to enter our own country. And so, after we had changed our plans to land on the Tuscan coast, we chose Nice as our destination, the first port of Italy; we arrived there around the twenty-third of June 1848.

Throughout all the misfortunes which had beset me in the turbulent life I had led, my hope that better days were to come had never wavered. Now, in Nice, more happiness than any man could ever want or be allowed to want was mine. Too much happiness indeed – I felt a kind of presentiment of disasters soon to come.

My wife Anita and our children had left South America some

months earlier and were already in Nice, together with my adored and now elderly mother whom I had not seen for fourteen years. Once again I embraced beloved relatives and childhood friends dear to me, all joyful to see me and at such an auspicious time! The brigantine was anchored; Anzani and Sacchi were safely disembarked, followed by the rest of the men eager to walk on Italian soil. I ran to embrace my children and my mother, whom I had caused so much anxiety with my wanderings. My poor mother! how fervently I longed to brighten and console your remaining days just as you desired to see me settled and at peace at home beside you. But how could I offer you such reassurance and consolation in your declining and grief-stricken years when our country was overrun by priests and thieves?

The few days we spent in Nice were passed in continuous celebration, but our brothers were fighting the foreigners along the Mincio and our idleness felt like a crime. We left for Genoa, where the inhabitants were no less welcoming: a steamer had been sent out to meet us and bring us to the city more quickly, but we had already left Nice and the boat searched for us in vain along the coast. The winds and currents had pushed us in the direction of Corsica, but we finally reached Genoa, where its people gave us a joyful and warm-hearted welcome while the city authorities greeted us with a cold reserve which betrayed their uneasy consciences. Here was our first experience of the tight-lipped smiles and the delaying tactics we were to meet again and again, wherever we encountered men who were accustomed to compromise and who felt constrained to establish free government not out of any faith or enthusiasm for human progress, but because they feared the people they ruled.

I had left Anzani with my mother in Nice, but his impatience and his fervour had led him to take the steamer to Genoa, despite his fatigue and weakness, and he was already in the city when we arrived. Anzani's arrival in Genoa (in 1848) marks the beginning of the opposition shown by Mazzini[2] and his followers towards me which continues to this day (1872). Their reason or pretext for such an attitude was my desire to march on to the battlefield on the Mincio and in the Tyrol with my comrades, for this meant joining forces with the King's troops who were fighting the Austrians. Yet the leading Mazzinians who tormented

5

poor Anzani when he was mortally ill by demanding that he should warn me of the consequences of my decision are the very same who are now to be found among the most loyal servants of the monarchy! I have to confess that when I heard Anzani, my beloved brother-in-arms, who had fought alongside me in so many battles, telling me 'not to abandon the people's cause' I was deeply aggrieved, even more than I was to be asked to 'make an open declaration of my republican beliefs'.

A few days later Anzani died in the house of Gaetano Gallino. All Italy should have mourned the passing of such a great patriot; if he had survived to lead our armies it is certain that Italy would now be free of all foreign domination. I have never known a more accomplished and honest man and nobler soldier than Anzani. No pomp accompanied his body as it travelled through Liguria and Lombardy to his final resting place in the family tomb in Alzate, where he had been born.

Milan

Our purpose in leaving South America was to serve the cause of Italy and to fight her enemies, whatever the political affiliations and beliefs were of those who were leading the people in the war for freedom. Most of our fellow-citizens thought the same and I was determined to unite our small band to those who were fighting in such a holy cause. Carlo Alberto[3] was the warrior who led the battle, the same man who had condemned me to death in 1834 – but I bore him no resentment: I made my way to Roverbella, which was then his headquarters, to offer him my services and those of my comrades. I met him and saw the distrust with which he received me; the hesitancy and indecision of the man to whom Italy's destiny had been entrusted made me grieve. I would have obeyed the King's orders as readily as I would have done in a republic, and I would have led the young comrades who put their trust in me along the same path of self-denial. My goal, which was, I believe, shared by most Italians at that time, was to unite the country and rid it of foreign powers. Those who gave Italy her freedom would earn her people's gratitude. I prefer not to disturb the dead in order to pass judgement on their behaviour: let posterity undertake this task. I will say only this: Carlo Alberto's position as King, the circumstances of the time, and the wish of the majority of Italians – all called on him to lead the war of redemption, a role for which he was found wanting. He did not know how to use the immense forces under his command; he was indeed the principal cause of their destruction.

My comrades were marching from Genoa to Milan, demoralised by the unfortunate and commonly held view at the time, doubtless encouraged by the enemy, that the presence of volunteer troops was redundant if not actually harmful; meanwhile I was racing from Genoa to Roverbella, from Roverbella to Turin and then on to Milan, in the vain hope of finding some way in which I could help my country. Only Casati, the leader of the provisional government in Milan, thought that he could use our help by putting us alongside the Lombard troops. I was entrusted with the task of organising the separate bands of volunteers, including my own small group of companions; this would have turned out well had it not been for Sobrero, the Minister for War in the King's government, and his malevolent interference – even now the memory of his equivocal manoeuvres and intrigues chills me.

I had caught a fever in Roverbella: this, together with my discussions with Sobrero (among other matters we disagreed on, he disliked our red shirts which in his opinion made us easy targets for the enemy), made Milan – the beautiful, patriotic city of the 'Cinque Giornate'[4] – intolerable to me. I breathed freely again when I left the city for Bergamo together with a band of badly clothed and inadequately armed companions, once more to try to organise the volunteers, a task for which I have neither the personal inclination nor the theoretical training. The men with me had been for the most part left behind or discarded by the volunteer troops fighting in the Tyrol and the long stay in Milan had sapped their strength and resolve.

Our stay in Bergamo was extremely brief. Measures had already been taken to defend the city and intense efforts were being made to enlist the support of the hardy local inhabitants from the surrounding valleys and mountains by sending out agents to recruit them; among the men in my band, Davide and Camuzzi were extremely effective in this, but their strenuous efforts came to nothing because of our hurried departure – a peremptory order arrived from Milan calling us back to join forces with the royal army in retreat from the Austrians and to take part in the battle which it seemed would, for good or ill, have to be fought in the city. At last we were to fight – we lost not a moment in setting out for Milan.

We left our baggage in Trecate in order to march more quickly. When we were approaching Monza, we received an order to deploy on the enemy's right wing, and immediately sent out mounted scouts to discover their movements and positions; once in Monza, however, the news both of the surrender of our forces and of the armistice broke.[5] Floods of fugitives soon filled the streets.

Armistice, surrender, flight – the news struck us down like successive bolts of lightning, spreading, in its wake, fear and demoralisation among the people and among the troops. Some of my men showed themselves to be shameful cowards and, abandoning their rifles in the town square, took to their heels in every direction; the others were angered and scandalised by such behaviour and were about to fire on them, but fortunately I and some of my officers managed to stop them and prevent complete confusion breaking out. Some of those who tried to escape were punished; others were degraded and expelled.

Faced with such a disastrous situation, I decided to go off and spend some time in Como, there to wait and see how things turned out; if nothing else could be done, then I would fight a guerrilla war. On the way from Monza to Como, Mazzini appeared under his flag 'For God and the People'. He joined us on our march to the town; when we arrived he crossed over into Switzerland while I planned my military campaigns in the mountains around Como. Many of his followers – or those who made out they were his followers – left Italy with him. This of course encouraged others to follow suit and reduced our numbers even further.

While in Milan I had made the mistake, for which Mazzini never forgave me, of suggesting to him that it was wrong to win and keep the support of young men by holding out the prospect of a republic to them, at a time when the army and the volunteers were engaged in fighting the Austrians.

The situation was quieter in Como, but the dismay caused by the disasters which had befallen Milan and the army was no less intense.

The good people of Como welcomed us as did the town authorities who provided us with as much as they could, especially clothing which my men badly needed. They were not in favour of trying to defend the town against the Austrians; it is true that it is situated on the shores of the lake surrounded by mountains, and would need many fortifications and men to defend itself against a stronger enemy. The day after our arrival in the town General Zucchi arrived, travelling in a carriage on his way to Switzerland. When the people of Como learnt of his arrival and of his intention to leave the country, they ran in indignation to the inn where he was staying, wanting to drag him out and beat him. I was told what was happening and managed to reach the inn, where I calmed down the crowd by asking them to remember the General's advanced age and his earlier illustrious deeds.

Return to Lombardy

A proclamation was immediately issued condemning the infamous treaty; our only thought was to return to Lombardy and fight its oppressors, whatever the situation there. When news of the armistice broke, Mazzini sent Daverio to us from Lugano promising men and arms so that we could continue to fight on – exactly what was needed.

Two steamers operated on Lake Maggiore, carrying passengers and goods between Italy and Switzerland; our first thought was to take possession of the two vessels and use them to get back into Italy. They made regular stops in Arona, which was near to us: a night's march brought us to the town where we seized one of the boats; the other vessel arrived during the day and we captured that as well. There were enough smaller boats for the transport of horses and other equipment; we took two small cannon with us on the steamers. The municipality of Arona provided us with the money and food we needed, and so we set out in the direction of Luino, towing the loaded boats behind us.

A stirring spectacle accompanied us on the journey along the western shore of the magnificent lake. Many Lombard families had left their homes to take up residence in this picturesque spot, one of the loveliest places in the world, and, knowing what we planned to do, they came out to greet us, cheering and waving flags and handkerchiefs and cloths. Their womenfolk – the beautiful women of Italy – leant from their balconies; their faces seemed ablaze with the desire to fly to the side of the noble warriors who still hoped to win back from the foreign oppressors the homes they had had to abandon. We responded to their cheers; their applause and our own sense of determination filled us with pride.

We crossed the lake and reached Luino: eight hundred of us disembarked, with a few horses. We left the cannon on board the steamers under the command of Tommaso Risso. The following day, we were getting ready to set out for the Varesotto region[6] from the Beccaccia, the inn where we had lodged in Luino, when I learnt that an Austrian detachment was advancing towards us along the main road from the south. Our troops had already set out on a road which provided a short cut to Varese: I immediately ordered the rear of the column to turn back, and sent a company to reoccupy the Beccaccia and the surrounding area to prevent it falling into the hands of the enemy. It was too late: the Austrians had already reached it and their large numbers easily drove back the few men I had dispatched. Our column had been divided into three corps; in the narrow road closed in between high escarpments there was no possibility of taking up a wider formation; if we returned towards the Beccaccia, however, there would be more room for manoeuvre and the second and third corps could form columns by sections.

I regarded the inn as the key position and therefore the objective of the battle, control of which we had to win or, failing that, abandon the field as if defeated. The inn consisted of a fortified house and various outhouses; it was also surrounded by hedges and stacks of timber. All this was held by the enemy and we had to win it back from them. Determined attack was our only option: the third corps started repeated waves of assaults, but, despite all the efforts of their commander Major Marrocchetti and his officers, they were repulsed. The second corps of bersaglieri[7] from Pavia, under the command of Captain Coccelli, was ordered to charge; while this was under way Coccelli and his company climbed over a wall which lay to our left and appeared on the enemies' right flank. These lads from Pavia fought with all the determination of experienced soldiers, even though it was their first battle; several of them fell in the attempt but they nonetheless came within bayonet range of the Austrians, who were astonished by their bravery and by Coccelli's sudden appearance on their right and took to their heels.

This victory left us in control of the Varesotto region; the country was ours to move around without hindrance. The good people of that region were roused from their sense of defeat and gave us an enthusiastic welcome when we entered the town of Varese. The hope I had cherished for so many years revived: the hope of involving my fellow-countrymen in a guerrilla war which, in the absence of an organised army, by itself would lead on to the liberation of Italy: the nation as a whole would take up arms, possessed by the deep and determined desire to free itself. So I detached from the rest the unit commanded by Captain Medici, made up of an elite group of young men, and others so that they could operate separately.

But Luino turned out to be our first and final success. The surrender of Milan, the retreat of the Piedmontese army, followed by the withdrawal of the various volunteer units from Lombardy had deeply demoralised the local people. It is true that our reappearance and our success at Luino had given them a new burst of enthusiasm, but their discouragement returned when they saw how few in number we were and how our soldiers deserted (encouraged by the very same people in Lugano who had promised us extra men and support!). All the while the Austrian forces were building up in every direction; they felt no sense of dishonour in sending huge numbers of troops against a small band of volunteers. We didn't linger in Varese and spent only a few days in the surroundings, every now and then moving on to avoid an encounter with the enemy which increasingly outnumbered us. Outside Sesto Calende, a Neapolitan captain from the volunteer contingent commanded by Durando accompanied by a few men and two heavy artillery pieces joined us: in different circumstances the artillery would have been a godsend, but as it was it proved an encumbrance since we could not risk fighting such a huge enemy on an open battlefield. I ordered the captain and his artillery back to Ticino while the few men who had come with him remained with us since they were good soldiers. Almost every night we had to change position in order to elude and deceive the enemy: I regret to say I've found that in Italy, especially at that time, the enemy had no difficulty in finding any number of traitors and spies among the populace, whereas we, even with bribes, could get hardly any information on their movements. For the first time I saw how little the national cause inspired the local inhabitants of the countryside. This may have been because they'd been moulded and exploited by the priesthood or because they had grown fat in the absence of their detested masters who had for the most part fled their estates in the wake of the foreign invasions.

On the road to Ternate we found ourselves closed off on all sides by enemy troops. It was truly difficult to escape from their grip and in a flat country would have been impossible; fortunately the mountainous terrain proved to be our salvation. Daverio's help in procuring guides for us was invaluable.

So we marched on resolutely towards the enemy troops, which seemed to get ever nearer. A deep valley lay between us. When our vanguard had reached the bottom of the valley it turned to the left, whereas the enemy was expecting an attack in the other direction; we marched towards Morazzone – in something of a hurry, it must be confessed – leaving the enemy several miles behind us. On the way, we gathered up the bread we could find in the surrounding villages which was carried by porters following the column in baskets strapped to their backs. Once we reached Morazzone at about five o'clock in the afternoon, the men stood in line – sideways because it was so narrow – in the main street; they were ordered to stay there and not to remove their rifles while their provisions and pay were distributed. When this was done, marching orders were given. I had eaten some bread and drunk a glass of wine sitting on the same bench where we had carried out the distribution when one of my officers who had prepared some soup approached and asked me to join their meal. We were on the ground floor of a house near to the Varese gate; suddenly we heard shouts coming from outside, from the gate. The Austrians had broken in, taking our guards, weakened by hunger or tiredness, by surprise. Night was falling: I leave the reader to picture the confusion which ensued among our men, with little experience of combat and demoralised. The only thing to do – there and then, without premeditation, and accompanied by just a handful of brave officers – was to draw my sword, go out and charge the enemy. Our shouts brought those who were escaping to a halt; they turned back to engage in hand-to-hand combat with their pursuers. Victory wavered between the two sides, with moments of complete confusion, but finally the brave Italians got the upper hand and drove the enemy out of Morazzone. Defences were set up, the roads were barricaded, and we occupied some of the houses on the edge of the village which were in danger of being attacked. Once they had been turned out of Morazzone, the enemy did what they always do, especially in Italy, a country that is so accustomed to expiation and martyrdom: they ruthlessly set fire to all the surrounding houses all the while bombarding the village itself indiscriminately. The fire spread rapidly from house to house with a terrifying noise, which the artillery fire on both sides only increased.

Driven off once, the Austrians made no attempt to attack us again and we couldn't risk attacking them in their positions. And yet, once all the circumstances had been considered, we had no option but to withdraw whatever the consequences, since it was certain that if we stayed we would find ourselves surrounded by overwhelming enemy forces in the morning.

After we had organised the men and attended as best we could to the wounded, some of whom we strapped to horses, we began to file out of the village by a narrow street which was out of sight of the enemy and which we had already barricaded. There were no guides to be found: we had to force an extremely unwilling curate to take us (who can be surprised at his attitude? Such vampires work for the foreigners in Italy). This priest, guarded by two of our men who marched on either side of him, was not of much help to us; a short distance outside the village he managed to run off despite his guards. The night was dark, lit only by the fires the Austrians had started. The march began in an orderly fashion and continued so for a short while. The question 'Is the rear keeping up?' passed down the line again and again, to which the answer came back on several occasions 'yes, yes, it's coming up'. Then the answer we got was 'no'. It was impossible to assemble the men without making a long halt, getting the aides near me, such as Aroldi and Cogliuolo, to go back, and then going back myself, in the direction of Morazzone. About sixty of us were left. After some delay, we needed to continue and get away from the main body of the enemy during the night.

In the course of that wearisome night march along paths which were almost impassable, about half again of the men were dispersed: thirty of us reached the Swiss border on the following evening. The rest had split up into small groups in order to cross over into Switzerland.

Inertia and Tedium

I was still suffering from the fever I had contracted in Roverbella, as I had throughout the whole campaign, and I arrived in Switzerland completely worn out. Yet I did not despair of making another attempt to enter Lombardy. The young men reunited in Switzerland had had their first experience of exile and were keen to undertake a new campaign at any cost. The Swiss Government had no wish to provoke the Austrians by supporting the uprisings in Italy. The Italian population in Ticino readily sympathised with our cause: we could hope for support from many of the individuals in the region where most of the Italian emigrants had gathered.

I had had to take to my bed in Lugano, when a colonel from the Federal Government came to tell me that, should we be ready to try our luck once more, then he, Luini by name, as an individual and not as a representative of the Government, together with various friends, would help us in every way they could. I discussed Luini's proposal with Medici, who was then the most influential advisor in the circle around Mazzini; his reply was, 'We can do better than that.' It was clear to me that Medici was simply mouthing his master's view of the matter, so I decided that any further stay in Lugano was pointless and left, accompanied by three comrades, for Nice, with the intention of staying at home in order to shake off the fever which continued to afflict me.

I reached Nice and spent some days resting with my family. I was more afflicted in spirit than in body: the peaceful stay at home did me good, and I left for Genoa, where public indignation at the country's humiliation ran high. There I made a complete recovery.

The march of events in Italy did not yet threaten complete disaster, yet it gave rise to serious forebodings. Lombardy was once again under the tyrant's heel. The Piedmontese army which had fought in its defence had not been destroyed: it had simply vanished, acknowledging the impotence of its commanders. It had won the support of the entire country and would have achieved miracles had it been under the command of a man capable of heading straight for the goal, undeterred by fears and dissensions: as it was, at the moment of conflict it had melted away. It retreated from Lombardy in total disarray but not defeated; and this was the case too with the forces stationed on the Adriatic coast.

In the duchies[8], which were still controlled by our armies, a wave of reaction was setting in, as it was too in Tuscany. In both these regions the peasants were taking up arms against a free government, urged on as usual by priests, spies and all those who favoured foreign rule. In the Papal States Rossi and Zucchi had been called upon to head the government and the army, in the belief that their well-established reputations would serve to hide the reactionary policies which were already in the ascendant.

But the people had seen the dawn of Italian unity and were angry when they realised it was a false dawn. On the eighth of August, a day which will live in memory, the Bolognese received the first contingent of Austrian troops, who had been called to the city by the priests, with gunfire and drove them back beyond the Po in a state of terror. The Neapolitans too put up a strong resistance to the tyrant, but were less successful. Sicily, which had acted as the bulwark and support of Italian freedom, made heroic efforts, but in the absence of a man who could direct them wavered in its choice of political institutions. In short, the whole country, so full of enthusiasm and energy, capable not only of resisting but of overcoming the enemy occupying its territory, was reduced to a state of prostration and inertia through the folly and the treachery of the men who ruled it: its monarchy, its intelligentsia, its clergy.

While I was in Genoa, Paolo Fabrizi came to find me with an

invitation from the Sicilian Government to go to the island. I willingly accepted and, together with seventy-two companions, both old and new and for the most part worthy officers, embarked on a French steamer bound for Sicily.

We stopped in Livorno. I didn't intend to land, but the reaction of the generous and excited populace when they learnt of our arrival made me change my mind and we disembarked. Perhaps I was wrong to listen to their urgings; they were concerned that we were neglecting what should be our principal course of action. They assured me that a large troop of men could be formed in Tuscany, whose numbers would be swelled by volunteers as we crossed the country; then we could march against the Kingdom of Naples by land and thus help both the Italian and the Sicilian cause. I agreed to the proposal, but soon came to see I had made a mistake. A telegraph outlining the proposal was sent to Florence; the replies were evasive. There was no outright disagreement with the Livornese plan, because they feared it, but anyone who understood something of the matter would have realised that the Government was displeased. However, we stayed in Livorno and the steamer left without us.

We remained in the town only for a short while. We were given some rifles, more because of the helpfulness of the leader of the townspeople, Petracchi, and other friends than from the Government. The increase in our numbers was negligible. We were told to march towards Florence where better results could be expected; in fact, matters got worse.

In Florence we were given a magnificent welcome from the inhabitants, but from their Government we met only with indifference and denial. I had to ask certain friends to help to feed the men. I thought a longer stay in Florence would be pointless and irksome and decided to continue on to the Romagna, where our prospects might be better and from where we could reach Venice more easily by way of Ravenna. But we ran into new and even worse problems in crossing the Apennines. On setting out we were supposed to have received the supplies we needed from the Tuscan Government; instead of which, we had nothing, apart from what the generous local people could provide – which fell short, however, of our requirements. The Government sent a letter to the mayor of a village on the frontier putting a limit on the aid which he could give us and ordering him to move us on as if we were so many tiresome adventurers. In such circumstances we reached Filigare on the border with Roman territory where the Papal Government had forbidden us to cross. In their enmity towards us at least the priests behaved consistently. Zucchi, the man we had saved at Como, and now the Minister for War in the Papal Government, came up from Rome in a hurry to ensure that these orders were carried out, while a troop of Swiss soldiers in the papal service came out from Bologna, with two artillery pieces, to block our passage.

The season of bad weather had arrived: it was November and the snow reached up to our knees. So we had left South America for this: to fight against the snow in the Apennines. The various Italian Governments, which I had had the honour to serve and whose territories I had crossed, proved incapable of providing my wretched yet valiant comrades with coats. It was distressing to see these worthy young lads in the mountains in such harsh weather: most were wearing only light clothes, some were in rags, all were hungry, yet they were in their motherland, which fed and fattened all the thieves and rogues in the world. We all contributed what money we had – mostly from the officers – to a common fund; with the help of the good innkeeper in Filigare we managed to spend a few miserable days in the place. In the meantime the Swiss troops took up their positions along the border and prepared to block our crossing, although they were ashamed of what the imbeciles in their Government had ordered them to do. We couldn't hold out for much longer in Filigare; the only solution was to move on. But where? We could retrace our steps to Tuscany… I had read the letter from the Government in Florence to the mayor which told him to get rid of us as quickly as possible: going back there we could either humiliate ourselves or prepare for conflict. We could go on into the Romagna: this would mean fighting those who were prepared to block our way. The dilemma which confronted us was created by the men who governed Italy – the very men who, so the Italian people hoped, would lead them to freedom!

The people of Bologna came to hear of our plight and their indignation was roused, and when the Bolognese are roused, it is never in vain, as the Austrians know only too well: their papal governors grew fearful. I was finally allowed to enter the city for talks with General Latour who commanded the Swiss forces in the service of the Pope. As Latour stood on the balcony of his house, the Bolognese shouted, 'Bring our brothers here or we'll drag you down.' I arrived in the city to the acclamations of the inhabitants; they were set upon getting rid of the foreigners and the reactionaries and I had to calm them down.

I suggested to Latour that we should be allowed to march across the Romagna to Ravenna, where we would embark for Venice. I asked him to speed up the arrival of a Mantuan company who were coming from Genoa with the intention of joining us and to provide them with supplies. In another meeting with Zucchi I also obtained his agreement that we could increase our forces with volunteers from the Romagna; several left under the command of Captain Bazzani from Modena for Ravenna where they would join us.

While I was in Bologna I met for the first time that great man, Angelo Masina: to know him was to love and esteem him. After the Roman division had withdrawn from Lombardy, where Masina had fought with great bravery, he had stayed in or around Bologna. He now found himself at the head of the Bolognese who had liberated their city from the Austrians so heroically on the eighth of August, managing to calm their anger at the cowardice and treachery of the priests and reactionaries in the city. He was at the same time and with characteristic energy assembling horses and men, partly at his own expense; he was organising a squadron of lancers, a group of men, handsome, elegant, and brave, which would have been the envy of any army in the world. Masina's charisma was such that he could both rouse and calm the crowd as needed. He and Father Gavazzi possessed great influence over the Bolognese and had been instrumental in getting us out of Filigare. He too was getting ready to leave for Venice; he was tired of inactivity and was also being pressed to leave by the priests and others who supported the foreigners. He was in Comacchio making his preparations for the voyage.

I reached Ravenna with a company of about one hundred and fifty men; Bazzini joined me there with fifty recruits. Once more we came into conflict with the priests who governed the town. The agreement with Zucchi was that we would await the arrival in Ravenna of the

Mantuan volunteers before setting out all together for Venice, but the priests were so alarmed and suspicious of my handful of poorly armed and ragged companions that they wanted only to get rid of us at the earliest possible opportunity. Latour told me to embark for Venice without further delay. I replied that I wouldn't move until the Mantuan volunteers had arrived. The papalists started to threaten us, but the people of Ravenna, like the Bolognese, treat such threats with contempt: they courageously started to gather together weapons and ammunition with the intention of fighting by our side if we were threatened with violence.

'Reciprocal fear rules the world' a friend of mine used to say – and he was right. Yet it is also true that the least frightened populaces are usually the least oppressed. This proved to be the case in Ravenna: the bullies did not dare, with all their swords and cannon and a thousand battle-hardened soldiers at their command, to face a handful of Italian patriots, wretched and almost enfeebled as we were.

The situation in which Masina found himself in Comacchio was similar. The Pope's men wanted him to leave immediately; he wished to take his time and join his march to ours and so resisted their menaces. Supported by the local populace under the leadership of the valiant Nino Bennet, he managed to prepare an imposing system of defence. So true justice prevailed at Comacchio as at Ravenna.

It was at this time that Rossi was assassinated in Rome:[9] he had faithfully served the interests of tyranny and in getting rid of him the ancient metropolis of the world showed itself worthy of its illustrious past. A young Roman had wielded anew the sword of Brutus and drowned the marble steps of the Capitol with the tyrant's blood! His death created a wave of fear among those who were persecuting us: not another word was said about our departure.

In the Papal States and Arrival in Rome

With Rossi's death, the authorities in Rome understood that they could not trample with impunity over the rights and the will of the nation. Men who were less unpopular were brought into the government, and we were granted leave to remain in Roman territory. But the authorities' distrust of us remained: even though we were now part of the Roman army, only after a delay were we given funds, assigned a destination, and above all provided with weapons and with the greatcoats we needed so badly for the winter which was now imminent.

In Ravenna the Mantuan volunteers arrived as expected; Masina joined us with his cavalry, few in number but a fine troop of men. All together there were about four hundred of us, some unarmed, most without uniforms and inadequately clothed. The town council in Ravenna, which was supporting us, gave us to understand that it would be better if we could move between different towns in turn so that they wouldn't have the burden of this expenditure alone. And so it turned out: after twenty days or so in Ravenna we said goodbye to its amiable and generous inhabitants and travelled between various other towns in the Romagna, welcomed by the local people and supported by the municipalities. I left the men in Cesena in order to visit the Minister for War in Rome and put the legion's miserable and vagabond existence on a more organised footing. I found out that the Pope had fled the city; with the Minister Campello, it was arranged that the Italian Legion (this was the name of the unit I commanded in South America and in Italy) would be incorporated into the Roman army and that as a consequence it would be supplied with all the necessary equipment and brought to Rome where its reorganisation could be completed. I wrote to Major Marrocchetti, who had been left in command of the men, instructing him to proceed towards Rome; I marched out to meet him on the way. I found the legion at Foligno; at the same time I received orders from the Government back in Rome to march with the men towards the port of Fermo and defend it. But Fermo was in no danger of attack: the incident proved to me that the new government continued to distrust us and wished to keep us away from Rome. I pointed out that my men still lacked the coats they had to have if they were to cross the Apennines in the snow, but to no avail; we had to retrace our steps again, back over the Colfiorito Pass in the direction of Fermo.

I realised of course what the Government was up to. The reason for sending us to Fermo was only to keep us away from the capital: they regarded us as revolutionaries and feared that our presence in the city would provoke the Romans into an uprising for which they were only too ready. That this was the Government's thinking was confirmed by the fact that I was ordered to keep the numbers of the legion down to less than five hundred men.

The same attitude prevailed in Rome as it had in Milan and in Florence. Italy had no need of soldiers; it wanted speech-makers and compromise-mongers, men who, in Alfieri's words, were 'now full of pride and now humble, but always contemptible'.[10] Our poor country alas has never had any shortage of such men. The real despots had simply handed over the reins of power, for the time being, to such charlatans in order to hoodwink and lull the people asleep knowing full well that such stuffed parrots would only make their re-entry easier when the tremendous counter-revolution, which was already in the making throughout the entire country, finally came.

So we crossed the Apennines for the third time, in the depths of winter (December 1848), without coats and beset by all the evils which tormented our country, not the least of which were the slanderous lies heaped on us by the priests who described us in the most lurid terms, poisoning the minds of the ignorant inhabitants against us. According to the necromancers[11], we were prepared to use every kind of violence against private property and families, we were wild hooligans without a trace of discipline. The people naturally took fright at our approach as though we were wolves or murderers.

Yet this attitude always changed once they saw my band of young men, fine-looking, polite, almost all the sons of cultivated families from the country's urban centres. It is a well-known fact that no peasants joined the volunteer troops I had the honour to lead in the Italian campaigns: they were too heavily under the influence of the reverend ministers of lies. My soldiers almost without exception came from distinguished families throughout all the different regions of Italy. It is also the case that there were always some delinquents among them, who had either wormed their way into the legion or been planted there by priests and the police in order to encourage crime and mayhem and thus bring the troop into disrepute, but their comrades maintained the legion's honour jealously and unmasked them.

When the legion had previously crossed out of the Romagna into Umbria, we had heard that the inhabitants of Macerata would close their gates against us, such was their fear of our arrival in their town; when we returned, however, along the same route on our way to Fermo, they let us know that they were now better informed and regretted their former decision, and would welcome a visit to make up for their former mistaken attitude. We had a harsh time of it crossing the Apennines, but the festive welcome we received in Macerata compensated for all our sufferings. Thanks to the goodwill of the local inhabitants and the contributions of the ministry in Rome, nearly all the men finally got some decent clothing.

While we were in Macerata the elections for deputies to the Constituent Assembly in Rome were being organised and the soldiers were called upon to vote.

The deputies for the Constituent Assembly! This was a truly impressive sight – to see the sons of Rome called once again to the *comitia*[12] after centuries of servitude, of prostration before the atrocious yoke of empire and the even more shameful burden of papal theocracy! The freedom of the redeemed motherland established without tumult or frenzy! Untainted by financial corruption, unmanipulated by prefects or police, a free vote took place, the sacred ceremony of the plebiscite was enacted, with not a single vote bought and not a single citizen forced to serve the interests of the powerful.

Be hopeful, my country! Never lose faith when foreign bullies and native thieves, like the cowards they are, pile affliction on you. Your brave young men are not yet all gone: the men who stood on the barricades in Brescia, Milan, Casale, on the bridge over the Mincio, on the bulwarks of Venice, Bologna, Ancona, Palermo, in the streets of Naples, Messina, Livorno, on the Janiculum Hill and in the Forum of the ancient capital of the world. They are scattered all over the globe, but all are stirred with love for you their motherland, unequalled among nations, and by the desire to save you – something the speculators and the compromisers who have sold off your limbs and your very blood will never understand, unless they should on the day when you are washed clean of the filth with which they have besmirched you! Never lose faith! Marked by the ferocity of the battles they have fought, they will appear to fight again at the head of your new generation; they will have been brought up to hate, they will be familiar with the massacres perpetrated by priests and foreigners, they will be re-emboldened by the memory of so much outrage and by the desire to revenge so much suffering in prisons and in exile. No one can tell how long Italy will languish, but all know equally well that the hour of her resurrection cannot be far away.

Proclamation of the Republic and the March on Rome

We stayed in Macerata until the end of January, and then left for Rieti, which we had been ordered to defend. The legion took the road over the Colfiorito Pass while I and three comrades went by Ascoli and the Tronto Valley along the border with the Kingdom of Naples in order to reconnoitre. We crossed the Apennines, through the rocky altitudes of the Sibilla, but the beauty of the landscape through which we journeyed was wiped out by the driving snow and the rheumatic pains which attacked me.

The hardy mountain folk greeted us and celebrated our arrival and accompanied us with enthusiasm. The crags echoed with the sounds of cheers for Italian freedom. Yet only a few days later, those same robust and vigorous people went out to fight against the Roman Republic, goaded on by priests, who had also supplied them with arms.

We reached Rieti, where clothes were finally provided for the whole legion. It proved impossible to obtain rifles for all the men, however, and so I decided to make lances for those who were without any weapon. Our numbers were increasing and we were better organised, but the ministry in Rome did not want soldiers. Just as it had restricted the legion to five hundred men, it now told me not to exceed one thousand; I already had rather more than that and so was obliged to cut the men's already meagre pay, including that of the officers, in order to maintain the whole legion. When this was announced, not a single complaint was heard among the ranks of those gallant brothers-in-arms.

We spent the time in Rieti training and building some defences along the border with the Kingdom of Naples to protect it against any possible incursions from the Bourbons, who were the openly declared enemies of Italian liberty.

I had been elected by the people of Macerata as a deputy to the Constituent Assembly and so was called to Rome to take part in it. On the eighth of February 1849 I had the good fortune to be one of the first of the almost unanimous assembly to proclaim, at eleven in the evening, the creation of the glorious Roman Republic, soon to be crushed by the Jesuits in their usual alliance with the European autocracies. My rheumatism meant that I had to be carried into the chamber on the shoulders of my aide Bueno.

I was a witness to the rebirth of the greatest of all republics, the Roman Republic, in the city which had been the greatest in the world! What a vision of the future, what hopes! The images and presentiments which had thronged my imagination as a child and as a young boy of eighteen when for the first time I had wandered through the magnificent ruins of Rome had not been idle dreams after all: nor had the hopes in the rebirth of the nation which had stirred in me, in the midst of the American forests and on storm-tossed oceans, and which had inspired me to fulfil my duties towards all peoples who suffer and are oppressed! We were all freely gathered there in the very same chamber where the ancient tribunes of Rome had gathered; nor were we unworthy perhaps of those distant ancestors, presided over as we were by the same spirit of the Republic which they were happy to acknowledge and to acclaim. The awesome voice of the Republic sounded once again in the chamber as it had done on the day when the kings were chased away for ever!

After the proclamation of the Roman Republic I returned to Rieti; towards the end of March I received orders to march with the legion to Anagni. In April we heard that the French had occupied the port of Civitavecchia – which could easily have been defended had it not been for the enemy's deceitfulness and our own stupidity – and intended to march on Rome. It was at about this time that General Avezzana went to Rome to take up the position of Minister for War. I did not know him personally, but everything I had heard about his character and his military career in Spain and America had made me respect him. His appearance on the scene in charge of the War Ministry filled me with new hope, which turned out to be justified.

Soon the order came to march on Rome, now under threat from Louis Napoleon's army. The reader does not need to be told how enthusiastically we marched to defend the venerable and ancient city. The legion now had about twelve hundred men; we had left Genoa with sixty. It is true that we had travelled through many regions since then, yet the authorities everywhere had spurned us, the priests had slandered us, we had been reduced to the direst straits and had been unarmed most of the time, which had demoralised the men and made it difficult to put the legion on a proper footing – with all these obstacles, it was a source of satisfaction that our numbers had grown so considerably. We reached Rome and put up in the abandoned convent of San Silvestro.

The Defence of Rome

We stayed there only very briefly, however, as on the next day we were ordered to set up camp in St Peter's Square from where we were moved to guard the stretch of city wall from Porta San Pancrazio to Porta Portese. The French were approaching and we had to be ready to receive them.

The thirtieth of April dawned: a day that was to reveal the glorious victory of the inexperienced young men who defended Rome and the shameful flight of the soldiers fighting on behalf of the priesthood and the reactionaries. Avezzana had devised a system of defence which was really worthy of the old warrior for freedom: he had untiringly seen to every detail and visited every place which had need of him. Beyond the stretch of walls between the two gates into the city I had set up strongly fortified outposts; for these I used the great residential villas Corsini and Vascello and other places which could serve as defence positions. These were vital: it was easy to see that if these prominently sited buildings fell into the hands of the French it would be difficult if not impossible to maintain the defence of the city. On the night of the twenty-ninth of April I sent out some men to reconnoitre the two roads which led to the gates; I also ordered two small detachments to wait in hiding by the edge of the road near enough to enable them to ambush some enemy scouts. And indeed, when dawn broke, I found an enemy cavalry soldier on his knees in front of me, pleading for his life; the taking of a single prisoner of war might be insignificant, but I was cheered and hoped his capture augured well for the coming day. France was kneeling before me, making honourable amends for her rulers' unworthy and shameful conduct.

The prisoner had been captured by the detachment under the command of Ricchieri, a young man from Nice, who had acted with great daring and presence of mind. They had forced a team of enemy scouts to flee, who, despite their greater numbers, had left behind several weapons in their panic. When the enemy is approaching, it is always useful to set up some ambushes on the roads which they are taking: it is possible to find out how far the head of the column has reached and to capture some prisoners of war.

From the commanding heights of the city the enemy could be seen approaching slowly and cautiously, marching in column along the road from Civitavecchia to Porta Cavalleggeri. When they came near enough to fire their cannon, they set up some artillery in key positions and sent some troops marching on resolutely to attack the walls. Their commander General Oudinot's strategy of attack was derisory: like Don Quixote launching himself against the windmills, he attacked the city as if it had no walls to defend it or as if they were guarded by children. This young scion of one of Napoleon I's marshals thought all he had to chase out of the place were four *'brigands d'Italiens'* and hadn't even bothered to acquire a map of the city. However, he soon realised that it was men, united by their republican faith, who were defending the city against the mercenary troops he was leading; these valiant sons of Italy calmly let the enemy approach and then repelled them with musket and cannon fire. More than a few of the French soldiers who had advanced nearer to the walls were felled.

I was observing the enemy attack from Villa Corsini and saw our spirited response from Porta Cavalleggeri and the surrounding walls. It seemed to me a good idea to attack the enemy on its right flank so I dispatched two units for this task who created much confusion among the French troops. The latter's superior numbers however forced them back on the support positions of the various villas just outside the city walls. The French approached these positions and were caught in the crossfire we launched on them; they halted their advance and took what shelter they could find behind walls and in the declivities of the surrounding terrain from where they returned our fire as hard as they could. The battle continued in this fashion for a while until we received reinforcements and were able to intensify our attack; the French began to fall back and finally turned and beat a hasty retreat. A burst of cannon fire from the walls and a sortie from Porta Cavalleggeri completed our victory; the enemy were crushed and didn't stop till they reached Castel Guido, leaving a number of dead behind and several hundred prisoners. The legion's morale was much cheered by their victory over more experienced troops, as their subsequent feats go to show.

On the following day I was ordered to keep the enemy under observation, so together with the legion and some cavalry troops I moved in the direction of Castel Guido, where we spent part of the day within sight of the enemy. In the afternoon a French doctor came to parley: I sent him to talk to the Government. Oudinot now saw that his forces were too weak to attack Rome and hoped to gain time with diplomatic initiatives while waiting for reinforcements to arrive from France. We could have taken advantage of his weakness and fear and driven him into the sea, and then we could have sorted him out.

In May the legion won glorious victories in the engagements at Palestrina and Velletri. In Palestrina Bourbon troops had arrived – some time before they had invaded Roman territory in order to assist the French, Austrians and Spanish armies – and were driven off resoundingly. Manara and his brave bersaglieri (Zambianchi, Marrocchetti, Masina, Bixio, Daverio, Sacchi, Coccelli, etc.) distinguished themselves in the conflict. The engagement at Velletri was a more serious affair: the Commander-in-Chief General Roselli was in charge of our troops, about eight thousand strong in infantry, cavalry and artillery, against the King of Naples himself with his entire army. We left Rome by way of Zagarolo to Monte Fortino where we took up our position in the rear of the Neapolitan army. Roselli had placed me in command of the main troops, but Marrocchetti was in the vanguard with the legion. I preferred to march with my companions-in-arms. As we went, I sought news of the enemy from the local inhabitants and sent what I heard on to headquarters. The scraps of information which I carefully pieced together seemed to indicate that the enemy was in retreat, and this turned out to be the case. When I reached the hills overlooking Velletri in the direction of Monte Fortino with the vanguard, I ordered them to halt; after surveying the territory, I divided the legion into two units to the left and right of the road for Velletri. The third regiment from the main army, which also formed part of the vanguard, remained partly in reserve on the road, with some troops distributed to right and left among the vineyards which bordered the sunken road. Two artillery pieces were placed in a prominent position to the rear of the third regiment, who started to march straight along the road; part of Masina's cavalry went ahead as scouts and part were kept back in reserve.

The enemy had already sent its baggage and heavy artillery back to Naples along the Appian Way, but as most of their troops were still in Velletri and since they knew how small our numbers were they wanted to attempt at least to engage us in a skirmish. An advance column was therefore sent along the road towards us, backed up by lines of marksmen among the vineyards along the side of the road; it fiercely attacked and broke up the advance lines in our centre.

Along the road, a vanguard of the enemy cavalry had charged the small number of our cavalry which were there as scouts; to support them I ordered the cavalry reserve to counter-attack. They bravely drove them back. But when they reached the top of the hill they encountered the head of the main enemy column coming along the road in our direction and naturally retreated under attack from the Bourbon cavalry. Our horses were young and not used to battle and they started off in panic. I thought that such a sight was unseemly in the presence of so many comrades and enemies and incautiously rode my horse across their path to block their oncoming rush; various of my aides and my valiant black batman Andrea Agujar did likewise. In an instant there was a sprawling mass of horses and men; our cavalry had not been able to rein in the headlong flight of their horses, which ran into us with such force that the horses were overturned and threw their riders, leaving all in a writhing heap on the sunken road. Even a single foot soldier couldn't have got through.

When they reached the scene, the enemy cavalry fell upon us with their sabres and we were only saved because of the general confusion. By now our legionaries who had been positioned in the vineyards on either side of the road on the orders of their officers started to fire heavily on the enemy; they managed to drive them back and rescue us from our sorry situation. A company of young lads on my right had seen me thrown off my horse and fell upon the enemy like madmen; I believe I owe my life to those brave youths since I was so bruised from the horses and men who had ridden and fallen over me that I could not move at all. When after much effort I finally got up I checked all my limbs to see that none was broken.

The charge of our soldiers on the right (the dominant and therefore the crucial part of the field) led by Masina and Daverio was driven forward with such impetus that they almost ended up inside Velletri together with the enemy.

Nearer to the town, I saw even more clearly that the enemy intended to withdraw. Quite apart from the news I had had about the equipment and heavy artillery being sent back, I could see quite visible beyond Velletri their cavalry echeloned along one side of the Appian Way.

I was sending back reports on all I observed to the Commander-in-Chief, but unfortunately the main body of the Roman army had been held up on the way to Zagarolo waiting for provisions which were being sent from Rome. My men instead had eaten while on the march, slaughtering the plentiful cattle which they found on the estates belonging to wealthy cardinals adjoining the road. Finally the General and the advance columns of the army arrived at four in the afternoon after we had fought all through the earlier part of the day.

I tried hard to convince them that the enemy was in retreat, but it was no good; on his arrival General Roselli ordered a skirmish and then made the troops take up their positions for a morning attack on the following day. But the enemy decided not to wait and decamped from Velletri during the night, making its soldiers take off their shoes and muffling the wheels of the gun carriages in order to retreat in silence.

Dawn broke on an empty town; from the town high on its hill the enemy could be seen in swift retreat along the Appian Way towards Terracina and Naples. The Roman forces withdrew to Rome with the general at the head. I had received orders to invade Neapolitan territory, via Anagni, Frosinone, Ceprano and Rocca d'Arce where I arrived with Manara's bersaglieri who were the vanguard. Masi's regiment, the Italian legion and a few cavalry were following us.

The valiant Colonel Manara was in pursuit of General Viale, who was in command of one of the enemy contingents and who did not stop for a single moment to engage Manara and his men. On our arrival in Rocca d'Arce, several delegations came from the surrounding villages to greet us as liberators and to urge us to go on, assuring us that we would have widespread support throughout the Bourbon kingdom. There is a tide in the affairs of nations as well as of men; this was one such moment which inspired leadership should have grasped.

I was of the opinion that we should go on to San Germano in the heart of Bourbon territory beyond the Abruzzi mountains, and was preparing for the journey; it would have been easy to reach and we would have been welcomed by the inhabitants who were very favourably disposed towards us. This fact, together with the demoralised Neapolitan troops, who had now been defeated in two battles and were ready, as I knew, to disband, with many of the soldiers wanting to return to their homes; the aroused ardour of my young men, who had had the best of every encounter with the enemy so far and were ready to continue fighting like lions, regardless of how many enemy forces there were; and Sicily still in revolt, encouraged by the defeat of its oppressors – all these reasons seemed to hold out the prospect of success if we pressed ahead boldly. Yet, in an ill-timed moment of vacillation and misguidedness, a new order arrived from the Republican Government telling us to return to Rome, which was once more threatened by the French: they attempted to sweeten the pill by graciously allowing me, if I so wished, to travel back to Rome by way of the Abruzzi!

If the person who had asked me to cross back over into Switzerland in 1848 after the surrender of Milan (and not only kept my volunteers there, but encouraged them to desert, even after our victory at Luino, by letting me know through his intermediary Medici that they had better plans) – if the man who had allowed me to march on to Palestrina and win, as I had intended to, and then, for some reason unknown to me, made me march to Velletri under the orders of the Commander-in-Chief Roselli – if this same personage, Mazzini, whose decisions went completely uncontested by the other two members of the republican triumvirate, had bothered to realise that I too knew something about fighting battles; had left General Roselli in Rome and given me the sole responsibility for the attack on Velletri as he had for Palestrina; and had then allowed me to invade the Kingdom of Naples, whose defeated army was incapable of any response and whose inhabitants were waiting for our arrival with open arms – how the circumstances would have changed! What a prospect would have opened up for a country not yet completely cast down by foreign invasion!

Instead of which, Mazzini called all the troops in the Republican State back to Rome, from its border in the south with the Kingdom of Naples up to Bologna in the north, and so offered them up in one appetising dish to the tyrant of France, who, if the forty thousand men he'd already sent were not enough, would have added one hundred thousand more to annihilate us with a single blow. Everyone who is familiar with Rome and its walls, which are eighteen miles in length, knows that the city is impossible to defend with only a few troops against a larger and better-equipped army, such as the French had in 1849. It was therefore pointless to employ all the troops of the army of the Roman Republic in the defence of the capital; the correct strategy would have been to deploy most of the forces in the numerous defensible sites throughout the state, enlist all the inhabitants and arm them, allow me to continue my victorious march southwards into Bourbon territory, and finally, after withdrawing all the defence troops from the capital, make provisions for the Government itself to leave Rome and establish itself in some central and well-protected location.

It is also the case that at the same time measures which should have been taken against the clergy to ensure the safety of the Republic were neglected: out of some mistaken sense of respect, the priests were left to conspire and plot and bring down the state.

Who knows what the consequences would have been if these

measures had been taken to save the situation? If we were destined to fail, then at the very least we would have failed after doing the best we could, after carrying out our duty; and we would certainly have capitulated after Hungary and Venice!

When I arrived in Rome from Rocca d'Arce and saw how the situation was being handled and how it would inevitably end in disaster, I asked to be made dictator, in exactly the same way as on other occasions in my life I had demanded to take sole control of a boat and steer it to safety through stormy seas. Mazzini and his colleagues were scandalised. Yet a few days later, on the third of June, when the enemy, which had deceived them, had captured the positions which commanded access to the city and which we tried in vain and with much bloodshed to retake, then – yes, then! – the chief triumvir wrote to me and offered me the position of Commander-in-Chief of the republican forces. I was in the thick of bloody battle on that unhappy day; I thanked Mazzini and chose to fight on.

Oudinot had successfully lulled the Republican Government with negotiations which gave time for his reinforcements to arrive; he now got ready for action and announced that hostilities would recommence on the fourth of June – and the Government chose to believe the perfidy of one of Louis Napoleon's henchmen. From April to June no thought had been given to building defences, especially in the crucial and commanding positions which lay just outside the city and which are the key to any attack on Rome. I recall that on the thirtieth of April, after our victory, Avezzana and I had agreed in a meeting at the Villa dei Quattro Venti that this key position together with several others beside it which were only slightly less important should all be fortified. But Avezzana was sent to Ancona and I was busy with other matters.

A few units were placed outside Porta San Pancrazio and Porta Cavalleggeri as advance posts, since the enemy was located on that side of the city towards Castel Guido and Civitavecchia. I returned from Velletri, grief-stricken at the ruinous collapse of my poor country's cause. The legion was back in the convent of San Silvestro; giving the battle-wearied troops a rest seemed to be the sole concern.

Oudinot had said that he would attack on the fourth of June, but chose to take us by surprise on the night of the second. We were woken in the early hours by the sound of gun- and cannon-fire in the area round Porta San Pancrazio. The alarm was sounded and, despite their fatigue, in a minute the legionaries were armed and heading for the place from where the noise of battle was coming. Their comrades who had been manning the outposts had been taken by surprise and either been killed or taken prisoner; the enemy had already gained control of the Villa dei Quattro Venti and other strategic positions by the time we reached Porta San Pancrazio. I immediately launched an assault on the villa in the hope that its defences could still be breached: if we succeeded, Rome would be saved; if the enemy could hold onto it, the city was lost. The attack was not well planned, but it was heroic: it was led by the first Italian legion, who were followed up by Manara's bersaglieri and then by various other corps, with the backing of artillery fire from the soldiers posted on the city walls, and it continued through the night. The enemy had appreciated the importance of holding the position and its best and bravest troops had occupied it; all the efforts of our finest men to seize control were in vain. The Italians led by the valiant Masina managed to enter the villa and engage in hand-to-hand combat with the French soldiers, beating back time and time again the experienced African troops they found there[13]. But the enemy was able to bring in fresh reinforcements to continue the battle and our soldiers found it impossible to prevail. I sent Manara's bersaglieri in to support them: they were few in number but they had fought gallantly alongside us in all our battles, and they were the best organised and disciplined corps in the city. The struggle continued for a while, but our men were finally overwhelmed by the enemy's superior forces and obliged to retreat.

The battle on the third of June 1849, one of the most glorious episodes in Italy's military history, lasted from dawn until night. Several bloody attempts were made to retake the Villa dei Quattro Venti. When it was dark I sent some fresh companies from the Unione regiment into the attack, supported by others. Again they fought their way bravely up to the villa and a fierce combat ensued; but again the enemy proved too much for them. Their commander together with many of his men was killed and they were forced to retreat. The first Italian legion comprising just over one thousand men lost twenty-three officers, almost all killed in action; as well as many of Manara's men and those from the Unione regiment, together with officers from other corps which I cannot now recall.

The third of June sealed the fate of Rome. The best officers and non-commissioned officers were either dead or wounded. The enemy had gained control of all the key positions; with all its men and all its artillery, it established its hold over them, as it did with the lateral strongholds, which it had won by surprise and treachery. It started to make the normal preparations for the siege as if it were confronted with an impregnable fortress – which showed that it was dealing with Italians who knew how to fight.

The corps, as I said, had lost their best officers and men; in the regular divisions, that is to say, the old papal troops, some had fought well at the beginning, but now that the situation was breaking down they started to show signs of inertia and reluctance, and to disobey the commands they were given. The superior officers in particular, who hoped for the restoration of the Papacy and whom the Republican Government wouldn't or couldn't eliminate, not only resisted orders but encouraged their men to be slack – which created many difficulties for Manara, my gallant chief of staff, and was a sure harbinger of disaster. A night sortie was attempted, but panic broke out among those who were leading the column and spread down the lines, making the whole enterprise futile. More and more of the outposts were abandoned because there were no troops to man them; only the Villa Vascello held out to the last on account of the bravery of Medici and his men. When it was finally abandoned, only a heap of ruins remained of what had once been an extensive edifice.

The situation got more and more difficult day by day. Our valorous Manara found it increasingly difficult to maintain contact between the front line and the rearguard positions which is essential for common security; the absence of such communication certainly made it easier for Bonaparte's mercenaries to enter through the breaches their cannon had opened up in the walls. Because these openings were so poorly guarded, the enemy was able to break through during the night with very little loss of life. If only Mazzini – and it is he who must be singled out for blame – had been as practically minded as he was prolix in thinking up movements and projects; if he had truly possessed the military genius he always believed he had; and if he had bothered to listen to some of those around him who might be thought, given their experience, to know something about these matters, he would have saved himself from many errors. In these particular circumstances he might not have saved the Italian cause, but he could have delayed the disaster at Rome for an indefinite period, leaving the city the honour of falling to the enemy last, after Venice and Hungary had capitulated.

The day before Manara met such a glorious death, I sent him to Mazzini with the proposal that we leave Rome and march with all our available forces and all the equipment and means of transport at our disposal towards the fastnesses of the Apennines. I cannot understand why we didn't do this. There is no lack of historical precedent for such a way of saving the situation: I myself had seen it in the Republic of Rio Grande, and another example occurred recently in the American Civil War. It is not true to say that it would have been impossible: I left Rome a few days afterwards with about four thousand men and encountered no obstacles. The people's representatives in the assembly, for the most part young and enthusiastic patriots, might have returned to their constituencies (where they were very much loved), roused the people's patriotic feelings and made it possible to try our luck once more. Instead I was told that all attempts at defence were becoming impossible and that the representatives should remain in the city. As far as the individuals were concerned, this was a courageous resolution and to their honour, but it was a poor decision for our nation's dignity and its future interests, and blameworthy when there were so many men still armed to fight and who in Hungary and Venice were still struggling against our enemies. In the meantime the city waited for the French to enter and to surrender up their arms to them, thus ensuring a grievous and dishonourable period of servitude. I, together with a band of trusted companions, decided not to submit but to take to the open countryside and once more try the chances of fate.

The American ambassador in Rome Mr Cass (2nd July 1849) knew how things stood and let me know that he wished to speak with me. I met him in the street. He was good enough to tell me that an American corvette was waiting for me in Civitavecchia if I wanted to use it, together with my other companions who might be at risk if they remained. I thanked this representative of the great republic for his generous offer, but told him that I had decided to leave the city along with any who wished to follow me and fight on for Italy's destiny which did not seem to me entirely beyond hope. I continued on towards Piazza San Giovanni, where I instructed my men to assemble in readiness for departure. On arrival I found most of them already there and the rest just joining them. Many soldiers from different corps and others too had heard about our plans and come to join us to avoid the humiliation of having to lay their arms down at the feet of Bonaparte's soldiers watched over by priests.

Retreat

Despite my urgings that she should stay behind, my good Anita had decided to come with me. When I described to her the discomfort, the privations, the dangers that lay ahead with enemies all around, this only seemed to strengthen her resolve; and it was pointless to observe that she was pregnant and should not travel. She went in to the first house she reached and asked a woman to cut her hair short; then she dressed in men's clothes and climbed up on a horse.

After I had surveyed from the top of the city walls the road I intended to take, to see if any enemy troops were there, I gave the order to march towards Tivoli and to be ready to engage with any enemy soldiers who might try to stop us. The march went smoothly and we reached Tivoli on the morning of the third of July. We spent some time trying to reorganise all the different parts which had come together to form the small brigade I was leading. The situation was not unpromising: most of my best officers were dead or wounded (Masina, Daverio, Manara, Mameli, Bixio, Peralta, Montaldi, Ramorino and many others), but several remained (Marrocchetti, Sacchi, Cenni, Coccelli and Isnardi). If the general mood among civilians and soldiers had not been so dispirited I could have gone on fighting for a good while and given the Italian people, once they had overcome their dismay and weariness, another opportunity to throw off the foreign yoke. Alas, it was not to be! I soon realised that there was no desire to carry on and wage the glorious war which destiny invited us to undertake. Setting off from Tivoli and striking north to attempt to rouse the people and stir up their patriotic ardour, I found not a single man willing to rally to our cause; not only this, but every night – as if they were ashamed of what they were doing and preferred to use the cover of darkness – the men who had followed me out from Rome started to desert. When I compared the fortitude and self-denial of the men I had known in South America with the timidity and effeminacy of my fellow-Italians, I was ashamed I belonged to such degenerate descendants of a once great people, town-dwellers incapable of fighting a campaign for a month if they had to do without their customary three meals a day.

When we got to Terni the valiant English colonel Forbes joined us with several hundred well-disciplined men. This courageous and honest soldier loved the cause of Italy as fervently as the best among us did. From Terni we continued to head north, criss-crossing the Apennines, but no one rallied to us. The numerous deserters abandoned their weapons, which we loaded onto mules, but there were soon so many and it proved so difficult to transport them with us that we had to leave them behind, along with ammunition, with local inhabitants who seemed trustworthy, in order that they could conceal them and keep them in reserve against the time when they would be weary of enduring shame and oppression.

Our circumstances were far from encouraging, but we could still be proud that we had succeeded in getting clear of Rome and the French army who had pursued us for a while, while we managed to keep ahead of the Austrian, Spanish and Neapolitan troops who were all around us. The Austrians looked for us everywhere. They must have known what poor condition we were in; no doubt they were jealous of the French successes and keen to add to their glorious victories in the north. They certainly knew our numbers were diminishing by the day from all the spies and priests and traitors who inhabit this land – a land which still tolerates them, to her great misfortune. The priests, moreover, who rule over the peasants, and are often local people themselves, and who are the best suited to go around at night, told our enemies everything about us, where we were and where we were going, while I on the other hand could find out nothing about them since the inhabitants who were on our side were too demoralised and frightened to risk compromising themselves, so that it was impossible to obtain guides, even for gold. The enemy forces were led by expert guides (I have seen priests, holding the cross aloft, leading the enemies of our country against us) and so always managed to find us at a certain hour of the day (we always moved on at night), but usually in well protected positions so that they did not dare to attack us. Yet their presence was a continual harassment and encouraged our men to desert. And so it went on like this for a while: the enemy, despite its immensely superior numbers, could not attack and defeat us.

As a result, few incidents occurred as we were marching to San Marino and only some insignificant skirmishes against the Austrians took place.

Two of our cavalrymen on reconnoitre were captured by peasants working for the bishop of Chiusi – a bishop, mark you – and I believe the town still has one today (1872). I asked for the men to be given back: I thought no good could befall them in the clutches of Torquemada's descendants[14], but the request was denied. So in reprisal I made all the monks of a nearby monastery march at the head of our column and threatened to shoot them all; the bishop refused to give way, saying that there was plenty of sackcloth in Italy to make new friars, and kept the prisoners. I thought it likely he wanted me to kill them so that he could pass them off to the ignorant masses as holy martyrs, so I let them go.

Once we reached San Marino I wrote the orders for the day sitting on the steps of a church just outside the city. It read like this: 'Soldiers, I release you from your duty to follow me. Return to your homes, but never forget that Italy must not remain forever oppressed and dishonoured!'

The Austrian general had sent a communication to the Government of the Republic of San Marino stipulating conditions which we found unacceptable: this produced a favourable response among the men who decided to fight on rather than submit to such ignominious terms. The agreement which had been proposed to the assembly in San Marino demanded that we lay down our arms in the neutral territory of the Republic so leaving us free to return to our homes; but we did not care to make any pact with the enemies of our country. For my part, I knew that it was not impossible to find a way out of San Marino and reach Venice, along with a small band of companions, and this is what we decided to do.

My beloved Anita's condition – her pregnancy was in an advanced stage and she was ailing – was a painful obstacle. I pleaded with her to stay and take refuge in San Marino, where she at least might be offered shelter and whose inhabitants had already shown such kindness towards us. To no avail: with manly courage and warmth of feeling she scornfully rejected all my warnings and cut me off by saying, 'You want to leave me.'

I planned to leave San Marino in the middle of the night and make for a port on the Adriatic from where we could sail for Venice. Many of the men with me, in particular several from Lombardy and the Veneto who had deserted from the Austrians, decided to go along with me whatever the outcome; I left the city with a few companions having arranged to wait for the others to join us at an agreed place. This arrangement caused some delays and I had to wait a considerable while before the others arrived. I had spent the previous day wandering round and trying to identify the more accessible stretches of coastline. As luck, in which I've always placed some trust, would have it, I came across a person who helped me a lot in this difficult task: one Galapini, a brave young man from Forlì, who was riding by in his cart, stopped and introduced himself and offered to guide me; he also did some reconnoitring of the enemy, running at top speed to where the Austrians were gathered, getting news out of the local people and passing it all back to me. Listening to what he found out, I decided to get to the town of Cesenatico, and Galapini found me guides who could lead us in that direction.

We reached the town at about midnight and found an Austrian patrol at the entrance; I took advantage of their momentary astonishment when they saw us by telling some of the men on horseback around me to dismount and disarm the guards, which they did immediately. We entered the place and had the run of it, having arrested some guards who certainly weren't expecting to see us during the night. One of the first things I did was to tell the local authorities to make a number of boats available, as many as we needed.

Yet my luck started to run out that night. A storm was rising over the sea: the waves were so rough and the currents so strong at the harbour entrance that getting out would be nearly impossible. But we had to leave: daybreak was approaching, the enemy was near, getting out to sea was our only means of retreat. My experience as a sailor stood me in good stead.

The men were put into thirteen small fishing boats. Colonel Forbes got in last of all, having spent all the time we were preparing to embark at the entrance into the town to ward off any enemy troops who might happen to approach. Once the boats had been kedged out to sea one after the other with all the men on board, the provisions which had been supplied by the town authorities were shared out. After instructions for the voyage had been given, telling them especially to keep together as much as possible, we set out towards Venice. It was already light when we left Cesenatico: the weather had changed for the better and the wind was favourable. If I had not been so anxious for Anita, who was in the most terrible state, I might have described our situation as hopeful – we had overcome many problems and were now on the way to safety – but her sufferings were intense and my anguish at not being able to do anything to help her even greater.

Our food supplies were limited, but we chiefly lacked water. My poor wife had a burning thirst, which was surely a symptom of her disease. I too was tired out and thirsty, but there was almost no water to drink.

With a favourable wind, we sailed along the Adriatic coast, keeping a certain distance from it, for the rest of the day. An equally serene night came on: there was a full moon. I had often gazed with reverence on the companion of those at sea, but now I saw it rising with displeasure. It was more beautiful than I had ever seen it before – too beautiful! It spelt disaster for us.

The Austrian fleet was situated east of the Punta di Goro: the Sardinian and Bourbon kingdoms saw fit to leave it untouched and in complete control of the Adriatic. I had heard from local fishermen that it was there, perhaps riding at anchor, but my information was uncertain. The first ship we encountered was a brig – called *Oreste*, I think – which came across us at sunset. It started to steer its way towards us. I tried to tell the other boats to head left out of the path of the moon's reflection on the water; it was easy in the moonlight for the enemy to spot us. But it was the clearest night I had ever seen, and the advice was futile; not only did the enemy keep us in their sights, but they started to fire off cannon and rockets to let the rest of the fleet know that we were near. I attempted to sail between the enemy ships and the coast, turning a deaf ear to the cannon fire aimed at us, but the noise of the firing and the approach of the other ships scared the rest of the men and they started to head back, at which point I did the same, not wanting to abandon them.

When day broke we found ourselves in the bay by the Punta di Goro, encircled by enemy ships. They continued to fire at us; I was grieved to see that some of our boats had already surrendered. Going back or going on were both out of the question: the enemy ships were much faster than our vessels. There was nothing for it but to head for the shore. Pursued by cutters and cannon fire, four of our boats reached land. All the rest had been taken by the enemy.

I leave my reader to imagine what that terrible hour was like. My wife was dying; the triumphant enemy was in swift pursuit; we had landed in a part of the country where we were almost certain to find more enemies, papal troops as well as Austrians, in the full throes of counter-revolutionary zeal. Despite all this we landed. I lifted my beloved companion in my arms out of the boat and laid her on the shore. I saw the perplexed looks on the faces of the men who were with me and told them to disperse singly or in pairs and try to find a hiding place wherever they could – to get away at all costs from the spot where we had landed since the enemy's cutters were about to arrive at any moment. I had to stay since I could not abandon my wife who was dying, so I hid in a nearby field of millet, with Anita and Lieutenant Leggero, my inseparable companion who had stayed with me even in Switzerland after the battle at Morazzone. My dearest one's last words were for her children. She knew that she would not see them again.

We remained in the field for some time, uncertain what to do. Finally I told Leggero to explore inland a little and see whether there was a nearby house; with his usual boldness, he set off immediately. I waited a while, but shortly afterwards heard voices approaching; I sprang up and saw Leggero with another man, whom I recognised instantly and with immense relief. It was Colonel Nino Bonnet, one of my most distinguished officers, who had been wounded at the siege in Rome, during which he had also lost his courageous brother. He had returned home to recover from his wounds. Meeting this comrade-in-arms here was the luckiest thing which could have happened to me. He lived on an estate in the area; he had heard the cannon fire and guessed that we were approaching to land and, with characteristic courage and intelligence, and at great risk to himself, had gone out to the shore to look for us and had found us. Once he had come to our aid, I submitted entirely to what he thought it best to do for our rescue. He suggested going to a nearby hut where my poor companion might find some succour. We set off, carrying Anita between us, and with great difficulty reached the place where the poor folk inside gave her the water to drink that she so badly needed as well as other things. From here we went on to a house where Bonnet's sister lived, who was extremely kind; then we crossed some of the valleys around Comacchio towards Mandriola, where we would find a doctor.

When we got there, Anita was stretched out on a mattress on a cart we had brought with us. I asked Doctor Zannini, who had himself arrived at that very moment: 'Please try to save my wife!' He replied that we should try to get her to bed, so each of us took hold of a corner of the mattress and carried her into the bedroom of the house, which was at the top of a narrow staircase. As I was laying her down on the bed, I thought I saw the signs of death on her face. I felt her pulse – there was no beat! The woman I loved so much, the mother of my children, was dead. And my children would ask after her when I next saw them...

I wept bitterly at her loss. She who had been my inseparable companion in the greatest adventures of my life was gone from me. I asked the good people of the house to bury her and, at their urgings, left straight away since I would put them at risk if I stayed any longer. I made my way shakily towards the village of Sant'Alberto, led by a guide to the home of a tailor, who was poor but honest and warm-hearted.

I owe my life to Bonnet: he was the first of a series of protectors without whom I would never have been able to make my way over the next thirty-seven days from the Po estuary to the Bay of Sterlino on the

Tuscan coast, where I was able to embark for Genoa.

From the windows of the house in Sant'Alberto where I was staying I could see Austrian soldiers walking around with their usual insolent air of being the masters. During my time in this small but excellent town I stayed in two houses, and in both I was protected and taken care of with a generosity which was certainly beyond the means of the owners. My friends thought it best to remove me from the town into the nearby pine forests, where I remained for some time, changing place continuously for safety's sake. Those who shared the secret of my whereabouts, mostly brave young men from the Romagna, managed to conceal me, as if wrapped in some magic cloud, from my persecutors, from the Austrians and, even worse, from the papal troops who were hunting for me. Their concern for my safety had to be seen to be believed: when they thought I was in danger they would come with a cart in the middle of the night to transport me miles away to a more secure hiding place.

The Austrians and the priests did all they could to find out where I was hiding. Various units of the Austrian army crossed and recrossed the pine forests in pursuit of me, while from the pulpit and the confessional the priests urged the local peasant women to act as spies for the greater glory of God.

It pains me to think I am unable to record for posterity the names of the generous inhabitants of the Romagna who assisted me and to whom I owe my survival. For this alone I would have to dedicate my life to the sacred cause of my country.

I spent several days in the beautiful pine forest round Ravenna, part of the time in a hut belonging to a certain Savini, a good-natured, honest and generous man of the people, and part concealed among the dense bushes in the undergrowth. On one occasion Leggero and I were stretched out in the bushes when we heard Austrian soldiers passing by on the other side. The sound of their voices disturbing the peace of the forest and our tranquil meditations was not a pleasant one. They passed very near to us, talking animatedly, no doubt about their chances of coming across us.

From the pine forest we moved to a house just outside Ravenna (I forget the name of the owner) where we were met with characteristic care and kindness. From Ravenna we were taken to Cervia and a farm run by a delightful man, whose benevolent expression has remained with me, although I have forgotten his name. We were there a couple of days before moving on to Forlì, and then set off towards the Apennines in the company of guides. We crossed out of the Romagna into Tuscany, where we encountered the same concern for our welfare and the same kindness. Her priests and all the disasters which have befallen her have divided Italy up, but she is destined to become one people. One Anastasio, I recall, welcomed us into his house in the mountains, and then we met a priest, a true guardian angel of the outlawed, who had sought us out in order to offer us a refuge in his home in Modigliana. This was Father Giovanni Verità and he was a true priest of Jesus Christ, not the figure used by the clergy to cover up their foul ways and errors, but the lawgiver and man of virtue. Whenever any Italian patriot outlawed by the Church found himself on the run in those parts, Father Giovanni made it his business to offer him protection and sustenance and ensured he was led out of harm's way. He had saved hundreds of men who had fled from the Romagna, where they had incurred the clergy's uncontrollable wrath, into Tuscany, where the Government was flawed, but still not as iniquitous as papal rule. I had met many such men who had been outlawed from the Romagna and all had praised this truly devout priest. We stayed with him for a couple of days; the widespread respect and affection in which he was held served to protect him and those to whom he offered his hospitality like a talisman. He himself then started to guide us over the Apennines, where the plan was to move from peak to peak to arrive at our final destination in the Sardinian states. One evening we had reached Filigare, where Father Giovanni left us a short distance outside the town while he went to look for a guide who could accompany us further. But a misunderstanding arose and we found ourselves separated from his company; he had sent us a guide but, perhaps because it was late at night and the man was sleepy, he got lost and arrived late. We entered the village, but Father Giovanni, impatient with the guide's delay in returning, had already left in order to find us himself and had taken a different road. Dawn was breaking and we found ourselves on the main road from Bologna to Florence.

44

We couldn't remain in such an exposed position so we decided to find a carriage and set off towards Florence, leaving, with much regret, the man who had up until then guided and protected us. So we went on along the main road and now in broad daylight. We came across a troop of Austrian soldiers marching from Florence to Bologna. We had to put a brave face on it and continued on towards the western slopes of the Apennines.

When we reached an inn on the left, our driver stopped and it seemed a good idea to get down and remain there a while, so we said goodbye to the driver, went into the inn and ordered some coffee. While we were waiting to be served, I sat down on a bench to the left of the door next to one of the long tables you find in inns. I was tired and had dozed off when Leggero tapped me on the shoulder to wake me and I raised my head to look into the not very benevolent faces of a number of Croats who had just burst into the inn. They may have belonged to the unit we had just encountered along the road or another one. I lowered my head again and pretended I had seen nothing. Once the inn was empty and we had drunk our coffee (the masters were served first), we left and crossed the road where we took refuge in a house belonging to some peasants. Once we had rested and taken our bearings we set off for Prato with the plan of reaching the border with Liguria from there. After marching for most of the day, we came to a valley where we found a kind of country inn and where we asked for a room for the night.

A young hunter from Prato was there: he seemed to know the place and its owners well. He had a decent appearance and a frank straightforward manner; his face had a kind of openness and directness about it which rarely deceives. I observed him for some time and made it clear that I wished to speak to him, and then approached him. After a few exchanges I told him who I was and I knew immediately that I had not been wrong to put my trust in him. He was moved when he heard my name and his eyes shone with eagerness to help me. He said: 'I'll go to Prato – it's a few miles off – and speak to some friends and then I'll come back here shortly.' And he was as good as his word. He soon returned and we followed him to Prato where his friends had arranged a carriage for us which would take us along the road to Empoli, Colle, etc., towards the Tuscan Maremma, where other trustworthy Italians would meet us and where we were likely to find a boat which could take us to the Ligurian coast.

Our journey from Prato to the Maremma was a truly strange one. We travelled mostly in a closed carriage, stopping every now and then to change horses; our halts in some places were very prolonged as the coachmen who were driving us were in much less of a hurry than we were to continue the journey, so the inquisitive had plenty of time to come up and take a look at the carriage. On occasion we had to get out and eat, taking care to conceal our faces and our unusual appearance. In the smaller places we naturally excited the curiosity of the idle who started to speculate on who we might be, ready to gossip about people they didn't know and who in those difficult times might be suspicious. In Colle – which is today a patriotic and enlightened place – we found ourselves surrounded by a throng of local people who showed every sign of distrusting and disliking our appearances which were such a contrast to those of the peaceable travellers they were used to seeing. But nothing occurred apart from some undignified verbal abuse which we obviously took care to ignore.

We reached our first real refuge when we got near the Maremma and were put up in the house of Dr Camillo Serafini in San Dalmazio. Serafini was a generous man and a true patriot, with a courage and imperturbability which were out of the ordinary. From there we transferred to the house of a certain Guelfi which was closer to the sea. In the meantime these generous friends were negotiating with a Genoese fisherman who could take us to Liguria, and one fine day several young men from the area carrying two-bore rifles, like the hunters we had known in Ravenna (and as keen and hardy and brave as they were too), came to Guelfi's house to find me. They gave us both a rifle like theirs and then guided us through the woods which lined the coast, a few miles to the east from the port of Follonica, where coal is loaded, in the bay of Sterlino. There a fishing boat was waiting for us. We embarked, touched by all the affection lavished on us by our young liberators. How proud I was to have been born in Italy, in this land of the dead, among people who – or so our neighbours say – have lost the ability to fight!

We sailed towards the island of Elba, where we had to take on board some equipment and provisions. We spent part of the day and one night in Porto Longone. Then sailing up the coast of Tuscany we reached the roadstead of Livorno, from where we continued in a westerly direction without stopping.

I was well aware that a frosty reception would be waiting for me from the Sardinian Government, and while we were in the roadstead at Livorno I thought of asking for asylum on board an English vessel which was anchored there. But the desire of seeing my children before I left Italy – for I knew I would not be allowed to stay – prevailed; in early September we landed safely in Porto Venere. This was followed by an uneventful journey on to Chiavari, where we were guests in the house of my late and dearly remembered cousin Bartolomeo Pucci, whose family celebrated our arrival, together with the town's sympathetic inhabitants and the many Lombards who had taken refuge there after the Battle of Novara. However, when General Lamarmora, who was the Royal Commissioner in Genoa, heard of my arrival, he ordered me to be transferred to the city escorted by a captain of the Carabinieri in civilian dress. I was not at all surprised by Lamarmora's reaction: it merely reflected the prevailing political view which made him the enemy of anyone, like me, who was tarred with republicanism.

I was shut up in a dungeon inside the ducal palace in Genoa, from where I was taken by night on board the war frigate *San Michele*, but I was treated with deference both by Lamarmora himself and by Persano, the gentlemanly commander of the frigate. I asked only to be allowed a day to go and see my children in Nice, after which I would return to be locked up in Genoa. My word was good enough for the General.

I was heartbroken when I saw my children, whom I would have to abandon for who knows how long. It is true that they were in good hands: my two sons were with my cousin Augusto Garibaldi, and my little Teresa was left with the Deiderys, who were like parents to her. I however had to go away indefinitely – yes, indefinitely, since I was asked to choose a place of exile. I decided on Tunis. My hope that my country would soon see better days led me to prefer somewhere nearby. An old childhood friend of mine from Nice, Castelli, lived in Tunis, as did Fedriani, a close friend of mine since 1834, who had been with me when I was first outlawed from Italy.

So I embarked for Tunis on the warship *Tripoli*, but the government there was under the control of the French and refused me entry. I was taken back and left on the island of Maddalena, just off Sardinia, where I remained for three weeks or so. From Maddalena I set out for Gibraltar on the brig *Colombo*, where the British Governor required me to leave within six days. I have always felt much affection for that generous nation, but I cannot hide my opinion that his decision was discourteous, unwarranted and unworthy. If a coward or a weakling had given such a kick to a man who was down, then it could have been borne with patience, but from a representative of the Government of Great Britain, the country which opened its arms to all, it was a bitter blow.

Exile

So I had to move on, even if that meant I had to throw myself in the sea. After talking with various friends I decided to cross the Straits of Gibraltar and seek refuge in Africa, from the Sardinian Consul in Tangiers, Giovanni Battista Carpenetti. He welcomed me and my two companions Leggero and Coccelli into his house, where we stayed for six months.

In Modigliana I had come across a benevolent priest, and now in Tangiers I found a royal consul who was generous and honest. I am profoundly grateful to both men. It goes to show that the old proverb which warns us not to judge men by the clothes they wear is true and that the categoric exclusions which certain people practise are mistaken. It is difficult to find perfection among humankind: let us try to be good; let us teach the masses, as far as we can, the principles of justice and truth; let us fight theocracy and tyranny, the embodiments of lies and evil, whatever form they take – but let us show compassion towards our own cruel human race, which among its other merits has the ability to generate one half of itself made up of emperors, kings, policemen and priests, who appear to be born with all the attributes of torturers for the glory and the good of the rest of us.

My life in Tangiers was tranquil and contented as far as it could be for a man exiled from his country and from his family. We went hunting at least twice a week and always caught plenty of game; a friend then lent me a small fishing smack and we went on trips along the coast, where the fish is also plentiful. My solitary and savage way of life was occasionally lightened by Mr Murray the British Vice-Consul and his hospitality. And so I whiled away six months, which were as serene as the previous six months had been stormy.

My Italian friends had not forgotten me, however. Francesco Carpanetto, who had, from the time of my return to Italy in 1848, showered me with favours and kindnesses, now proposed getting friends and acquaintances to contribute to a fund which would pay for the building of a ship which I could then captain, so enabling me to earn my own living. Such a project much appealed to me. I was unable to do anything in furtherance of my political mission; as a merchant seaman I could earn my own living and no longer be a burden on the generous man I was staying with. So I immediately accepted Francesco's proposal and got ready to go to the United States of America, where the purchase of the ship would go through. In June 1850 I left for Gibraltar, from where I sailed for Liverpool and then on to New York. For much of the crossing over the Atlantic I suffered a very bad attack of rheumatism and had to be carried off the ship like a trunk when we got to Staten Island. The rheumatic pains stayed with me for a couple of months, which time I spent partly on Staten Island and partly in New York itself, as a guest of my dear friend Michele Pastacaldi, in whose house I also enjoyed the company of the celebrated Eleuterio Foresti, who had suffered at the hands of the Austrians in the Spielberg prison.[15]

Carpanetto's plan couldn't be carried out because there were not enough contributions. He had sold three subscriptions of ten thousand lire each to the two Camozzi brothers in Bergamo and to Piazzoni – but what ship could you buy in America with thirty thousand lire? Maybe just a small coaster. As I was not an American citizen I would have had to take on as a captain someone who was, and that wasn't acceptable.

I had to do something. A Florentine friend of mine, Antonio Meucci, set up a candle factory and asked me to help him with the business. I accepted as soon as he suggested it. I couldn't have any financial interest in the business since I had no money (the thirty thousand lire had remained in Italy since it was not enough to buy a ship in America), and so I agreed to help in whatever way I could. I worked for Meucci for several months; although I was his employee he treated me with great kindness like one of his family. Yet one day I was tired of making candles and led by a restlessness which was part of my nature, I left the factory in search of other work. My seafaring days came back to me; I knew a few words of English and so I went down to the shores of the island, where I found several coasters busy loading and unloading cargoes. I went up to the first and asked to be taken on as a sailor; none of the crew working on the boat gave me so much as a glance and just carried on with their tasks. So I went to a second ship and asked again and got the same lack of response. Finally I tried another boat where they were unloading: 'May I help you with your work?' and got the answer that they didn't need extra men. 'But I'm not asking for charity,' I insisted. No reply. 'I just want to work to warm up a bit' (indeed it was snowing). Still no response. I was mortified. My thoughts returned to the days when I had commanded the fleet and the army – the ever-renowned army – in Montevideo. What good was that? I was surplus to requirements.

I swallowed my resentment and returned to work at the candle factory. It was fortunate I had not told my good-natured employer Meucci I wanted to leave; it meant that my disappointment was entirely private and so less irksome. I must add that it was not his behaviour towards me which had caused me to act in the way I did; he and his wife Ester always treated me with benevolence and kindness.

At last my friend Francesco Carpanetto arrived in New York. In Genoa he had started up a large business concern involving Central America. The *San Giorgio* – a ship he owned – had left Genoa with part of its cargo, and Carpanetto had then gone to England to prepare the rest of the cargo and send it on to Gibraltar, where the ship would pick it up. We agreed that I should accompany him to Central America and we got ready to go. In 1851 we set out on a journey to Chagres on an American steamship. From Chagres we travelled on in an American yacht to San Juan del Norte and there we took a piragua or canoe. We sailed up the River San Juan as far as Lake Nicaragua, crossed the lake and finally reached Granada, the busiest port on the lake. I travelled under the assumed name of Giuseppe Pane, which I had already used in 1834, to avoid curiosity and police harassment.

Carpanetto's business affairs depended on the arrival of the *San Giorgio* in Lima and he planned to travel on to that city to await the ship. So we returned to San Juan del Norte, went back to Chagres and then travelled up the River Cruz as far as Panama. During this voyage I was afflicted by a terrible fever which is endemic in that climate and in that marshy country. It struck me down like a thunderbolt: I have never been so ill in my life and if I hadn't had the luck to find some excellent Italians, including the two Monti brothers in Panama, and various kind-hearted Americans, I do not believe I would have recovered. Carpanetto too looked after me like a brother.

At Panama I embarked on an English steamship which would take us to Lima. The sea air was like a balm and gave me new strength.

At Lima we found the *San Giorgio* waiting for us and I received a very warm welcome from the wealthy and generous Italian community there, especially from the Sciutto, Denegri and Malagrida families. Pietro Denegri gave me the command of the 400-ton ship *Carmen* for a voyage to China. I set off shortly afterwards for the islands of Cincia to the south of Lima, where we took on supplies of guano destined for China; then I went back to Callao to make final preparations for the long journey. On the tenth of January 1852 we set sail for Canton. It took us ninety-three days to get there and we had favourable winds all the way. We sailed within sight of the Sandwich Islands and entered the China Sea between Luzon and Formosa in the Philippines. Once in Canton my shipping agent sent me on to Amoy since we didn't succeed in selling the guano in Canton. I returned to Canton: the return cargo was not ready so I went to Manila with various goods. Once I was back in Canton the ship's masts had to be replaced as well as the copper plating on the keel; when the cargo was ready we set out back to Lima. We sailed through the Indian Ocean and came out from the Indian archipelago through the Lombok Strait. We had had some problems entering the straits since the south-west monsoon was still active. Once in the Indian Ocean, a few parallels off beyond the straits, we met a steady east wind. We tacked to the left and continued like this as far as the fortieth parallel of southern latitude, where we met a west wind and sailed on through the Bass Strait between Australia and Van Diemen's Land. In this strait we landed on one of the Hunter Islands to take on fresh supplies of water. Here we found a group of buildings which had just been abandoned by an Englishman and his wife after his partner had died, as we learnt from a board put up over his tomb which also gave a brief history of the colony. The inscription read: 'The couple were afraid to remain alone in this deserted island and left it to move to Van Diemen's Land'. The main building in the settlement was a small one-storey house, not elegant but comfortable. A lot of work had gone into its construction; inside there were tables, beds, chairs, etc. It was certainly not luxurious, but it all had that air of ease and comfort which comes naturally to the English. There was an orchard, which was the most useful discovery for us, since we found fresh potatoes and other vegetables of which we took large supplies.

Desert island, how often has my imagination dwelt with delight on you, whenever I have been weary of civilised society, adorned with all its priests and its police; how often the image of your charming bay has floated into my mind's eye, where on first landing I was greeted by a flock of partridges, and where we slaked our thirst from a sparklingly clear stream murmuring through a woodland of centuries-old trees, and where we collected abundant water for the voyage back.

From the Bass Strait we sailed between New Zealand and Lord Auckland Land and then headed for the west coast of America. In the last few days of the voyage our provisions started to run out and as a precaution the crew were put on short rations. When we arrived in Lima we unloaded the cargo and then left in ballast for Valparaiso; once there, the *Carmen* was hired to transport copper from Chile up to Boston; we called at various ports along the Chilean coast (Coquimbo, Guasco, Herradura) and filled up the cargo in the hold with wool on top of the copper in Islay (Peru). From here we travelled south round the Cape Horn and after an extremely stormy journey through the high latitudes we arrived in Boston. In Boston I was ordered to go to New York, where I got a letter from the *Carmen*'s owner complaining about certain matters; I felt that I was being blamed unfairly so I left the ship. I stayed on for a few more days in New York in the company of my good friends Foresti, Avezzana and Pastacaldi; during this time Captain Figari arrived in the port intending to buy a ship and offered me the captaincy on its voyage back to Europe. I accepted and went with him to Baltimore where he bought the *Commonwealth*. We loaded a cargo of flour and grain and set off for London, which we reached in February 1854. From London we went to Newcastle to load coal for Genoa; we were in the Italian port on the tenth of May. I was ill again with rheumatism and was taken to the house of my friend in the city Captain Paolo Augier, who looked after me with great kindness for a fortnight. Then I travelled on to Nice, where I was finally able to embrace my children again after an exile of five years. During the period between my arrival in Genoa in May 1854 and my departure in February 1859 for the Italian mainland from the island of Caprera – where I had acquired a small property – there is nothing of interest to relate. I spent the time in seafaring and in cultivating my land on Caprera.

Return to Political Life

In February 1859 I was asked by La Farina, acting as an intermediary for Count Cavour[16], to go to Turin. The Sardinian Government was at that time in negotiations with France and disposed to declare war on Austria, and wished to win the support of the Italian people. Manin, Pallavicino and other distinguished Italians were trying to reconcile our democratic political vision with the Savoy dynasty in order to achieve, by bringing most of the national forces together, the dream of so many enlightened Italians down the centuries: the unification of our country.

Count Cavour, then all powerful, was of the opinion that I had retained some prestige among the Italian people and so called me to the capital. He found me a very willing listener to his idea of going to war with Italy's centuries-old enemy. It is true that I was less convinced by the ally he had chosen – but there was nothing to be done, it had to be accepted. It was hard to swallow, but it must be admitted: with France as an ally we would cheerfully go to war; without the French, we wouldn't even think of it. Such was the view of most of these degenerate descendants of a great nation – and all because they did not know – or did not wish to know – how to exploit the national resources which were just waiting to be used.

Cavour was the only member of the Government I saw in Turin. The idea of joining with the Piedmontese to go to war on Austria was not new to me – nor was the need to suppress my convictions for the sake of uniting Italy whatever that took This was what we had set out to achieve when we left Montevideo, and when I was told on Caprera of Manin and Pallavicino's fine idea of joining Victor Emmanuel to unify the country, I was of the same opinion. Was this not the same idea which had inspired Dante, Machiavelli, Petrarch and many others among our great men? I can declare with pride that I was and I remain republican; yet at the same time I have never believed the republican system to be the only possible one, which has if necessary to be imposed by force on the majority. In a free country where the virtuous majority of the people freely wish to live in a republic, then in those circumstances it is certainly the best political system. If I had to give my vote of allegiance as I had to in Rome in 1849, I would always give it to the republic, and I would always seek to convince the masses that this was the right thing to do. Yet the time today (1859) is not yet ripe for a republican system, either because our society is still too corrupt or because present-day monarchies have managed to ensure their own survival, and so, when the opportunity came for the nationalist forces working together with those of the monarchy to unite the country, then I gave the plan my unswerving support.

After staying a few days in Turin where the news of my presence would encourage Italian volunteers to enlist, I immediately saw the kind of people I was dealing with and what was wanted of me. I was pained but I had to accept the situation as the lesser of two evils: I may not have been able to achieve everything I wanted, but I could at least do something for my unhappy country. Garibaldi was to make a brief appearance – to be around, and yet not be around. The volunteers had to know that he was in Turin to enlist them, but he also had to live in hiding so as not to cast any shadow over continuing diplomatic negotiations. What a predicament! Volunteers, as many as possible, were to be enlisted, but only the smallest number – those who were least ready to fight – would be entrusted to my command. The volunteers were racing to join up, but they were not supposed to see me.

Two depots were formed at Cuneo and Savigliano, while I was relegated to Rivoli on the road to Susa. The task of directing and organising the troops was given to General Cialdini. Cosenz was given command of those at Cuneo while Medici went to Savigliano: both of them distinguished officers who formed the first and second regiments as the proud nucleus of the Cacciatori delle Alpi[17]. There was also a third volunteer regiment at Savigliano under Arduino, but on account of its commander this was not so effective.

A recruitment board had been set up at Turin to select the strongest and fittest young men between the ages of eighteen and twenty-six for the regular front-line troops. Those who were too young or too old or not up to standard were sent to the volunteer corps. As far as the officers were concerned a more straightforward procedure was followed and most of the men I proposed as officers were accepted. They were not all graduates of the military academy, but almost all of them lived up to my expectations and showed themselves worthy of the cause for which they were fighting.

In those early days several plans of action were drawn up by the Government. One was that I should be sent to fight on the borders of the Duchies of Parma and Piacenza and Modena and Reggio. If acted on, such a plan would have produced great results, but the idea was soon dropped doubtless because they did not want to run the risk of the local inhabitants joining up and increasing the number of volunteers under my command. They decided to send me to operate on the far left flank of the armies. I was still pleased to think that I would see Lombardy again and its fine people who had suffered so much under the yoke of foreign tyranny.

From the outset I was promised the frontier troops (and I don't think they meant the military guards). I was also promised several battalions of bersaglieri. However, it was far too many men, and I was never given any of these. On the contrary, seeing that an excessively large number of volunteers was joining up, General Ulloa was asked to form a separate division known as the Cacciatori degli Appennini; he was supposed to join me, but I saw nothing of him until the very end of the war. General Lamarmora, the Minister for War, had always been against the formation of volunteer forces and refused to recognise my officers, so that in order to give their rank some legal status we had to circumvent His Excellency and get warrants signed by the Ministry for Internal Affairs.

I put up with all this in silence: the important thing was to fight for our fellow-Italians against their oppressors.

The political situation was increasingly tense and Austria's arrogant behaviour showed that the open conflict we sought was near. The supply of arms to the volunteers was therefore given some priority and Cialdini spent time organising them. When the Austrians invaded Piedmont we were still not in a state of complete readiness, although we were always willing enough to march against them come what may.

We were to head for Brusasco on the right bank of the Po, and on the far right of Cialdini's division which had been entrusted with the defence of the Dora Baltea line. We were to defend the road that led from Brusasco to Turin. The ministry had had several cannon sent to the old castle in Varrone in order to control the road from Vercelli to Turin, or so it was said. I received orders to occupy and defend this position, which would have blocked my movements had the enemy advanced.

Several days passed at Brusasco, Brozolo, Pontestura. Those first marches helped to break the men in. We used our various halts for military exercises, to get the soldiers used to the different requirements of defending an outpost, of patrolling, etc.

Cialdini was then called to the defence of Casale and we were ordered to join him. On a reconnoitring sortie from Casale, we sighted the Austrian forces for the first time. The enemy made a mock attack on the outer positions of the town; under Medici's command the second regiment charged them and drove them off, giving them a taste of what the Cacciatori delle Alpi could do. A short while before the attack I had been called to see the King in his headquarters at San Salvatore. He welcomed me with kindliness and instructed me to go and defend the capital Turin against the possibility of a surprise attack by the enemy on the city; once the danger of an attack had passed, I was to move and harass the enemy troops on their right flank. So I returned towards Turin as far as Chiavasso. The King's written orders had also specified that I was to muster under my command all the volunteers who had remained behind in the various depots together with the regiment of the Cacciatori degli Appennini. I wrote to Cavour about the Cacciatori joining me, but he ignored the King's orders and fobbed me off with excuses to avoid sending me the men. My conviction grew that he wanted to limit the number of men under my command – the old ruse which Sobrero had tried in Milan in 1848 as well as Campello in Rome when he decreed that my legion should not exceed five hundred. Cavour wanted to limit me to three thousand. The three regiments were made up of six battalions, each of six hundred men, making a total of 3,600, but this number had been reduced to three thousand by the time we crossed the Ticino, because of the long stay in the depots and the marches which these young soldiers were not accustomed to.

The King – who, despite the basic fault of being a king, which made him responsible for a great deal of wrongdoing, was nevertheless no worse than many of the men who surrounded him in 1859 – ordered us again to march towards Lake Maggiore and take up a position on the enemy's right flank. No doubt the government clique around him was not pleased, but I was: I was free to move, and this was an invaluable asset. So I bade farewell to that brave old man General Cialdini, for whom I felt a real affection, and marched on to Chiavasso and from there to Biella. The people there gave my men a fervent welcome which was a good omen. We stayed a couple of days in the town and then went on to Gattinara. The enemy in Novara had heard I was moving in that direction and sent a small band of soldiers to cut off the ferry crossing on the River Sesia, but a patrol I had sent there to guard it fired at them and prevented their taking it. We crossed the river and marched on towards Borgomanero, where I made preparations for our passage across the Ticino river. At Castelletto we found barges ready on the river beneath the town; I made the second regiment under Medici cross over while the rest remained on the right bank. The crossing went off well, although it was difficult to steer the boats to the same point on the other side, as they were all carrying a lot of men and were heavy. Some were carried quite far downstream by the currents and there was some delay in reuniting the regiment on the Lombard bank of the river. At last we set off marching for Sesto Calende, where we arrested some of the people in charge and some guards and took possession of the harbour, where the rest of the brigade crossed over. I believe it was the seventeenth of May 1859.[18]

We were at last in Lombardy – and within sight of the power which had been building up its army for ten years to the point where it thought it could take what it had failed to take at Novara[19] without the risk of defeat. No doubt they dreamed of grasping the entire peninsula in their talons. There were three thousand of us and our baggage was light, since we had left the baggage train behind in Biella. The carts too had been left behind in Piedmont except for a few to carry our munitions. We also had some mules while our indefatigable chief field-surgeon Bertani had organised the ambulance.

From Sesto Calende I marched overnight with the troops to Varese. Bixio with his battalion set off along the shores of Lake Maggiore in the direction of Laveno, where his instructions were to stop on the road which led from there to Varese. De Cristoforis stayed in Sesto with his company to keep our lines of communication open with Piedmont; this valiant officer was the first to engage the enemy, just as he had been at Casale. The Austrians, who knew we were at Sesto, sent a large detachment on reconnaissance and found De Cristoforis and his men there. That valiant man did not stop to count the enemy numbers, but fought them with determination; after putting up a brave fight, he fell back towards Bixio's battalion – according to plan, since I knew it would be impossible to hold this very important position with so few troops. The Austrians showed their usual caution, however, and didn't take the town, withdrawing back towards Milan instead.

While this was taking place, the local people were beginning to rouse themselves, but there was no hope that they would rise up in one decisive and conclusive insurrection: they had been deceived too many times before and had suffered too much. The more energetic young men of the region were for the most part either in the Austrian army, enlisted in our regular forces, in exile, or among our volunteer troops. But they gave us a warm welcome, made every effort to meet our requirements and gave us information about the enemy's movements as well as acting as our guides when we needed this. The excellent women of the region were zealous in looking after our wounded.

It is hard to give a just account of the welcome we received at Varese when we arrived there the night after our crossing of the Ticino. It was teeming with rain, yet I am sure that every single person in the city – man, woman and child – turned out to receive us. To see the local inhabitants embracing the soldiers in delirious delight was the most moving sight. The whole city was bursting with enthusiasm and friendship; it had declared its colours and we would be obliged to defend it. Three thousand men against an immense Austrian army, however, are not much of a defence; moreover, in staying to protect the city, we lost the freedom to move rapidly and secretly, which was our best asset on the enemy's flank. Varese has some strongholds, such as Biumo, and if these had been fortified the city could have been defended from larger forces. We put up barricades at the main gates and armed some of the citizens with weapons they themselves had taken off the enemy.

Urban was in charge of the troops now heading to destroy us. The first news I got – enough to make anyone quake with fear – was that he was in command of forty thousand troops and advancing on Varese from Brescia. There were troops at Laveno and another corps coming from Milan. On the morning of the twenty-fifth of May, just after dawn, we saw the enemy column advancing on the city from the road which led to Como. I had sent Captain Nicolò Suzini and his company about a mile out of Varese to a building in the surrounding countryside which overlooked the road and from where he could stage an ambush; with great skill he engaged the enemy as they advanced, firing on them at short range, before retreating to our right. After this initial obstacle, Urban drew up his column of attack along the road; led by a few lines of marskmen it charged on our left. Our soldiers, who were stationed there in the positions we had previously prepared, met and repulsed the enemy with the sangfroid of veteran fighters; I sent two companies from the first regiment to support them. The encounter didn't last long: after firing at them point-blank, the brave Cacciatori of the second regiment, urged on by Medici and Sacchi, leapt out of their shelters and charged the Austrians with their bayonets, pushing them back down the road along which they'd advanced, although a good deal more quickly.

I guessed that the enemy's attack would not be confined to our left wing; in accordance with all the strategic rules for attacking a position like Varese, a simulated attack could be carried out on the main road to the left, but the main body of the troops should come in the opposite direction, from the high ground around Biumo to the north. However, Urban chose to take the bull by the horns – all the better for us, since it meant that, with our limited numbers, we were not distracted by a number of attacks on several sides as well as from the direction of Milan where considerable numbers of enemy troops were present. From the vantage point of Biumo, where I had set up my general headquarters, I had a perfect view of all the enemy's movements as well as our own; I sent Captain Simonetta (whom I could rely on to do a thorough job) with his guides to explore the area to the north behind me. Once I was certain that there was only to be the attack on our left wing, I came down from Biumo and ordered our soldiers to follow the enemy movements, while the rest of the brigade were to follow in good order. The enemy, along with the two pieces of artillery it had used to attack Varese escorted by a cavalry platoon, kept stopping at any new position but then retreated whenever we appeared – although it is a hard task, without cannon or cavalry, to pursue a fully equipped enemy. They only turned round to confront us once they had reached San Salvatore, beyond Malnate. A fierce gun battle took place, in which the Genoese carabinieri particularly distinguished themselves, with the enemy on one side of a ravine overhanging the road and our men on the other. More men were wounded in this confrontation than in the first since the enemy had the dominant position and were hidden by dense forest. Their advantageous position and their superior firing power made them overconfident: they sent an infantry unit to advance on our left, who charged us and managed to drive us some way back. But we had taken control of a farmstead which dominated that part of the battlefield: the men holding it saw reserves coming up and charged the enemy infantry with such force that they were driven down into the ravine and didn't appear again.

The enemy's position on the side of the ravine overlooking the road was a formidably strong one. To launch a frontal attack would have been foolhardy; instead I tried to find a way of getting round. This was not out of the question: we held the farmstead on our left; under its protection we could cross over the upper part of the ravine and come upon the enemy on their right, without their being able to do anything to stop us. I had decided on this course of action when, like a bolt out of the blue, I was told the news that a large enemy column was marching on our left towards Varese. I was truly mortified: could it be that Urban's retreat had been a trap? I was so angry at the thought that I immediately ordered Colonel Cosenz, who was in command of the reserve forces, to march on the city and defend it at all costs. With the brigade I marched towards the left in order to deceive the enemy, who couldn't know for certain if we intended to circumvent them. When we had reached an area concealed by the mountain, we turned left along a path that led to Malnate, where the men were gathering to march on Varese as quickly as possible.

I had been taken aback by the news that an enemy column was still marching towards Varese. The column had been sighted not just by peasants and soldiers in the rank and file, but superior officers had seen it too. Finally we were told that it had reached Varese – whereupon nothing more was heard about it. The enthusiastic acclamations which greeted our return to Malnate drove the mirage away like some black mist.

We gathered up our casualties together with those of the enemy and sent them to Varese. Justice would have been on our side if we had made the prisoners pay the price for the blood of our former companions who'd been murdered by the Austrians: Ciceruacchio, Ugo Bassi and many others; but they were looked after well, perhaps even better than our own men.

So we marched back to Varese in order to take a much needed rest. This had been the first battle for the Cacciatori delle Alpi, and they had outshone all expectations: young and untried as they were, they had fought a regular army which had been trained to despise Italians and in every engagement they had put them to flight. I was much encouraged by this first victory.

In terms of actual numbers, our losses were comparatively negligible, but they were nonetheless significant and painful, when one considered the type of individual we had lost. Most of the men I commanded were not merely from distinguished and cultivated families – that is the lesser consideration, since all social classes are called upon to pay their debt to their motherland – but their ranks also included celebrated artists who had enlisted as ordinary soldiers.

None of the wounded complained; the only cry that could be heard from those under the surgeon's knife was 'Long live Italy!'. When a people reaches this point, it is time for the Pope with his tiara, the foreign bullies and the domestic tyrants to pack their bags and leave.

I knew how important it was to attack an enemy, however strong, which had been shaken by an initial setback, and I did not want to lose the opportunity. So on the morning of the twenty-seventh of May we set out towards Como. Shortly after midday we arrived in Cavallasco, which was on the way. The men had had a long march and were tired, but the time was right: with night coming on, it was possible to attack even superior enemy forces at reduced risk, especially in the kind of mountainous terrain where our battles were going to take place and where the enemy's cavalry and artillery would have little effect.

So I allowed the men to rest, while I began to gather all the information I could on the enemy's position, the number of their troops, etc. In this way I learnt that a large number of their forces had occupied the stronghold of San Fermo: this therefore was the key to all the others, and I dispatched some companies under the command of Captain Cenni to encircle the enemy position on its right. Once these units had taken up their position, the second regiment would make a frontal attack. At the appointed time, Colonel Medici bravely charged from the front, while Cenni attacked the enemy's flank. The enemy fought back hard and courageously. They held a strong and dominant position, securely enclosed. The combat lasted for about an hour, after which, surrounded on all sides, the Austrians started to fall back and retreat. Some of them surrendered.

This first rapid success gave us control of all the key positions – an important gain because large Austrian reinforcements were on their way from Camerlata and Como to support their detachments in the mountains. The enemy had been beaten back, but in mountainous terrain they could always find a position to hold and defend against our soldiers, who were pursuing them too closely. The lie of the land also prevented us from getting an unimpeded view of the battlefield; often the sound of gunfire was the only sign that our men and the enemy were fighting on another part of the field. The large reserve forces of the enemy could be seen drawn up in formation on the plain below, together with twelve artillery pieces which they were unable to use.

After the battle and with night coming on I managed to unite our scattered troops and without delay set off down the zigzag road which led to Como. As we advanced the enemy retreated. We stopped in San Vito – one of the outlying villages – for news, but the inhabitants had taken fright and left. So we decided to go on and enter Como.

Here too the people were frightened; since it was dark, they had not been able to make out whose forces were invading the city and kept their doors and windows firmly shut. But when they recognised us by our speech and our accents as Italians – their fellow-countrymen – the scene which took place would have been worth seeing in broad daylight. In an instant lights came on all over the town, the inhabitants flocked to the windows and filled the streets. All the church bells were set ringing with a deafening noise – the enemy in retreat must have been terrified. The people went wild: men, women and children threw themselves on the soldiers with delirious hugs and tears and shouts. The few men on horseback at the head of the column had to hold on tight to prevent themselves being pulled off, especially by the young women of the place, who seemed to think that their beauty gave them the right to do what they liked with their liberators and fellow-countrymen!

There was no definite news to be had about the whereabouts of the enemy. Some said they were in one place and others elsewhere; there were rumours they were marching towards Camerlata. As it turned out, they were leaving as we were entering the town; they did not feel secure enough at Camerlata and so had continued on to Milan, in much disarray, leaving behind them in the depots in Camerlata an abundant supply of provisions and arms.

My poor valiant Cacciatori bedded down in the streets and squares of Como; they were exhausted and with good reason: they had left Varese in the morning, had marched all day, and then fought a battle, after which they had gone on marching half through the night – a prodigious achievement for young men unaccustomed to the rigours of marching. Their patriotic zeal was the only thing which kept them going. I had done it as a veteran, however. After organising barricades on the road leading out of the town towards Camerlata and casting an affectionate look on my weary companions stretched out in the open, I accepted an invitation to take a brief rest myself, if I remember rightly in the house belonging to the Rovelli family.

The enemy had been hit hard: fighting a series of battles at night in mountainous terrain it is likely that many of their men had been dispersed and that they were demoralised. This turned out to be true. And yet they had 9,000 men, twelve pieces of artillery, a decent number of cavalry, while we had less than 3,000 soldiers, only a few guides with horses, and not one single cannon. Moreover, Como was in a valley surrounded by mountains. If the enemy had any initiative, I thought anything could happen on the following day. My sleep was cut short by such worries; I rode out at dawn towards Camerlata to try to obtain news of the enemy forces. I was pleased to find out that they had already left the place: my men were too tired to face another battle that day. So we entered and occupied the village; my men were able to rest for the whole day, much to their satisfaction.

The fact that we held Como meant that we now received reinforcements of every kind – of money, men and arms. The muni-cipalities together with the captains willingly handed over the local steamers to us; with these, we could control the whole of the Verbano region. All the towns and villages around the lake had come out in support of us. There was a general call for arms in aid of the national cause, since weapons and especially ammunition, which we had used up in the battles we had fought, were in very short supply. We were moreover a long way from our base in Piedmont and communications were almost completely cut. A few courageous and patriotic individuals managed to get news out of Piedmont, but it would be difficult if not impossible to get supplies of arms and ammunition. So the idea occurred to me to move off again in the direction of Lake

Maggiore and at the same time attempt to take control of Laveno. The Cacciatori delle Alpi found themselves once more back on the road from Como to Varese.

I sent that brave and resolute officer Major Bixio on ahead (like Cosenz and Medici, he was one of the men I could rely on completely to carry out their duty) to observe Laveno. He didn't go ahead to lead the attack on the town, however, since when I got there it was suggested that the land attack could be reinforced from the lake; so I moved Bixio, who was an experienced sea captain as well as being a fine soldier, to take command of this part of the operation.

We didn't stay long in Varese and continued on towards Gavirate, spacing out the brigade on the road between Gavirate and Laveno. I could have attacked the town at night with all my troops, but I learnt that Urban was in pursuit at the head of much increased forces, and I certainly did not want to engage all my men in an attack on Laveno when I had a strong enemy coming up behind me. So I limited myself to a partial attack: two companies from the first regiment under Captains Bronzetti and Landi would carry it out. Marrocchetti with the rest of the battalion and Cosenz with the rest of the regiment would lend support if necessary. In the meantime, two small mountain howitzers and two small cannon arrived, brought by the brave Captain Griziotti.

The attack on Laveno did not succeed. Landi led the assault, and with about twenty men entered the fort at about one in the morning, but the rest of the company did not follow and, as he had been seriously wounded, he was forced to evacuate. Bronzetti had been given wrong directions by the guides and didn't arrive in time to support Landi. Our men were driven back into the open and the enemy behind their parapets could easily target them. If the rest of Landi's men had followed up his initial assault and he had been joined by Bronzetti's company, we could have occupied and held the fort. Once we were in possession both of the fort and of the steamers on the lake I could have taken Laveno without any problem and so re-established communications with Piedmont.

So the attack on the fort didn't come off and the attack from the lake also failed to take place because Bixio couldn't persuade the coastguards on the Piedmontese shore to go across with him. We had to start thinking of retreat. When the enemy realised at dawn that our attack had failed it started up a tremendous bombardment against the companies and the reserves in retreat. Uninterrupted fire was directed on us from the forts and the warships, as if they wanted to take revenge for the fright we had given them during the night. They fired rockets – the Austrians' favourite toy and a useless device which has never in my experience succeeded in harming man or beast – in overwhelming quantities.

There is a wooded hill to the south of Laveno, from which there is a perfect view of the town and its harbour. I had sent our small artillery corps up there. They were able to drive back the Austrians' steamers and enable us to make our retreat in good order.

That evening I learnt with much annoyance that Urban had retaken Varese. I was cut off from Como: there was no time to lose. We advanced rapidly through the Valcuvia and crossed the Valganna. At the end of the valley we came within sight of Varese, and with the vanguard arrived beneath the upper town of Biumo. Night was falling: we could launch an attack on the enemy without much risk. If things went against us we could fall back on the strong positions in the Valganna. From the mountains to the north of Varese which overlook the city I had been able to observe the enemy's positions. Their forces were large, although not as numerous as the locals believed – no fewer than twelve to fifteen thousand. I could make out their artillery which they had sited, as was to be expected, in the most dominant positions.

I had a strong desire to attack Urban and liberate Varese, but at the same time I knew that he was capable of taking revenge on the people of the town for the defeats we had inflicted on him. I decided not to attack and to lead the brigade back to Como.

There was an Austrian detachment at Malnate, so we couldn't take the main road from Varese to Como. We had to follow a more mountainous route, but led by some skilful guides which the Podestà[20] of Arcisate arranged for us and despite a torrential downpour of rain which never stopped, we were able to get through. My young companions thus had to endure another test of their fortitude and courage. We passed near to Malnate, but the storm was so bad there was no danger of coming across Austrian scouts. The column had become very stretched out and on one occasion I tried to halt the head of it so the others could catch up, but it was unthinkable – only by marching could my men get some protection from the rain and from the cold. It was a long and hard march: only with the utmost difficulty, especially for the rear of the column and the carts, did we manage to get across some of the most swollen streams and torrents.

We finally reached Como, where we were welcomed by the inhabitants with their usual kindness and where we soon forgot the dangers and discomforts we had experienced. We had arrived in time, since the town was increasingly anxious that we were so far off. The Austrians and the priests had spread all sorts of lying rumours of enemy forces massing in every direction. The town authorities had withdrawn onto the lake, as had some companies which I had left in the town before leaving for Laveno. The wounded too had been transferred with some difficulty to Menaggio. All this had frightened the townspeople; if the enemy had appeared in the short period we were absent, Como would certainly have fallen again to the Austrians.

I learnt all this from a courageous and beautiful young woman who appeared like a vision before me in a carriage on the road to Varese, while I was marching with the brigade to attack Urban's troops in the town. She had left Como to find me, to let me know the condition the town found itself in, and to implore my return.

Once in Como, and with the enthusiastic help of the inhabitants, we started to erect defences on all the dominant positions in the town and its surroundings. But then the battle which was fought at Magenta[21] changed the situation completely. The victory electrified the public and made our circumstances a lot easier and Urban's much more difficult – if we had had a few thousand men more we could have forced him to surrender. But the brigade had no more than two thousand men who were fit to fight, and I could not risk an engagement which might result in our defeat by issuing forth onto the road that a far larger enemy would take. I did not intend to remain idle, however: I decided that we should undertake operations on the line between Lecco, Bergamo and Brescia: this terrain would be more suitable for our kind of fighting and for our now limited numbers. Part of the brigade began to embark on the steamers bound for Lecco. While this was going ahead I received a message from General Fanti asking me to operate, if possible, in conjunction with his troops against Urban. I don't know who was responsible for this communication, but I never saw the messenger nor was I asked to send a reply, so I continued to move towards Bergamo, leaving the allied forces to go in pursuit of Urban, who was now retreating towards Monza and the River Adda.

From Lecco we marched to Bergamo, where we found the Austrians. We captured an enemy officer who had been going round extorting 12,000 *zwanzigers* from the local inhabitants with the threat of destroying their houses if they didn't comply – the usual courteous behaviour we had come to expect from these kindhearted masters who are always ready to put their threats into force. This time they were paid in the same coin Camillus used to pay the Gauls in Rome – with steel.[22]

As we approached Bergamo in the early morning we heard from the citizens that the enemy was abandoning the city, but we couldn't march fast enough to catch them up. We entered the town, where we found cannon and ammunition, although the enemy had tried to destroy everything. A curious incident occurred shortly after we had taken control of the town: news arrived from the local railway station that a contingent of one thousand men was leaving Milan to reinforce the Austrian occupation of the town. I assembled the brigade round the station, hiding the men in ditches and in houses and at the best vantage points in the surrounding area. The news was true: a train carrying Austrian troops was on its way – but they were warned by a signalman at Seriate, two miles away, that we were in possession of the town. They halted in Seriate, uncertain what to do. Bronzetti and his company had been sent to reconnoitre in the area; they boldly charged the enemy – ten times larger – and put them to flight.

We did not stay long in Bergamo. We heard that the enemy were extorting money from the towns and villages in the plain below and so we marched down to protect the poor inhabitants from such threats. Then we made our way towards Palazzolo, where I had sent Cosenz and his regiment on ahead. Once we were there I heard that the enemy was on the road from Brescia, so we hurried on; the town had already been evacuated but, since the enemy was still in the vicinity, feared a reoccupation. They had sent messengers to me with news of the situation, asking me, on behalf of all the citizens, to come to them. My poor Cacciatori had arrived at Palazzolo completely worn out after so many forced marches, but I knew that with their enthusiasm they would not let me down. I asked the officers if they thought the men were capable of continuing on to Brescia that very same night, and with one voice those champions exclaimed 'To Brescia! On to Brescia!' By eleven at night, they were on their way with their usual gaiety and non-chalance, heedless as ever of discomfort and fatigue. Cacciatori delle Alpi! My young and brave companions! Now, as I write this account of you, the only token of my affection which I can offer, you are beset by the fault-finding and envy of those who did nothing or almost nothing for Italy while you acted like true patriots for your country!

On the road between Palazzolo and Brescia we came across the enemy. If we had attacked them our arrival in Brescia would have been delayed, and, in any case, there was scant possibility of victory against a much larger force. So we had to avoid them by taking another road to the left, in good conditions and not much longer than the one we were on. The inhabitants knew we were arriving and sent out transport for those who were too tired to continue marching. On the following morning we reached the town, where we found the entire populace gathered to welcome us, just as they had at Bergamo, but with something in their enthusiasm which was unique! Palermo, Genoa, Milan, Brescia, Messina, Bologna, Casale! – when all the cities of Italy decide to treat the enemy as you did, then our land will truly be free and respected by all.

Just as at Bergamo, we found plenty of cannon and ammunition abandoned in the castle. We stayed several days so that the men could rest and then set off for Rezzato and the River Chiese, which we thought the enemy would cross in its retreat. But it was still present at Castenedolo as was shown by the numerous patrols around the provincial road we were taking, which led from Brescia to the San Marco bridge over the Chiese.

While in Rezzato, I received a command from the King's headquarters to occupy Lonato, adding that as support I would be sent two cavalry regiments and an artillery battery under the command of General Sambuy.

With the enemy holding Castenedolo in such strength, I could not cross the Chiese at the San Marco bridge and tried to find out if the river was passable higher up. With the information I received, I decided to rebuild the bridge at Bettoletto, which the Austrians had destroyed some days earlier.

I was overjoyed to receive the order from the King, but from the outset it also caused me problems, on account of the cavalry regiments and the artillery which were to join us and support our operations. If I marched with the entire brigade towards the Chiese river, I would leave the road behind us unprotected and the arriving artillery and cavalry would be at risk. So I decided to leave the first and second regiments spread out along the road, facing the enemy in Castenedolo and keeping them under observation, while I went on ahead to the river to start to rebuild the Bettoletto bridge, with part of the third regiment, the company of Genoese bersaglieri, the four pieces of artillery and our scouts. We had almost finished the bridge when I was told that the enemy had attacked the two regiments we had left behind on the road; I immediately stopped work on the bridge and rode back at a gallop. The first regiment under the command of Cosenz and Turr had repulsed the enemy as far as the main body of its forces in Castenedolo; there the enemy numbers proved too great for them and they were obliged to retreat. It was in this rather disordered state that I came across them when I reached the battlefield. Turr was on the left flank and had been wounded and carried off. Together with my aides, Cenni, Trecchi and Meryweather, I got the Cacciatori to regroup and charge the enemy again, but they were once more obliged to retreat since the Austrian forces were so much larger and were attempting to encircle our troops. However, we managed to retreat in good order under the protection of the second regiment. The Battle of Tre Ponti was the fiercest and hardest fought in which the first regiment, who took the honours of the day, had yet taken part, while the second regiment fully lived up to the reputation it had gained in previous engagements. The companies of the third regiment showed that they were worthy to fight alongside such valiant comrades.

We were obliged to fight this battle in such unfavourable conditions because we had been honoured with the command from general headquarters; we had had to divide the brigade leaving two thirds behind in order to protect the cavalry and artillery, which were supposed to arrive but in fact never made an appearance. For the first time in the campaign I was in contact with the king's general command headquarters yet it was no cause for celebration. Did our commanders know that the Austrian Emperor's general headquarters were at Lonato, in the thick of an army of two hundred thousand men? If they knew, why did they send me to Lonato at the head of one thousand eight hundred men? And if they didn't know, that doesn't say much for the Kingdom of Sardinia's military staff, which no doubt has many defects, but a shortage of spies is not one of them. It was all a trap into which I and my band of valiant comrades were intended to fall since certain distinguished military strategists found us so annoying!

I finally came to be convinced that general headquarters were playing games with us, and they weren't lighthearted ones: I realised that the idea of occupying Lonato was not to be taken seriously and that I would do better to follow my own plans and not wait for any orders from the oracles on high. In the evening after the battle I related the events of the day to General Cialdini, who said to me: 'You're heading for trouble if you listen to such men.' I was to rely on myself and my companions in planning my future moves and trying to keep out of the way of the enemy, which had its entire army near at hand, as events were soon to show.

During the Battle of Tre Ponti I had noticed that the enemy kept advancing on its right; I deduced, correctly, that they were trying to cut us off from the regiment which was by the river. So I sent an order to Colonel Arduino that he was to abandon the bridge, which was already completed, and withdraw in the direction of the mountains around Nuvolento. Arduino overreacted to my order: not only did he withdraw to Nuvolento, but he sent the artillery via Gavardo towards Brescia, and then, along with the infantry, took the mountain paths and withdrew in the same direction.

After I had given orders to Cosenz and Medici to assemble their men in pre-arranged places I set off on horseback to reach Arduino in order to put him in contact with the other units on the mountainside, good positions from which the larger forces of the enemy could be held back.

I was without my aides because Cenni's horse was dead and the others either had horses that were tired or were being used, so I went on alone asking anyone I encountered for news. Very few inhabitants had not fled or hidden away to escape persecution and pillage from soldiers, either those from our own forces or the enemy's. In any case the glories of war hold little interest for the country folk of Italy who, when they have not actually been hostile to us, have always been indifferent to the battles fought on their soil.

The men I was searching for seemed further away with each piece of news I gathered and I owed it to the stamina of my horse, which had galloped all day, if in the end I found them. Without it, I would have had to postpone my search until the next day, much to my annoyance. In the evening the brigade remained spread out between Rezzato and Nuvolento. In the meantime the King's army was advancing along the Brescia road. General Cialdini, with whom I was on friendly terms, had done all he could when he first heard of the engagement at Tre Ponti to come on ahead; he said he had sent some of his light infantry to support us, but either they were too exhausted to finish their march or they turned up after the battle was over.

We remained like this for several days. Our presence and the approach of the King's army reassured the people of Gavardo and Salò; as the bridge over the Chiese had now been rebuilt I decided to cross over to Salò. So we brought the whole brigade together again at Gavardo and crossed the river during the night. Bixio and his battalion was ordered to occupy the town on Lake Garda while the rest of the brigade remained in the surrounding hills, waiting until the following morning before entering the place. At the same time as I decided to march on Lake Garda I had also requisitioned several barges from Como and Iseo, which arrived in Salò at the same time we did. We stayed in the town for several days; the most notable incident while we were there was the destruction of an enemy steamer. One came every day to spy on us, entering right into the harbour, and backwards, with its prow always facing the harbour entrance so that it could get away quickly if necessary. I observed this daily manoeuvre and asked the commander of the army which was now at Gavardo for a detachment, and half a field battery including two howitzers. When they arrived

I positioned them at the entrance to the harbour on the right; the place could not have been more suitable if it had been built on purpose. The gunners were perfectly positioned on the edge of the lake, hidden by undergrowth, which completely concealed them from outside but which allowed them to fire in any direction on the lake. I sent the Genoese bersaglieri to the left of the harbour to hide there among the bushes ready to ambush the boat. The steamer duly arrived moving backwards as usual and came within range of the bersaglieri troops who started firing on it with their precision rifles. The steamer moved off to escape them over to the other side of the harbour, where it encountered the battery which had been concealed there. After a few shots from these brave gunners fire broke out on board which proved impossible to extinguish. The boat tried to make for the opposite shore as quickly as it could, but to no avail and it sank while still a short way off. It saddens me that I cannot now recall the name of the skilful artillery officer who was in charge of the operation.

The King had placed me under the command of General Cialdini, who ordered me to march with the brigade into the Valtellina. I sent Medici on ahead; he gathered together all our detachments who were in the vicinity of the valley and pushed the Austrians back towards the Stelvio. I followed with the rest of the brigade crossing the lake from Lecco to Colico on steamers. We took control of the Valtellina as far as Bormio, where Medici, pushing on towards the Stelvio, forced the enemy forces to leave Lombardy. In this new kind of combat, among the ravines and precipices of the snow-covered Alps, our young Cacciatori gave new proofs of their valour and fortitude against an enemy force which was largely made up of men from the Tyrol, who had the advantage of knowing the place and being used to the climate.

So we were masters of the Valtellina while Cialdini at the head of the army's fourth division held the Val Camonica and the Val Trompia as far as Lake Garda. Colonel Brignone from the same division occupied the Val Camonica.

Was the fourth division, without a doubt one of the finest in the army, separated from the rest because there was a real fear that a large Austrian force would appear from the Tyrol? Or was it sent away to weaken the army and ensure they wouldn't fight so well in the decisive battle which was looming on the Mincio river? Or were they meant to keep an eye on the ever-increasing numbers of the Cacciatori and curtail their independence of action, which the King may have welcomed but certain others in high places didn't. Louis Napoleon was as cunning as a fox and might well have wanted to cut the Italian army down to size with the mere pretext that one of its best divisions was needed in the Valtellina. And the number of the Cacciatori had increased, as if by magic and in less than a month from eighteen hundred men – the number left after the Battle at Tre Ponti – to twelve thousand, and continued to grow, much to the concern of those men with uneasy consciences, who were alarmed by the volunteer forces despite their assertions they were useless.

Whether the fear of an Austrian invasion from the Tyrol was real or assumed, preparations for one were apparent as soon as I reached Lecco, where I found a unit from the French military engineering corps under one of their officers, laying mines along the main road which led from Lecco to the Valtellina. The officer was supposed to have discussed with me beforehand how to proceed. I had had no information that the enemy was advancing in the area and asked him to stop the destruction. I believe Cialdini had received orders to destroy roads and bridges in the valleys; these orders were transmitted to Brignone in the Val Camonica and to me in the Valtellina. Brignone obeyed reluctantly and carried out some explosions; I got some engineers to identify the appropriate sites in case of need, but destroyed nothing: in the absence of any signs of a large enemy invasion, I thought it premature and excessively cautious to destroy the bridges and roads which were so vital to the wretchedly poor inhabitants of the valleys.

In the meantime the great battles of Solferino and San Martino were fought, to be followed by the peace Treaty of Villafranca[23], which many saw as a calamity but for me was a stroke of good fortune.

By the time of the armistice and the Treaty of Villafranca the Cacciatori delle Alpi numbered more than twelve thousand men, divided in five regiments, occupying the four valleys of the Valtellina, Camonica, Sabbia and Trompia, up to the border with the Tyrol. Cialdini had withdrawn northwards to Brescia. In addition to our five regiments, the Cacciatori degli Appennini had finally turned up; despite the orders from the King Cavour, had done all he could to prevent them from joining us earlier – and now the war was over, he sent them.

The armistice and the peace which followed it were unsuited to the Cacciatori. These were generous spirited young men who had left the responsibilities and pleasures of civilian life behind to take part in the struggle for their country; the enforced leisure of garrisons and barracks was not for them, or the excessive discipline of the regular army in peacetime. It was obvious from the start that the Cacciatori would be fish out of water in the permanent army, never out of the hostile eye of Lamarmora, the minister responsible for the army. But there was news of conflict in the central Italian states: the Duke of Modena was said to be ready to return to the Duchy and after the massacre they had perpetrated in Perugia the Pope's Swiss troops were eager to continue on into the Romagna[24].

In Central Italy

The people of central Italy wanted the Cacciatori delle Alpi to help them in their struggle against their rulers. The volunteers were held in high esteem and rightly so. They were independently minded and it was unlikely that they would remain for long under the command of the King. They didn't need much encouragement to move against petty tyrants and priests.

Montanelli and Malenchini both spoke to me of the matter – they had gone round the states and come back to see me and to convey to me the wishes of the Governments of Florence, Modena and Bologna – that I should come to central Italy where I would be given the command of their troops. When I told Montanelli that I would resign from the King's army and come without delay he embraced me with emotion. Malenchini then arrived with a letter from Ricasoli asking me to come to central Italy and take command of the army, or a part of it: I sensed a certain diffidence in this last phrase, but in fighting for my country I have never laid down conditions so I made no comment. Malenchini told me however that both Farini, with whom he had spoken in Modena, and Pepoli, whom he had seen in Turin, had assured him that they would give me the command of all the troops they had at their disposal.

I tendered my resignation from the King's army and set off from Genoa to Florence. There my initial suspicion hardened into conviction: once again I was dealing with the kind of men I had had to face on my first arrival in Italy. In Montevideo I had fought for six years at the head of a heroic army; I returned to Italy with my sixty-three companions, where I spent various months going from Nice to Turin, from Turin to Milan, from Milan to Roverbella and back again to Turin, before I was given the command, with the rank of colonel, of some of the remnants left in the barracks, just before the surrender at Milan, when the war was heading for disaster (it was because it was heading for disaster that I was given the command). I had come all the way from South America to serve my country, even as an ordinary soldier – all the rest didn't much matter. But it was important to me to see that Italy was fittingly served and not left in the hands of gangs who were unworthy of her. In Rome a so-called minister, Campello, had kept me and my volunteers away from the capital and had warned me not to exceed five hundred men. In Piedmont at the beginning of 1859 I was put on display in order to attract volunteers, but when they flocked to the call the ones aged between eighteen and twenty-six were sent to join the front-line troops while I was left with the under- and over-aged, and the incapable, with whom I was forbidden from appearing in public in order not to upset the course of diplomatic negotiations. And once we were on the battlefield I was denied the support of the very volunteers who had enlisted in order to join me.

In Florence I quickly came to see that it was the same old story: they began to ask me – thinking they were flattering me, the wretched cheats! – if I would be prepared to accept General Farini as the supreme commander. I should have agreed to nothing and returned home, but the country was threatened. Besides, I was not in the habit of demanding something in return for fighting for such a great cause. So I accepted the command of the Tuscan division. As I entered the Palazzo Vecchio the good people of the city cheered me on much to the displeasure of their rulers who asked me to calm them down and leave as soon as I could for Modena, where the division's general headquarters were located.

In Modena I met Farini. He was welcoming and transferred the forces of Modena and Parma to my command. He was a man of superior intelligence and was sharp-witted. Like his fellow-governors in these beautiful provinces he rather enjoyed his power and was certainly not too keen on sharing it with a man of popular acclaim. From the outset Ricasoli seemed more straightforward and less devious than Farini; it was unfortunate that he too feared and disliked me, an antipathy which lay behind his criticisms of me for hotheadedness, etc. As for Cipriani in Bologna, he was a passionate supporter of Napoleon III and was therefore unlikely to have much in common with me. In fact we openly disliked each other from the moment of my arrival in the region; no risk there that he would entrust his own troops in the Romagna to my command. What popularity I enjoyed among the people was the real reason these men had asked me to come, and the hope that some of this popularity would rub off on them – as will be seen.

This said, in central Italy in the last few months of 1859 a hundred thousand young men would have rallied to me and the course of European diplomacy would have taken a more favourable direction; or with just the thirty thousand who were then in the Duchies and in the Romagna the fate of central Italy could have been decided in a fortnight – what in fact happened with the Thousand[25] a year later. The rulers would have remained to administer their provinces; they would have been secondary to the action, it is true, but they would still have played a glorious role in supporting our operations. But this was not their view of the situation: so they joined forces to put me down and render my actions ineffective. Petty egoism led Ricasoli and Farini to act like this whereas Cipriani was probably taking orders from the man whose last wish – I may be mistaken – is to see a united Italy come into being. (1859).

So I spent several months doing little or nothing when so much could and should have been done. I was bored by having to organise the troops – I have always disliked the business of being a soldier. I've had to fight on occasion because I was born in a country which was not free, but I've always done it with repugnance and in the conviction that mutual butchery, to speak plainly, is a crime.

I was restricted to dealing with the Tuscan division so I did what I could to improve their condition.

What really concerned these gentlemen was how to dispense with me as a person while still managing to use my reputation, for they needed this to ingratiate themselves with the people. They thought they'd found the solution by appointing me the second-in-command of the troops belonging to the League. The League was made up of three provinces, the governments of which didn't dare to call themselves Italy for fear of displeasing their masters. These are the ways and means our poor humiliated country has to adopt on the road to unification!

So a good deal of unscrupulous plotting now began to take place with the aim of making life difficult for me and wearing me down. Fanti refused to accept my valiant officers from the Cacciatori delle Alpi, whom I had summoned with the consent of the Government in Modena, although he was prepared to accept anyone else. My poor men who had flocked to me as soon as they knew I was in central Italy to join the existing forces there and form new ones were treated very badly. They arrived from the remotest parts of Lombardy, barefoot, inadequately clothed, tired and worn down by the journey and found themselves rejected for service on account of the slightest shortcomings – of age, of physical condition, of height, etc. And do you think they were ever asked if they had eaten or if they had the money to buy food and to return home? Not once!

Cipriani, working in conjunction with Fanti, sent me off to Rimini to arm two merchant vessels with cannon; I was accompanied by his brother, who carried the key to a secret code which he used to communicate with his brother so that I knew nothing of what passed between them. While I was in Rimini, orders and instructions were given to General Mezzacapo who happened to be my subordinate. I was only too aware how difficult my position was; I swallowed this bitter pill in the hope of being able to doing something to help my unfortunate country. The love the local people and my soldiers showed me made up in part for the abuses I had to endure from such a cowardly gang.

I thought that I could mend the situation and be helpful by trying hard to be friends with Fanti and to win him over to my side; I soon realised that I was deceived and that my good faith was being abused.

Papal rule was much resented in Ancona, in the Marche and in Umbria and before my arrival the people there had agreed with Cipriani that they would rebel. My journey to Rimini to prepare the two ships was part of the plan and I had been instructed to encourage an insurrection. My presence among the people of Rimini was an incitement. Yet it was obvious – above all with Cipriani – that the main aim was to appear to be doing something while at the same time actually doing nothing or indeed actively hindering progress. All kinds of subterfuges were used with me. One idea – which came from either Cipriani or Fanti – was to make the volunteers sign a commitment to remain in service for eighteen months. From the outset of the campaign in 1859 the volunteers had agreed to serve for a term of six months after the conclusion of hostilities. Not one of those brave young men would have murmured a word if they had been called upon to serve for ten years had the war continued so long. But I knew very well that a fixed term of eighteen months, whatever the circumstances, would be unacceptable and told Cipriani and the Commander-in-Chief. My remarks went unheeded and we almost lost the entire division under Mezzacapo because of the measure. I was in Bologna and was called to go and see Mayer, who headed the local administration in Forlì, and Malenchini; both were seriously alarmed by the desertions and the requests for leave among the troops stationed on the front line of Cattolica. I raced there and managed to stop the forces disintegrating any further, but while I was doing my utmost to achieve this, Mezzacapo, possibly acting under orders from Fanti, did everything he could to undermine my efforts by insisting on the eighteen-month rule. He did it to annoy me and also perhaps to diminish my reputation in the eyes of those who knew me only by repute. I asked for the oath of service to be suspended temporarily, but to no avail.

Meanwhile unrest continued among the inhabitants of the Marche and in Umbria. Brigadier Picchi, that noble veteran fighter for Italian liberty and a native of Ancona, kept in constant touch with the oppressed peoples. There were also moves afoot to involve the Kingdom of Naples and Sicily. If the governors and the generals had been more supportive – they couldn't have been more obstructive if they'd been paid directly by the enemy – we could have made the attempt and marched triumphantly down to the South, much more easily and overwhelmingly than we did the following year. But I received the following instructions from Fanti: 'If you are attacked by papal troops, drive them back across the border and invade their territory; if there is an insurrection in a town like Ancona or over a whole district, go in to support the uprising'. The first outcome was impossible since the papal troops would never attack us and the second was also highly unlikely, since the enemy had stepped up its vigilance over the local people. Despite this, arms were being smuggled into Ancona and the Marche and the people's courage remained high. If the order had been given to march ahead the young soldiers who formed the vanguard would have shouted for joy at the thought of going to free their fellow-Italians. While I was busy preparing for operations, behind my back my subordinates were being instructed not to obey my orders. Mezzacapo for example received a dispatch from Fanti telling him that no one should move without his orders and to pass this on to General Rosselli. But it was not only men like Mezzacapo and Roselli who received such instructions; my own chief of staff was told to report to Colonel Stefanelli who had been put in charge of the Tuscan division.

Such was my situation in central Italy when General Sanfront was sent by the King to Rimini. He found me baffled and angry at such lack of support; if he hadn't come I don't know what desperate remedy I might have adopted. I returned with him to Turin and had an audience with the King. The conclusions we reached were that he would advise Fanti to accept the resignations of the Governments in Florence and Bologna, that the continued presence of Cipriani in the Romagna was harmful, and that I should act for the common good as the commander of the forces of central Italy as I saw fit. He did not however give me his permission to invade the Papal States, just as a year later he did not give his consent to the Sicilian expedition or to crossing the Straits of Messina, or, some years after that, to the march on Rome which ended at Aspromonte – an attitude only to be expected from someone in his position made uneasy when faced with revolutionary demands. I felt satisfied when I left Turin and I lost no time in going to Modena and letting Farini and Fanti know in no uncertain terms what the King had said. But my opponents had not been dormant: Fanti received a telegraph from the War Ministry telling him not to accept the resignations. In the meantime pressure was being put on Victor Emmanuel to get him to change his mind.

The first thing to do in central Italy was to get rid of Cipriani, by fair means or foul, and I told Fanti and Farini so. If we were to invade the Papal States, an opponent like Cipriani could not be left to create obstacles in the way of a national campaign. They all agreed since all of them, especially Farini and Fanti, were interested in seeing Cipriani out of the way. Fanti was not a man to oppose the King's wishes, but Napoleon, Cavour, Farini, Minghetti were all too busy pursuing their own interests to lend him any support. So once again the good intentions of the King were being thwarted (unless it was all a trick) and Cavour was bullying him into compliance, as had happened at the beginning of the war when the King ordered the regiment of the Cacciatori degli Appennini to join my forces but who then didn't show up until hostilities were over.

That sly old fox Farini steered a middle course. When Minghetti asked me who would take Cipriani's place, I replied: Farini. There were two advantages to Farini replacing Cipriani: first, the Romagna would be united with the Duchies of Parma and Modena under a single government. The second was that Farini was intelligent and patriotic and would support, as Cipriani never had, a push towards national armament and unification. From the moment of my arrival in central Italy, I had understood the kind of man Farini was: as an Italian I trusted him, while I had less reliance on him as a personal friend. But at the end I realised that he had not treated me in good faith. My last words to him in Bologna were: 'You've not been straight with me,' and as this angered him I added, 'and the blame for the mess we're in lies mostly at your door!' Yet I must also admit that his government in Modena was an effective one and so it was when he ruled Bologna. In Modena he and Frapolli managed to achieve what no one else did in other parts of Italy: they worked energetically to arm, to organise, etc. Yet despite this he was still less than open with me: while he agreed on the division of responsibilities between us – he would be in charge of the administration while I looked after the troops – from the expressions on his pallid face you could see that other thoughts were passing through his mind, that he had had contrary impressions from elsewhere, and that he was ready to act according to the way the wind was blowing out of Piedmont – and that wind was no longer favourable to my cause. My opponents had won the King over to their point of view; no doubt Paris had also played its part – Cipriani's departure and my role as commander of the forces in central Italy were certainly not looked on kindly in those quarters. If I had been in my opponents' shoes I would simply have said, 'Garibaldi, we don't need you any more,' but these men were incapable of acting so straightforwardly. Instead they tried to ward me off with all sorts of hindrances and stratagems.

My reputation among the soldiers and the ordinary people – or so it seemed to me – enabled me to act regardless of what my opponents thought. I was certainly not scared of launching myself once more on the tide of revolution, which would probably lead to success but in starting such a revolution on my own authority I would have had to dissolve every bond of discipline in the soldiers and in the people. There was also the prospect of French intervention in the south at Rome and in the north at Piacenza, etc. Ultimately it was the holy cause of my country which restrained me from adopting this course of action since by acting in this fashion I could have compromised it. I was waiting for some sign from the King – as we had agreed – which, even if it had not explicitly authorised my actions, would have tacitly allowed them, leaving me all the responsibility for the undertaking, and giving him the option of stopping me if necessary. I was ready to submit to anything and to undertake anything. But no sign ever came.

Eventually I sent Major Corte to see the King and I was summoned to Turin. When I saw him, I was immediately aware of a change in his attitude since we had last spoken. He was as good-natured as always, but made it clear that external pressures obliged him to maintain the status quo. His advice to me was to keep my distance for a while.

He wanted me to accept a position in the Sardinian army which I declined with thanks. I did accept the gift of a fine hunting rifle from him: he sent Captain Trecchi with it when I was already on the train to Genoa. From Genoa I went on to Nice where I spent three days with my children, returning to Genoa to catch the steamer which left for La Maddalena on the twenty-eighth of November 1859.

I was ready to leave and my luggage was already on board ship; I was in my friend Coltelletti's house when a deputation of leading Genoese citizens led by the mayor arrived. They informed me that in such circumstances my departure would be inopportune. So I agreed to remain and stayed as a guest in Leonardo Gastaldi's villa in Sestri for a few days. There was talk at the time of forming mobile national guards. Colonel Turr told me that the King wished to see me about the matter. So I went to Turin and saw the King as well as the Minister Rattazzi, who certainly did not inspire me with confidence. With both of them I agreed that I would take responsibility for organising the guards in Lombardy. I was pleased with this outcome for two reasons: the first was that it would give me an opportunity to train up a good body of men who could then form part of the army which would be needed for the war Italy would inevitably have to fight again, while it would also enable me to offer a place to many of the comrades-in-arms from the Cacciatori who had ended up homeless and hungry. I stayed in Turin to await the official nomination; while I was there a group of distinguished patriots – Brofferio, Sineo, Asproni and other liberal deputies in the parliament – came to see me. They wished to use my presence in the city to try to mend the rifts which had occurred in the progressive party. The conflict between the various groups only harmed their cause. At first I didn't think that I would be able to help; I was in any case opposed to any association which did not reflect the entire nation and so I turned them down. It would have been better if I had stuck to this decision. They pleaded with me, arguing that great good would come of it if I were successful, and so finally I accepted. The idea was to establish a new association incorporating all those which already existed, to be called 'Nazione Armata'. So far so good: various members belonging to these different associations came and saw me and all agreed on the idea and were happy with it. A meeting of the association 'Libera Unione' was supposed to set the seal on the agreement, but all those who had seemed perfectly happy with the idea of the merger when they came to see me now advanced proposals which were directly contrary to it, and with one pretext or another, declared reconciliation to be out of the question. I have long believed – with ever growing conviction – that Italians need to be whipped into agreeing with each other.

It was all wasted effort – worse than that, since the foreign ambassadors, encouraged, or so it was said, by Cavour and Napoleon III, then at the height of their power, took advantage of the Government's weakness and demanded an explanation. As a result, the whole cabinet, apart from Rattazzi, resigned. The pretext for their intervention was the new association *Nazione Armata*, the mobilisation of the national guards and, if I may be excused the presumption, my own poor self as I had become implicated in all of this. The idea of the formation of the *Nazione Armata* thoroughly frightened these wretched diplomats, whose only concern was to keep Italy weak. May this teach my fellow-citizens a lesson: if we wish to transform ourselves from timid rabbits into lions capable of terrifying our bullying neighbours we truly need the *Nazione armata*, a nation of two million people in arms (and all the priests set to do something useful like draining the Pontine marshes).

So I was summoned again to see the King who told me that all these plans had to be dropped.

I was on Caprera when I first heard of an insurrection in Palermo: the news was uncertain, at first saying the rebellion was spreading fast and then that it had been crushed at the outset. Yet rumours of an uprising continued to circulate: one had certainly occurred, whether it had been suppressed or not.

Friends on the mainland told me what had happened. They asked me about a subscription scheme, called 'A million rifles', which had been started to raise money for the purchase of arms.

Rosolino Pilo and Corrao got ready to leave for Sicily. Knowing as I did the attitudes of the men who ruled northern Italy, and still seeped in the scepticism in which the recent events of 1859 had left me, I advised them to wait until they got more positive news about the uprising. With my middle-aged caution I tried to chill their youthful fervour and resolve. But it was written in the book of fate: chill caution, sage advice, carefully weighing up the pros and cons – all this could not stop the onward march of Italy's destiny. I advised them to wait and yet they went and in a glimmer of hope we heard the news that the insurrection was still alive. I advised them to wait, yet is it not the duty of all Italians to fight wherever their fellow-citizens are struggling against tyranny?

I left Caprera for Genoa; in the houses of my friends Augier and Coltelletti all the talk was of Sicily and what we should do. In Augusto Vecchi's Villa Spinola we started to lay the plans for an expedition.

It was Bixio without a doubt who played the leading role in this remarkable enterprise: it was his courage and his resourcefulness, his knowledge of the sea and of Genoa, where he had been born, which were invaluable in organising everything. The Sicilians among us – Crispi, La Masa, Orsini, etc. – were fervent supporters of the idea, as were the Calabrians. All agreed that whatever the circumstances and whether we succeeded or not, we must go to support the Sicilians in their struggle.

Some depressing news almost stopped us setting out. A reliable source in Malta sent us a telegram saying that all was lost and that the leaders of the attempted revolt had all fled to Malta. The whole project was almost entirely called off, though I must admit that the Sicilians among us didn't falter for a moment and remained prepared to go off with Bixio to try their luck or at least find out what was really happening on the island. And in the meanwhile Cavour's Government started to set its traps and obstacles which were to dog us to the very end. Cavour's men could not say outright that they did not want an expedition to Sicily; public opinion would have condemned them and the popularity they'd acquired by using the country's money to buy off men and newspapers would have been shaken. So I could continue to make preparations to help our Sicilian brothers with little fear that I would be arrested and encouraged by the warmth of feeling among the general populace in support of the islanders' courageous resolve.

The Sicilians' desperation and their firmness of purpose, recalling their ancestors who rose up during the Sicilian Vespers,[26] could only serve to drive forward the insurrection. La Farina had been sent by Cavour to keep an eye on us; he appeared to have little confidence in the undertaking and took it upon himself to try to dissuade me from going, saying that as a native Sicilian he knew the people of the island and was sure that once Palermo was lost, the insurgents, whoever they were, would give up too. And yet La Farina also provided us with an official piece of news which only confirmed us in our determination: we were told that in Milan fifteen thousand good rifles were waiting to be distributed, as well as funds to be disbursed. Besana and Finzi were in charge of the subscription scheme, 'A million rifles'. I summoned Besana to Genoa to bring the money which was available; before leaving Milan he had left orders that the rifles, ammunition and other military equipment there should be sent on to us. At the same time Bixio was negotiating with Fauché, who managed the Rubattino steamship company to arrange our journey to Sicily. Things were going well: thanks to Bixio and Fauché and the enthusiasm of the young men who rallied to us from every part of the country we found ourselves ready to embark after only a few days, when an unforeseen incident not only threatened to delay us but to stop us going altogether.

The men who had been sent to collect the rifles in Milan found two royal carabinieri placed on guard at the gate of the depot where the guns were stored, who stopped them taking a single weapon, on the orders of Cavour. This new obstacle was frustrating and annoying, but it didn't succeed in preventing us. As we couldn't take possession of the arms which were ours, we began to look for others and would undoubtedly have been successful when La Farina stepped in and, with the condescending generosity of those in high places, offered us a thousand rifles and eight thousand lire both of which I accepted without rancour. We were deprived of our own good rifles, which remained behind in Milan, and were obliged to use the very defective weapons La Farina had offered us. The comrades who fought by my side in the glorious Battle of Calatafimi, when they come to tell their story, will no doubt describe how we fared against the excellent rifles of the Bourbon army with these useless weapons in our hands.

All this delayed our departure; we had to send many of the volunteers home because we did not have enough boats to carry them all and to allay the suspicions of our police surveillants, both French and Sardinian. But our determination not to abandon our Sicilian brothers carried us through. The volunteers were recalled and they came back immediately, mostly from Lombardy. The Genoese had remained ready to leave. Weapons, munitions, provisions and what little baggage we had were put on board a few small boats. Two steamers to carry the volunteers had been arranged: the *Lombardo* commanded by Bixio, and the *Piemonte* commanded by Castiglia. On the night of the fifth of May they left the port of Genoa to pick up the men who had been divided up into two groups, the first waiting at La Foce and the rest at Villa Spinola. There were the usual annoying problems. Boarding the steamers in the port of Genoa, taking charge of their crews and forcing them to help these pirates, lighting the fires in the engine rooms, getting the *Piemonte*, which was ready, to tow the *Lombardo* which wasn't, and all taking place by the light of the full moon – these actions are more easily narrated than performed. They need cool heads, skill, and luck. Two Sicilians, Orlando and Campo, were both ship's engineers and were of great help.

By dawn everyone and everything was on board. The faces of the Thousand shone with the exhilaration of the risks they had run, of the chances they were taking, and the knowledge that they were fighting for the sacred cause of their country: a thousand men, mostly from the

Cacciatori delle Alpi, the same men whom Cavour had abandoned in the remoter parts of Lombardy in the wake of the retreating Austrians, and to whom he had denied the reinforcements which had been commanded by the King; the same soldiers who, when they had to turn in their need to the Ministry in Turin, had been received and driven away like lepers; the same thousand men who had come twice to Genoa ready to face certain danger – who would always come whenever they were called to lay down their lives for Italy, with no thought of reward other than their own good consciences. What a beautiful sight they were! my young veterans of the fight for Italian freedom. Their faith made me proud and ready to undertake anything.

From Quarto to Marsala

The two steamers arrived in the harbour at Quarto. The embarkation was quickly completed, since all the boats to carry the men across to the steamers had been prepared beforehand. When we were all on board and ready to set off for Sicily, another incident occurred which stopped the boldest in their tracks and almost put paid to the entire journey. Two smugglers' boats had been loaded with ammunition, percussion caps, and small firearms and it had been arranged that we would find them along the stretch of coast towards Monte Portofino and the lighthouse in Genoa. We kept a look out for them for several hours in that area, but failed to spot them.

Ammunition and percussion caps: the loss was very serious. Who would undertake to fight without ammunition? And yet, after we had spent the whole morning searching everywhere for the boats, and stopping at Camogli to take on oil and sawdust for the engines, we decided to trust in the fortunes of our motherland and headed south. In order to get a supply of ammunition we would need to stop at a port along the Tuscan coast. We chose Talamone.

Here I should pay tribute to the authorities in Talamone and Orbetello for their warm and generous welcome, singling out Lieutenant Colonel Giorgini, the principal military commander there, without whose help we would never have been able to get everything we needed. We found not only ammunition there but also cannon as well as supplies of coal: all this made the rest of our journey much easier and less unpredictable.

We were on our way to Sicily, but it seemed a good idea to send a diversionary detachment from the coast into the Papal States and the Kingdom of Naples; by so doing we could keep the enemy's attention occupied for a while and deceive them as to where we were really heading. I proposed the idea to Zambianchi who agreed. He would certainly have been able to accomplish more if I had been able to give him more men and equipment; as it was, he had to undertake the difficult task with just seventy men. After this we set off for Sicily, headed for the island of Marettimo, on the afternoon of the ninth of May.

We had a good voyage, apart from two unpleasant incidents both involving the same individual, a man who seemed determined to want to drown himself but managed on both occasions only to cause us a good deal of trouble without obtaining the desired result. He had thrown himself off the *Piemonte*, but despite the steamer's speed we were able to rescue him. In less time than it takes to write this, the steamer was brought to a halt and a small boat let down into the water; with not a moment to lose and heedless of danger a sailor then threw himself into the boat and following the signals of those on board rowed in the direction of the drowning man. At moments like this, when speed and courage are required, Italian sailors are second to none.

The would-be suicide had changed his mind on contact with the cold water and the threat of imminent death: he started swimming like a fish in the direction of his rescuers. The same thing happened again on the *Lombardo* and this time his madness almost proved fatal for our expedition. His first attempt had taken place on the *Piemonte* in Talamone. Since there was so little space on board for them to lie down and rest, our men had disembarked to stretch out on land. This madman had been taken off first and entrusted to the local military commander, but he somehow managed to smuggle himself back onto the *Lombardo*. He made another attempt to drown himself on the evening of the tenth, the day before we reached Sicily.

On that evening I had hopes of coming within sight of the island of Marettimo and so had stoked up the engine of the *Piemonte* to increase the steamer's speed. Because of this and because the man had thrown himself overboard once again, the *Lombardo* got left behind. As it turned out, we didn't manage to sight Marettimo; my thoughts immediately turned to the other steamer, which I had last seen at sunset and which was now just a small puff of smoke on the horizon. With night coming on, I suddenly felt uneasy and regretted my decision to steam ahead. Becoming separated from the *Lombardo* was a disagreeable setback and it was my fault. So I turned the boat round and headed back towards our companion vessel. It got darker and my fears grew; the minutes seemed like hours. I knew nothing of the incident of the man jumping overboard which was the reason for their delay. At one point I thought I had lost track of them – I cannot describe what I felt and how I cursed myself for the crazy impatience which had driven me on to see if I could reach Marettimo. But at last the *Lombardo* appeared. It would have been difficult to miss each other since we were moving closer together, but I had had a moment of real panic.

And now, to cap it all, another mishap occurred. When night had come on, in the same position as the *Piemonte* there were various other unknown vessels which were visible. Bixio on the *Lombardo* had seen them, but he'd not been able to make out who they were because they were too far off. When he saw us bearing down on him at top speed, instead of waiting for him to catch up, as we had always done before, he took us for an enemy steamer and so began to move off as fast as he could in a southwesterly direction. I was desperate. I immediately saw the mistake and tried every type of signal, including lights, which we had agreed not to use in order not to arouse the suspicions of other ships, but even these did not work and I had to chase the *Lombardo* until it disappeared into the dark. We finally managed to catch up with it: my shouts were heard and the sound of my voice recognised above the noise of the wheels, and the crisis was over. We travelled on together for the rest of the night; when morning came we were in sight of Marettimo and headed south to land on the island.

During the voyage the men had been divided up into eight

companies, each under the command of the most distinguished officers on the expedition: Sirtori was named as chief of staff; Acerbi was the chief paymaster; Turr, the aide-de-camp. We distributed the weapons and the few uniforms which we had been able to gather together before we left.

We at first planned to land at Sciacca, but the day was already far advanced and we were afraid we might encounter enemy battle cruisers. So the decision was made to head for the port nearest to us: Marsala. It was the eleventh of May 1860. As we approached the west coast of the island we could make out sailing ships and steamers. In the harbour of Marsala there were two warships at anchor, which turned out to be English. We arrived in Marsala at about midday; as we entered the harbour we found merchant vessels from various countries.

Fortune was really on our side and leading the expedition; we couldn't have made a better choice of landing. The battle cruisers from the Bourbon fleet had left Marsala that very morning. They had gone off towards the east whereas we were arriving from the west; they could be seen off Capo San Marco as we entered Marsala. This meant that by the time they got within firing distance of us, all the men on the *Piemonte* had already disembarked while those on the other ship were just beginning to get off. The presence of the two English warships must have given pause to the commanders of the enemy ships, who were obviously impatient to start bombarding us, and so we had time to complete the disembarkation from the *Lombardo*. Albion's noble flag once more served to prevent bloodshed and this seagoing race, who have taken me to their hearts, once again, and for the hundredth time, afforded me protection.

However, the view put about by our enemies that the English had deliberately planned to help our landing in Marsala with their own ships is untrue. The British flags, so widely respected and so authoritative, which fluttered from the two warships and on the roof of Mr Ingham's firm in the town, made the Bourbon mercenaries hesitate, almost as if they were ashamed in their presence to fire their huge guns on a small band carrying only the wretched rifles with which the Italian monarchy sees fit to equip its volunteers. Nonetheless the Bourbons still sent over a hail of grenades and small shot, despite the fact that over three-quarters of the volunteers were already on the quay; luckily no one was hurt. The enemy carried off the empty *Piemonte*, but they left the *Lombardo* which had run aground.

The inhabitants of Marsala were astonished at the unexpected turn of events and celebrated our arrival, while their governors and the town's magnates looked on with tight-lipped smiles. No cause for surprise there: the kind of people who are used to making calculations about everything are hardly going to welcome a small band of desperate men intent on improving society by rooting out the cancer of privilege and deceit which corrupts it, especially when this handful of men, unsupported by three-hundred-bore cannon and battleships, challenge what was thought to be an overwhelming power, like that of the Bourbons. Before such men commit themselves to any undertaking, they check to see which way the wind is blowing and who has got the biggest battalions; once this has been ascertained, the victors can be sure of their ungrudging support, even their enthusiasm. Is this not the story of human egotism in every country?

But the poor inhabitants of the town welcomed us with applause and with warmth. All their thoughts were for the sense of sacrifice, the arduous and generous mission which had led this band of valiant young men from afar in support of their Sicilian brothers.

We spent the rest of the day and the following night in Marsala. I was not familiar with the island and its inhabitants and I relied on Crispi's services; this honest and extremely able man was a native Sicilian and provided invaluable help with essential matters such as administering the island and dealing with its people. There was talk of setting up a dictatorship to which I had no objection: I have always believed this to be the right expedient in a crisis, the life raft when nations find themselves adrift in turbulent currents.

On the morning of the twelfth, the Thousand left for Salemi. It was too far to reach in one march and we stopped for the night at a farmstead in Mistretta. The head was not there, but his brother, a young man, courteously and generously made us welcome. The next day we marched on to Salemi, where the inhabitants received us enthusiastically. Here the local fighting units known as *squadre* joined us together with several other Sicilian volunteers. On the fourteenth we occupied the village of Vita; on the fifteenth we came within sight of the enemy for the first time. They had occupied Calatafimi and having heard that we were approaching had spread out across the hills known as the 'Pianto dei Romani'[27].

Calatafimi

When dawn broke on the fifteenth of May we had taken up our positions on the hills outside Vita; shortly afterwards the enemy started marching in columns out of Calatafimi towards us. The heights surrounding Vita face the so-called 'Pianto dei Romani' hills where the enemy columns took up their formations. These hills slope gently towards Calatafimi; the enemy were able to climb them easily and once at the top occupied all the summits; the descent on the side facing Vita however is very steep. We were on the facing hills to the south and so I was able to see all the enemy positions quite clearly; they on the other hand could hardly make out the line of marksmen formed by the Genoese carabinieri under the command of Mosto which was protecting our front line, as all our companies had been placed behind in echelon formation. What little artillery we had was placed on the road to our left; Orsini, who was in command, still managed to fire a few well-aimed shots. In this fashion both our side and the enemy were in possession of extremely strong positions, facing each other over a wide stretch of rolling countryside, with a few houses scattered here and there. It was to our advantage then to stay where we were and wait for the enemy to make the first move.

The Bourbon troops numbered about two thousand men with several artillery pieces. Sighting only a few of our men, not in uniform and together with local peasants, the enemy boldly sent several lines of bersaglieri forward, backed up by some support troops and two artillery pieces. When they came within firing distance they started to fire their rifles and cannon, all the while continuing to advance on us. I had ordered the Thousand not to fire and to wait for the enemy to approach. There were already several casualties among the Genoese line and they sounded an American reveille on their bugles which had the seemingly magical effect of stopping the enemy in their tracks. They suddenly realised they were not dealing with the local *squadre* they were accustomed to: their soldiers and the artillery made a movement backwards. This was the first sign of fear shown by the despot's army in the face of the men they were in the habit of referring to contemptuously as 'filibusters'.

At that point the call to charge was sounded and the Thousand moved forward, led by the Genoese carabinieri who were followed by an elite corps of young volunteers, eager for the fight. The plan was to put the enemy vanguard to flight and capture their two cannon, an aim which these heroes accomplished with élan. Going on to attack the enemy head-on in their almost impregnable positions was another matter, but the volunteers were fired up and there was no stopping them. Our trumpets sounded out 'halt', but they didn't hear, or chose not to hear, like Nelson at the Battle of Copenhagen.[28] They thrust into the enemy's vanguard with their bayonets and drove them back deep into their lines.

There was not a moment to be lost in following up this brave attack. I gave the order to charge and all the men of the Thousand, together with the brave Sicilians and Calabrians who had joined us, moved swiftly forward towards the enemy. They had by now abandoned the low-lying terrain between us and regained their positions on the summits of the hills, where their reserves were stationed. From here they defended themselves with a tenacity and valour which would have been better employed for a better cause.

The valley which lay between us and the enemy positions was the most dangerous part for our troops to cross; a storm of artillery and musket fire rained down on us, wounding many of our men. Once we had reached the foot of the hill on top of which the enemy was positioned we had some cover from their fire; a lot of men had been lost, but those who remained were able to catch up with and join the vanguard.

The situation was crucial: we had to win. The steep southern flank of the hill had been divided up by the local farmers into terraces for cultivation, as is often seen in hilly terrain, and we started to climb the lowermost terrace under a hail of gunfire. I cannot remember exactly how many terraces there were, but certainly there were quite a few to climb before we could get to the top. Each time we had to climb over onto the next terrace, in the process becoming visible to the enemy above, we were met with a tremendous round of firing. Our men were under orders to fire as little as possible because the decrepit old rifles the Sardinian Government had seen fit to supply us with refused to fire. Once again the men from Genoa came to our aid: they had good weapons and were well-trained shots and they enabled us to maintain our part in the action.

We climbed up the terraces swiftly, driving the enemy soldiers upwards, and sheltering for a moment under the wall of the terrace above to regain our breath and prepare ourselves for the next assault. We finally made it to the top where the Bourbon troops made a last stand, resolutely defending their position even to the point of throwing stones down on us when they ran out of bullets. We launched a final charge over the top: our most valiant men were massed under the bank of the topmost terrace. They got their breath back, saw how far they would have to run before engaging in hand-to-hand combat with the enemy and then threw themselves forward like lions, confident that victory for the great cause for which they were fighting was within their grasp. This huge push forward broke through the Bourbon troops and they fled, not stopping until they got to Calatafimi which was some miles away from the field of battle. We pursued them to just outside the entrance into the town which was in a strongly defended location.

When you fight, you need to win: this is true in all the circumstances of war, but it's particularly true when you are at the start of a campaign. Our victory at Calatafimi was insignificant in terms of material gains – a single cannon, a few rifles and a handful of prisoners – but its overall effect was immense, in spurring the local population on and demoralising the enemy. Our 'filibusters' whom the enemy held in such contempt had routed several thousand men from the finest troops in the Bourbon army, under the command of a general capable, like Lucullus, of consuming the entire produce of a single province at one dinner, together with all their artillery and other equipment. The victory had been achieved by an army made up of 'filibusters' or rather middle-class civilians, sporting no stripes or epaulettes, and without the need for such military trappings since they were inspired by the love of their country.

The first important result of our victory was the enemy's evacuation of Calatafimi: we were able to occupy the town on the following morning (16th May 1860). The inhabitants of Partinico, Borgetto, Montelepre and other villages fell on the enemy as they withdrew. Everywhere local *squadre* were formed, which then came to join us; the general enthusiasm among all the towns and villages in the area knew no bounds.

The enemy troops on the run did not stop until they reached Palermo, where their arrival alarmed the Bourbonists and cheered the patriots. Our casualties and those of the enemy were left in Vita and Calatafimi. We had suffered many serious losses. Many men among the Thousand had fallen at Calatafimi as our Roman ancestors had done, fighting the enemy with their naked swords, struck down in front, with only the cry of 'Long live Italy' on their lips. I have experienced other battles which were fought even more ferociously and desperately, but never have I seen such a brilliant body of soldiers as my band of bourgeois filibusters at Calatafimi.

It was a decisive victory in the 1860 campaign. We needed to start the expedition with just such a brilliant military feat. It demoralised the enemy who, with the vivid imagination characteristic of the people of the South, began to tell wondrous tales of the Thousand, such as having seen bullets bouncing off our men as they advanced, as if they were wearing bronze breastplates; it gave new hope and energy to the Sicilians, who had previously been oppressed by the vast numbers of the well-armed Bourbon troops. The battles at Palermo, Milazzo, and the Volturno saw many more men wounded and killed, but in my opinion Calatafimi was the decisive event. It convinced our men that we would carry off the final victory. When a campaign begins with the good omen of such a resounding victory, then one carries on winning!

On the seventeenth of May, we reached the important town of Alcamo, where we were enthusiastically received. At Partinico the inhabitants went wild when we arrived. They had been very badly treated by the Bourbon troops before the Battle of Calatafimi; when these same troops returned to the two towns, in disarray and in retreat, the local people set upon them with fury, killing as many as they could and chasing the others on to Palermo. It was a wretched sight: we found their corpses lying in the streets being eaten by dogs – the corpses of Italian men slaughtered by their fellow-Italians. If they had been brought up as free citizens, then they could have fought for their oppressed country; as it was, and as a result of the hatred in which their masters were held, they had been torn apart by their own brothers, with a frenzy which would make hyenas recoil.

From the beautiful plains of Alcamo and Partinico, our column wound its way up to Borgetto on the high mountain pass of Renda, from where there is a view of Palermo, the delightful queen of the island, in the valley of the Conca d'Oro. If among Italy's hundred cities there were half a dozen like Palermo, the foreigners would have departed our shores long since and the Governments with their police and their spies would be in retreat – or carried off by the devil.

Renda dominates the road leading from Palermo to Partinico and would be a very strong position were it not for the hills to the south and west which form part of the irregular chain of mountains surrounding the fertile valley in which the capital is situated. The town has become notorious in the history of the Sicilian campaign: while the Thousand were there it poured with rain for two days. None of the men had any protection against such weather, but they showed they were as capable of putting up with such discomforts as they were of fighting bloody battles. After two days under this downpour in Renda – there was nowhere to take shelter and so little wood to make fires that we had to chop down telegraph poles – we descended to the village of Pioppo, just above Monreale. This was not a good position, however, for such a small force as ours.

On or about the twenty-first a skirmish with the enemy, in which there had been a brief exchange of gunfire, convinced me that we needed to find a better protected position, above the crossroads in Renda so that we could keep our communications open along the road we had taken from Partinico and to San Giuseppe in the south. In this good tactical position we would have an advantage over the enemy. But then it occurred to me that the road from Palermo to Corleone would be an even more advantageous option: it would enable us to operate over a wider area as well as to make contact with the numerous *squadre* coming from Misilmeri, Mezzojuso, Corleone and the area around, where I had sent La Masa to bring them together. So I decided to march by night from Renda to Parco on the Palermo-Corleone road. We started out before nightfall, but the path was difficult and we had to carry cannon and equipment on our shoulders while incessant rain and thick fog made this the most uncomfortable march I have ever undertaken. The day was already far advanced when in ones and twos the head of the column arrived in Parco. Only with enormous effort did we manage to get the cannon into the town by the evening. However, the rain and the fog also meant that the enemy knew nothing of our march until some time after our arrival in Parco.

The town of Parco is dominated by strong positions which we occupied and on which we started to build defences protected by our cannon. Because of the surrounding mountains, however, it is possible to encircle these positions.

On the twenty-fourth of May two large columns of enemy forces marched out of Palermo. The first went down the main road from the capital to Corleone and the interior of the island, passing by Parco; the second column followed the road to Monreale for a while and then crossed the valley, passing threateningly behind us and then to our left on its way towards Le Portelle and Piana dei Greci.

The prospect of a frontal attack did not make me flinch, even though the enemy was much larger, but their approach to our rear through the mountains which overlooked our position made me decide to retreat before they arrived. I therefore ordered the cannon and baggage to be taken down the main road while I, together with a small group of the local insurgents known as *picciotti* [29] and Cairoli's company, went to meet the second enemy column on its way to Le Portelle as it tried to cut off our retreat.

Our strategy succeeded like a dream. I got to the hills before the enemy were able to occupy them: a few gunshots stopped them. So I found myself at Piana together with all my forces, in control of the road to Corleone and to the interior of the island, and with complete freedom of movement. We spent the remainder of the day in Piana dei Greci resting. While we were in Piana I decided to get rid of the cannon and baggage so that our freedom of movement towards Palermo could be unimpeded. We would join up with the *squadre* which La Masa had gathered together and brought to Gibilrossa. When night came on, I had Orsini take charge of the transport of the cannon and baggage on the Corleone road. With the rest of the men I took the same road for a while, but then branched off to the left in the direction of Misilmeri along a forest path which was fairly easy of access.

Just as I had hoped, the movement of the cannon along the Corleone road deceived the enemy. On the twenty-fifth their forces under the command of Van Meckel and Bosco continued on to Corleone under the belief that they were in pursuit of our entire army when in fact all they were following was Orsini accompanied by only a handful of men. It must be said, to the honour of those brave islanders, that only in Sicily could such a strategy succeed: it was not until two days after our entry into Palermo that the enemy commanders found out we had hoodwinked them and gone on to the capital while they thought all the time we were in Corleone.

In the meantime, I led my column through the Cianeto forest, where we slept. On the following day we reached Misilmeri, where we were enthusiastically received, and on the twenty-sixth we were in Gibilrossa where we met up with La Masa and the various *squadre*. After conferring with La Masa and the other Sicilian leaders, both from Palermo and the rest of the island, the decision was taken to launch an assault on the capital. At nightfall on the evening of the twenty-sixth we began our march on Palermo. We descended along a concealed pathway which leads from Gibilrossa down to the road to Porta Termini.

Various mishaps occurred during the night which held us up. The track was narrow and impracticable and the column of about three thousand men was forced to stretch out into a very long single file so that it was impossible to move up and down it in order to keep it together. One of the horses broke loose and shots were fired which caused general alarm. At a certain point those at the head of the line took the wrong turning and we had to stop while we all got back onto the right path. All this meant that when we came within sight of the enemy outposts at Porta Termini it was already broad daylight.

The Assault on Palermo

At the head of the march there was a vanguard, selected from the best men among the Thousand and led by Tuckory and Missori. They marched on heedless of the numbers of the Bourbon mercenaries facing them or the barricades and cannon they had put in position round Porta Termini. They stormed the outposts and forced the enemy to abandon them, driving them back to the Ponte dell'Ammiraglio, where they continued to pursue them. The rest of the column and the *squadre* followed hard on their heels trying to rival their heroism.

The enemy in large numbers put up a fierce resistance at every point, their artillery bombarded us from land and sea, a battalion of their cacciatori fired on their attackers at about half the distance of a rifle shot from the dominant position of the monastery of Sant'Antonino – to no effect. Victory favours the courageous and the just, and after a short while the centre of Palermo fell to our Italian freedom fighters.

The inhabitants were completely unarmed and couldn't face the tremendous bombardment which was taking place in the streets: not only from the artillery being fired by the troops and from the forts, but also from the Bourbon warships whose guns targeted the main streets and raked them with its missiles. As everyone knows, when men can bombard a city with impunity, they do it with increased savagery.

However, under the direction of Colonel Acerbi, that brave veteran of all the Italian battles, the local people soon took to building barricades, those bulwarks of the city streets which make tyranny's mercenaries quake. They then procured weapons of all kinds from knives to hatchets and crowded into the streets in a mass which no troop of men, however well organised, could hold back.

I rode into the city from Porta Termini to Fiera Vecchia and then Piazza Bologna; here I saw that it would be difficult to gather together the men who were scattered all over the city so I dismounted and found a gateway to stand in. I was placing the saddle of my horse Marsala and my holster on the ground, when one of the pistols was hit and went off. The bullet grazed my right foot and took a piece of my trousers away. 'Joys never come singly,' I thought to myself.

In conjunction with the revolutionary committee in the city, it was decided that I should set up my headquarters in the Palazzo Pretorio in the very centre of Palermo. There were not many armed men in the city whom we could use since the Bourbon authorities had taken care to keep the population unarmed, but it must be said that despite the bloody combats on the streets and the ferocious bombardment from the ships in the harbour, the Castellamare fort and the Royal Palace, the citizens' enthusiasm never faltered. Many joined us with daggers, knives, roasting spits and iron utensils of all kinds since they didn't have rifles. The *picciotti* in the *squadre* fought bravely too and made up for the men we had lost from the Thousand. The local women were awe-inspiring in their patriotic fervour. Amidst the chaos of bombs and rifle-fire they cheered and applauded and waved us on. They threw chairs, mattresses, furniture of all kinds down into the streets for the barricades, and many came down to help build them. The sudden audacity of our entry into the city had taken the populace by surprise, but once their initial amazement had worn off they grew braver and more intrepid by the day.

The barricades rose up as if by magic: Palermo was soon hedged in by them. There were perhaps even too many, but their presence encouraged the local people and panicked the Bourbon troops. The work involved in erecting them kept everyone busy and increased their enthusiasm.

One of the greatest problems we faced was the shortage of ammunition. However, we found some gunpowder factories. Work continued day and night making cartridges, but there were never enough for the continuous fighting which went on against the enemy troops which occupied the principal positions in the city. The soldiers and especially the *picciotti* who fired all the time kept running out of bullets and complaining to me about the lack of them.

Despite this, the enemy had been confined to the Castellamare fort, the Palazzo di Finanze and the Royal Palace, and a few adjoining houses, while we were masters of the whole city. The main body of the enemy was located in the Royal Palace, where their chief General Lanza was to be found; they had no possibility of communicating with their ships in the harbour or with their other positions in the city. Various of the *squadre* had taken control of the gates into the city from the surrounding countryside. Lanza and his troops in the Royal Palace were increasingly cut off and began to run out of food. The building was spilling over with their casualties. So Lanza decided to make a series of proposals to me, the first of which concerned the burial of the dead, whose corpses were beginning to decay, and the transfer of the wounded soldiers onto a ship so they could be taken to Naples. A twenty-four-hour truce was called to carry this out. By God, we needed one: we were having to make gunpowder and cartridges which were being used up as soon as they were ready. Here I must add that not once in all this time, when we would have sold our blood for a handful of cartridges, were we given any arms or ammunition from the warships in the port and the roadstead, including an Italian frigate. If I remember rightly we managed to buy an antiquated iron cannon from a Greek vessel.

The reappearance of Van Meckel and Bosco at the head of five or six thousand well-trained men after they had spent time trying to find us on the road to Corleone almost made Lanza change his mind and could have spelt disaster for us. They had thought that they would catch up with us and drive us off, but found out instead that we had given them the slip and entered Palermo behind their backs: they approached the capital livid with rage and launched a fierce attack on Porta Termini.

The few forces I had at my disposal were scattered all over the city; it was unlikely that there would be enough men to stop the enemy pouring in. Nevertheless the few men who were in the area round Porta Termini put up a brave defence, and though they were forced to withdraw as far as Fiera Vecchia, they fought every inch of the way.

I heard that the enemy was advancing in that part of the city and assembled some of our companies and set off. On the way I was told that General Lanza wished to continue our negotiations on board an English admiralship, the *Hannibal*, which was in the roadstead of Palermo, under the command of Admiral Mundy. I left the city in charge of General Sirtori, my chief of staff, and went on board the *Hannibal*, where I found Generals Letizia and Chretien, who had been sent to negotiate with me on behalf of the Commander-in-Chief of the Bourbon army.

I cannot now recall precisely the proposals which Letizia made to me. I do remember that they concerned an exchange of prisoners, transferring the enemy's casualties on board one of their ships, allowing provisions through to the Royal Palace, assembling all the enemy forces at the Quattro Venti, an area of the city where there were large buildings next to the sea, and finally a demand that the city of Palermo make a formal declaration of respectful obeisance to the Bourbon King Francis II[30]. I listened patiently to the articles of the proposal, but when the last clause was read out I immediately rose up in indignation and said to Letizia that he must by now be well aware he was dealing with people who knew how to fight and that I had nothing further to say. He asked for a twenty-four-hour truce to enable the casualties to be transferred, which I agreed to, and our discussion was at an end.

I observe in passing that as the leader of the Thousand I had up until then been treated as a filibuster; suddenly I was 'Your Excellency' and remained so in all our subsequent negotiations, much to my scorn. Such low tricks are to be expected from the powerful when they find themselves in trouble.

The situation was far from encouraging. There was a shortage of arms and ammunition. Part of the city had been destroyed by bombardment. The enemy's best troops were inside the city and the rest were in control of its strongest positions. Their fleet could target the streets with their artillery, backed up by the cannon in the Royal Palace and the Castellamare fort.

I returned to the Palazzo Pretorio where I found Palermo's leading citizens waiting for me. They scrutinised my face with that penetrating look so typical of southerners, trying to read on it the results of my meeting. I told them about the enemy's proposals and they did not seem dispirited when they heard them. They told me to speak to the people who had gathered outside the building and so I went out onto the balcony to do so.

I have never been subject to discouragement even in circumstances which were perhaps worse than these and I was not discouraged now, but when I considered the enemy's strength and numbers and compared them with our restricted means, I was somewhat at a loss what to do, whether it was worth persevering with the defence of the city or whether I should assemble all the forces and take once more to the open country. But this was a nightmarish thought and I quickly put it out of my mind: it would mean abandoning Palermo to a furious and vengeful military rabble. I was annoyed with myself for letting the idea even occur to me. I went out to face the people of Palermo and I told them about the enemy's proposals and my acceptance of them. When I came to the last demand they had made, however, I said that I had rejected it with contempt. A roar of indignation and approval rose up unanimously from the noble-hearted crowd. That roar decided the fate of millions, the liberty of two peoples, the fall of a tyrant!

It gave me new strength: from that moment on I felt not even a twinge of fear, hesitation, uncertainty. Soldiers and citizens threw themselves into decision-making and activity. The number of barricades multiplied. Every balcony and loggia was covered with mattresses for defence and heaped with stones and projectiles of every description to be thrown at the enemy.

Gunpowder and cartridges were manufactured with feverish haste. Some old cannon appeared from out of nowhere; they were assembled and positioned in suitable places; other cannon were purchased from merchant ships in the port. Women of every class went down into the streets to urge on the workers and the soldiers. The English and American officers from the ships in the port gave us their revolvers and their hunting guns. Some of the Sardinian officers were also sympathetic to our cause while the crew of the Italian frigate wanted to fight alongside us and threatened to desert. Only those who obeyed the cold calculations of the Government in Turin remained unmoved, impassively looking on as one of the noblest cities in Italy was threatened with destruction. No doubt they were waiting for their instructions or already knew what they were: to spit on us if we were defeated and to embrace us as friends if we won.

But the enemy realised how determined we and the city were... When it is a matter of defying a people who are determined to fight to the bitter end, it cannot be done with impunity. Despotism in any case is prey to self-deception: its proconsuls grow fat – small wonder then that they hesitate to draw their sword when the mob erects its barricades.

Before the twenty-four hours of the truce were up, a new messenger from the enemy announced the arrival of General Letizia. He asked for three further days of truce, since one day was not enough to transfer the casualties on board ship. I granted his request; and in the meantime we didn't lose a minute in building up stocks of gunpowder and cartridges and continuing work on the barricades. The *squadre* near the city added to our forces and threatened the enemy from the rear. Orsini, with the cannon which he had taken to Corleone and accompanied by more *squadre*, had now arrived back in the city. Our situation improved day by day as the desire of the Bourbon troops to attack us dwindled.

In another discussion with Letizia he asked that the troops in the Royal Palace and at Porta Termini should be withdrawn to assemble at the Quattro Venti and on the jetty. So much the better for us.

The suspension of hostilities and the withdrawal of the enemy forces towards the sea made the people of Palermo confident and bold, so much so that some of our redshirts had to be stationed in the outposts to prevent the Sicilians from coming into contact with the Bourbon troops, such was the natives' hatred of them. The places where the enemy troops had been assembled were too confined for them to remain there long and at last they left, evacuating the city completely.

The Thousand and all who had defended Palermo had shown their mettle. Not once had they wavered; if need be, they were ready to be buried under the ruins of that beautiful city. It must be admitted that the outcome was magnificent, beyond all our expectations.

It was a day of national celebration when the Bourbon troops left Palermo; the mood of rejoicing was increased even further by the release, as agreed, of all the political prisoners from the city's leading families from their detention in the Castellamare fort. The sight of these men who had been condemned by the Bourbons to suffer in horrible prison cells filled the whole city with joy, and the welcome they were given was moving. I had set up my headquarters in a wing of the Royal Palace, from where I could see the whole of Via Toledo and its continuation as far as Monreale. I could bask in the spectacle of their fervour. The freed men were carried in triumph towards the Royal Palace through an immense crowd, wild with happiness that these dear fathers and sons and brothers were at liberty. They were so profusely grateful to me that my eyes filled with tears.

After this a more restful period ensued: the Thousand above all had need of it. Those poor youngsters who came from the best families, many of them still at university or graduates, unaccustomed to discomfort and privation – all without exception were vowed to heroic struggle and martyrdom for the liberation of our own land from enslavement to the foreigner. Perhaps justly enslaved: in the past it had conquered and ruled the known world and so incurred blame, since in order to achieve this it must have earned the hatred of the countries which it too had in the past plundered and dominated.

The Thousand had suffered seasickness – for the most part they weren't sailors – to plunge into the strife and bloodshed of battle. Along paths which were almost impassable they had marched to Palermo, where, with the help of its people, they chased out an army of twenty thousand men from the best Bourbon troops and liberated the whole of Sicily in twenty days.

The enemy had gone off to prepare for the battles to come and we too had to get ready to meet them again. We started to enlist recruits in Palermo and all over the island, now that the Bourbonists had left. We negotiated for the supply of arms from outside the island. An iron foundry was established in the capital and work continued without let up on manufacturing gunpowder and cartridges. Palermo, which had been the parade ground of Bourbon despotism, was transformed in the space of a few days into the seedbed of fighters for the cause of Italian liberty. In the cool of the early morning it was a fine sight – one which consoled the heart of an old veteran whose lifelong dream had been to see his country liberated – to watch those vigorous young descendants of the old Roman Trinacria[31] doing their military exercises with such keenness and concentration. And the whole of Italy could have gained her freedom if inertia and malice had not sapped the mood of national heroism in those glorious days.

This time in Palermo was also used to initiate useful social projects. The large number of young boys who lived on the streets, where for the most part they fell into bad ways, were gathered up and admitted to schools where they could be taught to become upright citizens and soldiers. The condition of a number of charitable establishments was improved and food was provided for the poorest people in the city as well as for those who had suffered during the bombardment and the fighting generally. A dictatorship to govern the island was set up; various distinguished Sicilian patriots participated in this, most notably Francesco Crispi, who had fought with the Thousand.

The national forces were formed into three divisions and took the name of the Army of the South, which then set off to the east to complete the work of emancipating the island.

The expedition led by Medici with three steamers and about two thousand men reached Castellamare, a few miles to the west of the city, before all the Bourbon troops had finished their embarkation. Other contingents arrived from all over Italy. We soon had enough men to be able to form new detachments which were then sent to different parts of the island to proclaim the new Government in Palermo – not a difficult task since it had already been everywhere acclaimed – and to seek out any enemy forces which had remained behind. One of the three new divisions, commanded by General Turr, set off for the interior of the island. The second division, under the command of Bixio, went to the southern coast, while the third, under Medici, went to the northern coast. They had orders to unite all the volunteers who offered their services and assemble them at the Straits of Messina.

General Cosenz also arrived in Palermo with two thousand men, followed by others who had been sent by the various committees which had been set up all over Italy to organise military support for Sicily, and which were under the general direction of Bertani in Genoa. Cosenz and his column also left for Messina to support Medici who was threatened by a large division of about four thousand Bourbon troops and artillery under the command of Bosco. The enemy had left Messina in order to try and keep the lines of communication open between that city and Milazzo and also to see if they could launch an attack on Medici's men who were in control of several of the surrounding villages. They found them and attacked, but were driven back towards Milazzo, occupying the low-lying country to the south of the town and harassing the local villages.

We needed to get rid of Bosco's troops which were now the only ones who held part of the island. Medici had kept me informed of the enemy forces and their movements; when Colonel Corte arrived in Palermo with two thousand men, I immediately transferred a number of them over to the steamer *City of Aberdeen* on which I joined them. We set off and arrived the next day in Patti. Once I'd met up with Medici and Cosenz, who had yet to be joined by the brigade marching along the northern coast, we decided to attack the enemy at dawn on the following day.

The Battle of Milazzo

That man[32] was being malicious and dishonest who wrote that the victories won by the free Italians over the Bourbon troops were 'easy': I have been in several battles in my time: the battles which were fought at Calatafimi, Palermo, Milazzo and Volturno did honour to the militiamen and the soldiers who took part. And in Milazzo, out of the five or six thousand men we had, over a thousand were wounded and had to withdraw, which goes to show that we did not come by our victory quite so easily.

As I wrote, Medici had marched with his division along the northern coast of the island towards the Straits of Messina, while Bosco, with an elite corps comprising infantry, cavalry and artillery and outnumbering us, had blocked the main road to Messina by occupying the town of Milazzo and its fort. Some skirmishes had already taken place in which our men had performed with their usual skill against Bosco's fine troops, armed with excellent rifles.

Once Corte's two thousand men had arrived and Cosenz's division was approaching, we decided to launch an attack on the enemy. When dawn broke on the twentieth of July the sons of Italian liberty were locked in combat with the enemy to the south of Milazzo; the enemy's strong positions gave them the advantage. They knew the countryside well and had taken care to exploit all the natural and man-made defences it offered them. Their right wing was arrayed in front of the imposing fortress and was protected by the heavy artillery placed there; it was sheltered by rows of prickly pears, which formed a susbstantial trench and behind which Bosco's cacciatori with their good-quality rifles could fire on our badly armed soldiers.

Their centre with its reserves was positioned on the road to Milazzo along the coast; in front they were protected by a thick boundary wall in which they had made many loopholes. The wall was surrounded by a dense thicket of reeds which made a head-on assault impossible. So that the enemy, in a secure position and well armed, was able to observe and fire on our men as they moved through the inadequate cover of the reed thicket.

Their left wing was in control of a row of houses and was positioned to the east of Milazzo like a hammer; an assault on their centre would meet with lethal firing from this flank.

Our ignorance of the terrain was the principal cause of the heavy losses we sustained and many of the charges we made against the enemy's centre were wasted. My initial plan had been to attack the enemy while it was still dark by sending a massed column of men to break through the centre and split it, separating off the left wing and capturing it if possible, in this way trying to reduce the advantage of its superiority in terms of artillery and cavalry. But the plan proved impossible because there was a delay in bringing together the various troops from the different positions which they were occupying; when the battle began the sun had been up for some time.

My main strategy was to close off the enemy's centre and right wing in the town of Milazzo, where so many men together with the garrison would not have been able to hold out long; to this end I moved the larger part of our forces over to the centre and left of the enemy, where they launched a vigorous attack. The battlefield was a perfectly level stretch of country, covered with trees, vines and reed thickets so that it was impossible to make out the enemy's positions. I climbed up on to the roof of a house to try to see something, but in vain; I ordered a charge on the road for the same reason, but this too yielded no results.

There were many dead and many wounded after our charges on the enemy's centre; our young soldiers were driven back, having failed to draw the enemy out from behind the protection of the loopholes, from which came a hail of gunfire. This unequal and fiercely fought conflict lasted until midday. By that time our left wing had retreated several miles and we were exposed on that side. Our right wing and centre which had come together in the face of the common danger managed to hold on, but with considerable difficulty and heavy losses.

But we had to win: this conviction with all the force of fate behind it was what drove us on through that extraordinary campaign, where in the most serious battles such as Milazzo and the Volturno we were on the losing side for most of the day, but where we stayed firm and refused to give up hope and so managed to defeat enemy forces which were larger and better equipped than ours. May these so-called 'easy victories' serve as an example to our sons who will be called upon to maintain Italy's honour on future battlefields.

We had to win! Our losses were greater than in any of the battles we fought in the South. The men were tired. The enemy's losses were limited in comparison, their soldiers were still fresh and unscathed, their positions formidably strong. And yet we had to win.

As I have said, all the conditions of the battle favoured the enemy until the afternoon; our noble fighters had not only not advanced one step, but had actually lost ground, especially on our left. 'Try to keep going as long as you can,' I said to Medici who was commanding in the centre. 'I'm going to gather together some of our men and try to attack their left flank.' This decision was the turning point. The enemy, attacked on its flank behind its defences, started to give way; we charged them head on and managed to seize a cannon which had caused us much grief by firing continuously along the road.

The enemy made a brilliantly executed cavalry charge to rescue the cannon and forced our men to retreat somewhat. I was caught in the charge and had to leap into a ditch by the side of the road and defend myself from there with my sabre, but not for long. Missori arrived at the head of the detachments which had previously captured the cannon, and with his revolver took over from me and rid me of my opponent from the enemy cavalry.

The enemy was closely pursued by our brave men and at last fell away and hurriedly retreated towards Milazzo under attack from the whole of our line. Our victory was complete. The artillery firing from the fortress could not cover the enemy's retreat; paying no attention to the bullets raining down on them, our men made an assault on Milazzo and took it before nightfall. They encircled the fort and barricaded all the streets which were exposed to its guns.

Our triumph at Milazzo was bought at a high cost. Our dead and wounded far outnumbered those of the enemy. It was one of the most lethal encounters we had had to face; the Bourbon troops fought bravely and held their positions for many hours, but despite this, the dynasty was now doomed. The results of the battle were extraordinary: the enemy were trapped in Milazzo and were soon forced to withdraw and crowd into the narrow spaces of the citadel, which we surrounded with barricades and where they soon surrendered, on the twenty-third of July 1860. Supplies of artillery and ammunition, plenty of mules to transport the cannon, and the fortress itself were ours. We were masters of Milazzo and the rest of the island, except for the fortresses of Messina, Augusta and Siracusa, and we immediately marched on the straits. Medici found no resistance at Messina and was able to occupy the town. We fortified the Punta del Faro. Our steamers could now move freely along the coast between Palermo and Messina.

When we had occupied Palermo, we had acquired some merchant steamers; with these and the *Veloce*, a warship belonging to the Bourbon fleet which we also obtained, we now had a small fleet which we could use for all our requirements. The Straits of Messina from the Faro to the town were under our control.

Bixio and Eber's columns arrived from Girgenti and Caltanissetta, and a fourth division was formed under the command of Cosenz. We had grown used to having small forces, but now over a short time we had amassed a considerable army.

In the Straits of Messina

Now we were at the straits we had to cross over: once more Sicily would form part of the Italian family. The diplomats wanted us to desist, but how could we abandon the work of rebuilding our country and leave it half completed? Calabria and Naples were waiting for our arrival with open arms. And there was the rest of Italy which remained subject to the foreigner and the priest. We had to cross over, despite the Bourbons on the other side and all those who backed them.

Through the mediation of one of our supporters in Calabria we entered into negotiation with some soldiers garrisoned in the important fortress at Fiumara on the eastern shore of the straits. I ordered Missori and Mussolin to make an overnight crossing with two hundred men and try to take the fort. But the attempt failed, either because our intelligence was faulty or the guide took fright or for some other reason. The men disembarked and found themselves face to face with an enemy patrol, which they routed but who were able to raise the alarm so that our soldiers were forced to take refuge in the mountains. This was not a good beginning: we had to abandon the plan to cross the straits at the Faro and find some other part of the coast instead.

It was at this time that Bertani came over from Genoa to tell me that he had assembled five thousand men in the city and sent them to Aranci on the western coast of Sardinia. This plan had been devised by men like Mazzini, Bertani, Nicotera and others who supported our operations in the south, but also wanted us to make a diversionary attack on the Papal States or on Naples (they may also have felt some resentment at having to obey the dictatorship set up in Sicily). I did not want to reject out of hand the plan of action which these gentlemen had thought up so the idea occurred to me of joining the five thousand men at Aranci and leading them in an attack on Naples. I left Messina with Bertani on board the *Washington* bound for Aranci; once we arrived, however, I found that most of the men had already left for Palermo leaving only a remnant behind in the Sardinian port, so I changed my plan. Some of the men who were left got on the *Washington* with us; we called at La Maddalena for coal, and then stopped at Cagliari, Palermo and Milazzo before arriving back at the Punta del Faro. I found that Sirtori had already arranged for two of our steamers, the *Torino* and the *Franklin*, to navigate round the island from north to west and then along the southern and eastern coasts as far as Taormina. This was a sensible and fortunate decision. When the two ships got to Giardini, the harbour at Taormina, Bixio embarked with his division and they made an uneventful crossing to Melito on the Calabrian coast.

Bixio was going to set out on the day I arrived back at Faro, so I disembarked at Messina, took a carriage to Giardini and got there in time to join the *Franklin* and accompany the crossing over to Calabria. A curious incident took place as we were preparing to leave. I had found Bixio and his men together with the Eberhard brigade boarding the two ships. The *Torino* was a magnificent vessel in good condition and already had many men on board; the *Franklin* on the other hand was sinking and was almost completely waterlogged, with the ship's engineer complaining that the ship couldn't leave in such a state. Bixio was very annoyed and was preparing to leave on the *Torino* alone. I had been on the *Franklin* and had got almost all the officers on board to dive into the sea and look along the sides of the ship to see if they could discover the hole through which the water was coming in; while they were doing this, I also sent someone back on land to obtain some animal dung in order to make liquid manure. With this I was able to caulk the ship, at which the ship's engineer calmed down and, once he knew that I would be coming with them on the *Franklin*, allowed the rest of the men to embark. At ten in the evening we left for the Calabrian coast which we reached without mishap.

On the Mainland

Towards the end of August 1860, at three in the morning of what promised to be a fine day, we reached the beach at Melito. By the time dawn broke all the men were on land with their equipment and baggage; if it hadn't been for the fact that the *Torino* had run aground and couldn't be moved, despite all the efforts made with the *Franklin* to tow it, we could have started the march towards Reggio. At three in the afternoon three Bourbon warships appeared and started to bombard the men on shore and the ships and everything else within range. They tried to drag the *Torino* out, but didn't succeed, so set fire to it instead. The *Franklin* had already left and so was safe.

The next morning at three o'clock, we set out on the march to Reggio. Along the road we passed Capo dell'Armi; we spent the afternoon resting in a village on the road between here and Messina's beautiful twin town, Reggio. The enemy ships kept a watch on us. When evening came on we set off again. When we were still some way off the city, we turned right onto unfrequented tracks in order to avoid the enemy's outpost along the road who would be expecting our arrival. Colonel Antonino Plutino and other patriots from Reggio acted as our guides. We made various stops during the night to rest and regroup; then at two in the morning we launched an assault on the city.

Our attack from the hills to the east was unexpected and met little resistance. After firing on us and wounding Bixio, Plutino and a few other officers and soldiers, the Bourbon troops shut themselves up in the forts. We cut off the enemy outposts and took some of them captive.

During the night an incident occurred which should have been avoided at all costs – young soldiers should learn it as a rule. During a night operation I have always forbidden the use of guns; I repeated this warning during the night march. My young comrades were drawn up on the main square in Reggio after pursuing the enemy into the forts; despite my warnings a shot rang out – perhaps accidentally, from the files or, some said, from a window – and the whole column consisting of two thousand men let off their rifles, without a single enemy in sight. I was on horseback right in the middle of the square formation which the men had been ordered to keep in the piazza and had to leap down quickly; one stray bullet caught my hat.

We were in control of the city; at daybreak I told Bixio that I would leave him in Reggio and go up onto the hills to reconnoitre. I wanted to see if there were any remaining enemy forces outside the city and also to find out if the Eberhard column, which had stayed behind, was approaching. As soon as I got up onto the hills I saw an enemy column, two thousand strong, advancing from the west on the very hills where I was standing. On leaving Reggio I had brought a small infantry company with me as well as my three aides, Bezzi, Basso and Canzio – there were only a few of us compared with the enemy and everyone had to carry out more than one task.

I placed my small forces on the highest summit, where there was a house belonging to a local peasant. I warned him to leave since I thought hostilities were likely and I was not wrong. The column under the command of General Ghio was getting nearer all the time. I put my soldiers in a position of defence and sent down to the city for reinforcements. The situation was uncertain: the enemy was large and we were few. If they decided to charge us head-on rather than employing their usual tactic of firing as they advanced then resistance would be impossible and the outcome of the day would be put in jeopardy. Reggio is on the sea surrounded by hills; the Bourbon troops had control of the hills and the forts: we were facing disaster. Yet once more victory was on our side: Bixio sent reinforcements, which were not numerous but came up rapidly, and we held our position; now we had enough men to charge the enemy who abandoned the field and retreated towards the north.

The consequences of the battle at Reggio were important. The forts surrendered after putting up a shortlived defence; once inside them we found huge quantities of food and weapons. In Reggio we had gained an important base for our operations on the mainland.

In the morning we gave pursuit to Ghio's troops, who surrendered on the following day, leaving us a quantity of small arms and several field batteries.

All the forts overlooking the Straits of Messina surrendered to us, including Scilla where Cosenz's division had landed on their way to join Bixio and his men and to help in Ghio's defeat.

Our progress through Calabria turned into a triumphal march; we moved swiftly on. The inhabitants were brimming over with warlike fervour: many of them had taken up arms against their Bourbon oppressors. In Soveria the Bourbon division of eight thousand men commanded by Vial surrendered and left us immense supplies of cannon, muskets, and ammunition, while the Caldarelli brigade together with Morelli's Calabrian column gave themselves up in Cosenza.

I moved swiftly ahead always in advance of our columns who, despite forced marches, could not keep up with me, and after a few days I arrived in Naples.

Entry into Naples

The entry into the city was more like some miraculous phenomenon than an actual event. Together with a few aides I passed among the Bourbon troops who were still in control; they presented arms and treated me with the greatest respect, more than they showed at the time to their own generals.

The seventh of September 1860: no Neapolitan will ever forget that glorious day. It was the day on which a hated dynasty fell, once described by a great English statesman as 'the curse of God', and on its ruins rose a sovereign republic governed by the people, a state of affairs unhappily destined never to last long. On this day a son of the people accompanied by a handful of friends, who called themselves his aides-de-camp, entered the proud capital city, acclaimed and supported by half a million inhabitants; with a single fervent and irresistible will they paralysed an entire army, unseated a tyrant, and recovered their sacred rights. Such was their force it could have moved the whole of Italy and set it on the road of duty; such was their roar it could have cowed the country's greedy and insolent rulers and toppled them in the dust. Although the Bourbon troops held all the fortresses and the main positions in the city, from which they could have wreaked destruction on the huge crowds, their enthusiasm and appearance was so formid-able that the soldiers stood meekly by.

I entered Naples while the Army of the South was still far off towards the Straits of Messina. The Bourbon King had abandoned the city on the previous day and fled to Capua. He left his monarchical nest still warm, to be taken over by the freedom-loving local populace and the richly woven carpets in his palaces were trodden by the rough boots of the city's proletariat. Such events should teach a lesson to those governments who boast they are dedicated to the improvement of the human condition, while in reality are only helping the egoism and arrogance and stubbornness of the privileged classes; even when the lion of the people roars in despair at their very doors and with good reason seeks to tear them apart in wild anger, born of the hatred which they themselves have sown, they remain utterly impervious to reform.

Another circumstance which favoured our cause was the tacit approval of the Bourbon fleet: if they had been entirely hostile towards us, our progress towards the capital would have been much slower. As it was, our steamers were able to transport our unmolested troops quite freely up the whole length of the coast to Naples, an impossible undertaking if the fleet had fought against us.

As in Palermo but to greater effect, the party of Cavour's supporters had been exercising their influence and I found many obstacles placed in my way. When the news arrived that the Sardinian army had invaded the Papal States, their arrogance grew insolent. Underhand dealing was second nature to them and they had tried every ruse. They had flattered themselves that they could stop us at the Straits of Messina and confine our operations to Sicily; it was with this intention that they had called on our generous ally – or should I say our master since he dictated all the terms? – who accordingly dispatched a vessel from the French navy to the Faro. It was the English Foreign Minister, Lord John Russell, who stepped in to help us and vetoed France from interfering in our affairs. But what hurt me most in their machinations was the discovery that certain comrades who were dear to me and whose loyalty I would never have doubted had a hand in them. Incorruptible men, swayed by the hypocritical, terrible pretext of necessity. The necessity of being cowards! The necessity of abasing oneself in the mud before some ephemeral image of power instead of heeding and understanding the vigorous, forceful, virile will of the people who wish to *exist* at any cost and are prepared to destroy these insect-eating icons and bury them back in the dung from which they sprang.

These gentlemen and their like caused me much grief when they stepped in to act as protectors after we had carried off the victory; if we had been defeated they would have treated us with contempt, just as they treated Francis II. I bore it all however for the sake – and only for this – of the sacred cause of Italy. One example of their behaviour: two battalions of the Sardinian army arrived. Their support had not been requested; their real purpose was to make sure of their hold on Naples and its wealth. However, I was told that if I so wished they would be placed under my command. I did so wish, and I was told that first the ambassador's approval would need to be obtained. I went to the ambassador who told me that this was a matter for the Government in Turin!

The brave men I commanded fought and won at the Volturno river not only without the help of a single soldier from the regular army, but without the support of any of the voluntary units of young Italians who wanted to join us from all over the country and which Cavour and Farini either prevented from leaving or imprisoned.

In Palermo too the Cavourians plotted and schemed and tried to spread distrust of the Thousand among the populace and encourage them to vote for an untimely annexation.

I had to leave my army on the Volturno on the eve of the battle in order to go to Palermo and calm the inhabitants of the city down. My absence led to the Army of the South's defeat at Caiazzo, the only defeat we suffered throughout the whole campaign.

Before the Volturno Campaign

Before leaving for Palermo, I had advised Sirtori, my worthy chief of staff, to get small units of our men to attack the enemy's lines of communication. This he did; it seems however that the person who was given responsibility for leading the attacks decided to go further, in the belief that our valiant soldiers could undertake anything after the series of victories they had won.

A decision was made to take the village of Caiazzo to the east of Capua on the right bank of the Volturno. The position was fairly defensible, but was only a few miles from the main body of the enemy forces who were camped also to the east of Capua. The enemy numbered about forty thousand men and was growing larger every day.

In order to take the village an initial sortie was made on the left bank of the Volturno, in which we lost several good soldiers: we had no cover and the enemy's rifles were of better quality. On the nineteenth of September the operation took place and Caiazzo was occupied. I arrived back from Palermo in time to witness the terrible spectacle of our men being mown down: as was the custom of volunteers, they had marched vigorously down to the riverbank, but then a hail of bullets forced them to turn and flee as there was nowhere they could shelter and they were shot in the back. This was the result of the sortie that had been organised to draw the enemy's attention and occupy Caiazzo. On the following day huge Bourbon forces attacked Caiazzo and the few men inside it were forced to evacuate, fleeing in a rush towards the Volturno, where many were either shot down by the enemy or drowned as they tried to cross the river. The operation was more than merely imprudent; it showed a severe lack of military skill on the part of the commander who organised it.

The Bourbon army, crushed by its many defeats in Sicily and Calabria and in Naples, withdrew behind the Volturno, basing itself at Capua, which it fortified and filled with provisions.

When the first columns of our army arrived on the outskirts of Naples they were sent off to Avellino and Ariano in order to quell some reactionary uprisings there which had been fomented by the clergy and other supporters of the dynasty. Turr was given this job and did it very well. Once the disturbances had been suppressed I ordered Turr and his division to occupy Caserta and Santa Maria. As the rest of the army arrived in Naples they stayed in the capital only very briefly before being sent on towards Caserta. Bixio's division occupied Maddaloni, taking control of the main road which goes to Campobasso and the Abruzzi and forming the right wing of our small army. Medici's division occupied Monte Sant'Angelo, which overlooks Capua and the Volturno river, with reinforcements of newly formed troops under the command of General Avezzana. One brigade from Medici's division, under the command of General Sacchi, took control of the northern slope of Monte Tifate which descends to the Volturno. All these troops formed our centre. Turr's division in Santa Maria was our left wing. The reserves were stationed in Caserta with Sirtori in charge of them.

On the first of October, in the low-lying country around Campania's ancient capital, the sun rose on the terrible confusion of a fratricidal battle. It is true that there were many foreign mercenaries fighting on the enemy side: Bavarians, Swiss and all the others who have grown used to thinking of Italy as a holiday resort or a brothel. With the guidance and blessing of the clergy, such a mob has always had a predilection for butchering Italians, who have in turn been taught by the priests always to submit. But most of the enemy soldiers on the slopes of Monte Tifate were, like ours, the sons of this unhappy land, driven to massacre each other: they were led by a young king who was the son of a criminal[33] whereas we were fighting for our country and its sacred cause. Since Hannibal defeated the proud Roman legions, Campania has never witnessed a more ferociously fought conflict: for many years to come the local oxen pulling the plough over those gentle slopes will stumble against the human skulls of those who were felled on that day by the ferocity of their fellow-men.

When I returned from Palermo I took to going up daily to the village of Sant'Angelo, from where the whole enemy camp could be seen to the east of Capua on the right bank of the Volturno; from these observations I understood that they were preparing to go on the offensive and join battle. Their numbers had increased and some partial advantages they had over us made them overconfident. On our side we built some useful defences at Maddaloni, Sant'Angelo and especially at Santa Maria Capua Vetere, which was on the plain and the most exposed.

At about three in the morning on the first of October I and some of my staff took a train from Caserta, where I had set up my headquarters, to Santa Maria where I arrived before dawn. I was getting into a carriage to go to Sant'Angelo when I heard a burst of gunfire coming from the left. Milbitz was in command of the troops there; he arrived and told me: 'We're under attack in Sanammaro – I'll go and see what else is happening.' I ordered the carriage to drive at top speed. The noise of the guns increased and extended gradually along the whole front line as far as Sant'Angelo. At first light I arrived at the road to the left of our forces in Sant'Angelo, who were already fighting; as we drew up a hail of enemy bullets greeted us. The coachman was killed and the carriage was riddled with bullet holes; I and my aides had to get out and force our way through with our sabres. I soon found myself in the midst of Mosto's Genoese soldiers and Simonetta's Lombard unit, so there was no need for self-defence: those brave men saw we were in difficulties and charged the Bourbon troops with such force that they were driven a good way back, leaving the road to Sant'Angelo clear for us to continue. The enemy's penetration of our lines and their movement to our rear were carried out with great skill and at night: they clearly knew the terrain very well.

Between the roads that descend towards Capua from Monte Tifata and Monte Sant'Angelo there is a network of deep lanes sunk in the volcanic tufo. Perhaps they were used in ancient times to keep lines of communication open during a battle; the rainwater flowing down from the surrounding mountains has certainly worn them away and made them deeper. A large force, even one which comprised infantry, cavalry and artillery, could move along one of these lanes completely out of sight. As part of the Bourbon generals' carefully prepared battle plan, various battalions had been moved along them during the night, managing to get above and behind our lines on the steep upper slopes of Monte Tifate.

Once I was free of the combat I'd temporarily found myself involved in, I went on with my aides in the direction of Sant'Angelo, thinking that the enemy troops were only on our left. As we climbed up, however, I soon realised that their forces were also behind our lines and had control of the upper slopes. Without a moment's delay I assembled as many of our soldiers as there were around me and set off up the mountain roads in an attempt to outflank the enemy and get above them. At the same time I sent a Milanese company to take control of Monte Tifate and the village of San Nicola on its summit, which rises above all the hills round Sant'Angelo. These men together with two other companies from Sacchi's brigade, who had come over promptly at my order, blocked the enemy's advance; the Bourbon troops scattered and many were taken prisoner. With this I could continue up to Monte Sant'Angelo where I had a view of the whole battlefront extending from Santa Maria to Sant'Angelo; the battle was raging, with our men sometimes gaining the upper hand and sometimes giving way as the enemy forces charged them.

All my observations from Monte Sant'Angelo in the days preceding the battle had told me that an attack was imminent: I had not been taken in by the enemy's various reconnaissance sorties on our right and left wings, the principal purpose of which was to get us to move our forces out of the centre, where it was planning to concentrate its assault. It was a good thing I had not been deceived since on the day of the battle the Bourbons used all their available troops on the field and in the fortresses to launch, as luck would have it, a simultaneous attack on all our positions along the whole length of our line. There was determined fighting everywhere from Maddaloni to Santa Maria Capua Vetere.

At Maddaloni the outcome hung in the balance until Bixio succeeded in driving back the enemy; they were forced to retreat at Santa Maria, where Milbitz was wounded. In both places they left behind prisoners and cannon. Eventually after fighting which continued for more than six hours we drove them back at Sant'Angelo, but here the enemy forces were so numerous that a large column remained in control of the lines of communication between the village and Santa Maria. The result was that I had to join the reserves I had asked Sirtori to organise, and who were supposed to come by train from Caserta to Santa Maria, by going round to the east of the road, reaching the village after two in the afternoon. The reserves from Caserta were just arriving: I drew them up in a column of attack on the road leading to Sant'Angelo, with Milano's brigade at the head, supported by Eber's brigade, and a part of Assanti's brigade in reserve. I found Pace's Calabrian men among the trees on my right and ordered them to attack, which they did with equal fervour.

As soon as the head of the column emerged from the dense thicket which lines the road leading out of Santa Maria, at about three in the afternoon, they were sighted by the enemy who started throwing grenades. There was a shortlived moment of panic, but the young Milanese bersaglieri who were marching in front when the order to charge sounded threw themselves on the enemy, quickly followed by a battalion from the same brigade which charged the enemy lines without firing, as I had ordered.

The road from Santa Maria to Sant'Angelo is situated to the right of the road from Santa Maria to Capua at an angle of about forty degrees so that as our column advanced along the road its deployment was always to the left where the enemy was positioned behind natural defences. Once the Milanese and the Calabrians were engaged, I sent the Eber brigade to join the attack to the right of the Milanese. How good it was to see these Hungarian veterans and their comrades from the Thousand march off calmly and cool-headedly, maintaining good order as if they were on manoeuvres. The Assanti brigade followed up the advance; the enemy soon retreated towards Capua.

At the same time as this attack on the enemy's centre was taking place, Medici and Avezzana's divisions attacked on the right, and the rest of Turr's division on the road to Capua on the left. At about five in the afternoon, after putting up a determined fight, the enemy was forced to retreat in confusion inside Capua, protected by the cannon in the fortress there. At the same time Bixio sent me news of his victory over the enemy's right wing. I was able to send a telegraph to Naples: 'Victory along the whole of the line.' We had fought and won a battle of key importance.

Fighting in the Old Town of Caserta

When I returned to Sant'Angelo in the evening, tired and hungry as I had eaten nothing all day, I had the good luck to find my Genoese carabinieri installed in the parish priest's house. It was fortunate I found them: I ate a good supper followed by coffee and was glad to go to bed and get some sleep, I can't recall where. But I was destined to get no rest – as soon as I lay down I was told that an enemy column of four to five thousand men were in the Old Town of Caserta and threatening to move down to Caserta. Such news had to be taken seriously: I gave orders for the Genoese carabinieri to be ready at two in the morning, with three hundred and fifty men from Spangaro's troop and sixty local people from the slopes of Vesuvius. At the agreed time I marched at the head of these combined forces on Caserta, down the mountain road which passes through San Leucio. Before we got to Caserta, Colonel

Missori, who'd been instructed to find out the enemy with some of his guides, informed me that they were spread out on the hill round the Old Town of Caserta and on the slopes stretching down towards Caserta. I soon saw this for myself. At Caserta I agreed a plan of attack with General Sirtori; I did not think they would be bold enough to launch a direct attack on my headquarters, but I turned out to be wrong. With Sirtori I arranged that all the available forces to be found in the vicinity should be assembled; with these we would march on the enemy's right flank to attack their troops in the upper stretches of the royal park at Caserta. In this way the Bourbon troops would find themselves between us, Sacchi's brigade at San Leucio, and Bixio's division which I had ordered to attack from the direction of Maddaloni. From the hill on which the Old Town of Caserta stands, the enemy could see that there were not many troops in Caserta and decided to occupy the town. It is probable that they had not yet learnt the outcome of the previous day's battle. They launched a vigorous assault on the town with about half their men. So as I was marching under cover round their right flank, two thousand of their troops came hurtling down the hill on our headquarters. They might well have seized them if it had not been for the quick thinking shown by Sirtori and a handful of our men who were with him who managed to fight them off. I continued meanwhile towards the enemy's right flank, together with General Stocco's Calabrians, four companies from our regular army and some other units. We found the enemy in battle formation on the hill, ready to follow up the attack on the town below. Our sudden appearance took them completely by surprise. They put up little resistance and we were able to chase them back almost as far as the Old Town of Caserta. Once there some of them made a stand, firing on us from the windows and from some ruins where they'd taken shelter, but they were soon surrounded and caught. Those who fled to the south were caught by Bixio's division which, after its glorious efforts and success in Maddaloni on the previous day, was racing to join us in the new battle. Those who were taken in the north surrendered to Sacchi, who had been ordered to follow my column. The enemy had certainly given us cause for alarm, but only a few of their troops managed to get away. These were the same troops which had on the previous day attacked and killed the small battalion commanded by Major Bronzetti at Castel Morrone; this brave band of men had kept them locked in conflict for most of the day and so prevented them from approaching to our rear during the battle. The two hundred martyrs of Bronzetti's battalion may well have saved our army.

As we have seen, what decided the fate of the Battle of the Volturno was the arrival of the reserve troops on the field at three in the afternoon. If the enemy had held these reserves back at Caserta, the eventual outcome of the battle would at the least have been uncertain. All this goes to show that the Bourbon generals' tactics were not so bad; in the chances of war, luck or the intervention of some other higher power is needed.

With the victory at the Old Town of Caserta on the second of October 1860 the glorious series of battles fought in the 1860 campaign was concluded. The troops sent by Farini and others from the north to put a stop to our revolutionary activities were welcomed as brothers; this army completed the rout of the Bourbons from the Kingdom of the two Sicilies. In an attempt to improve my fellow-soldiers' circumstances I asked for the Army of the South to be incorporated into the national forces; this request was unjustly refused. The fruits of conquest were welcome, but the conquerors were not.

I resigned the dictatorship which had been conferred on me by the people into the hands of Victor Emmanuel and proclaimed him King of Italy. I asked him to make provision for my gallant brothers-in-arms, which was all that concerned me on my departure, keen as I was to regain my solitude. So I left those generous-spirited young men who had trusted in me and followed me across the Mediterranean, making light of mishaps, discomforts, dangers, facing the prospect of death in ten ferocious battles with only the hope of the reward they had reaped in Lombardy and in central Italy: the praise of their own consciences and of the world who witnessed such extraordinary deeds. With companions like these, to whom I owe most of my successes, no undertaking however arduous would ever deter me!

A tree is judged by the quality of the fruit it bears, and individuals are judged by the benefits they can bestow on their fellow-human beings. Being born, existing, eating and drinking, and dying – insects do all this as well. In times like those in 1860 in southern Italy men are truly alive and live their lives in the service of others. This is the real life of the soul!

'Leave it up to others' – this is what those who are inclined to do nothing, except to make sure they keep their snouts in the trough of the public exchequer, usually say. This was the thinking behind the monarchy's veto on the expedition of the Thousand: it didn't want us to go to Sicily; it didn't want us to cross over into Calabria; nor, later, the Volturno. We went to Sicily; we crossed the Straits of Messina and then the Volturno – and if we hadn't Italy would now be worse off.

'You must proclaim the republic!' Mazzini and his followers cried, as they continue to do today, as if these learned fellows, accustomed to viewing the world from behind their desks, know the people's moral and material condition better than we do, who had the good fortune to lead them and guide them to victory.

Nothing good can be expected from either the monarchies or the clergy – so much is obvious, increasingly so as each day passes. But it is totally false to say that we should have proclaimed the republic from Palermo to Naples in 1860. Those who say this don't do so because they believe what they're saying; they say it out of the partisan hatred they have nursed continually since 1848.

We had the monarchy's veto in 1860 and we had it again in 1862. It seems to me that overthrowing the Papacy is as important, perhaps more important than toppling the Bourbons. And that is what the by now customary band of redshirts intended to do in 1862: to overthrow Italy's fiercest and most implacable enemy and to reclaim its natural capital, with no other purpose and no other ambition than doing good to our country. It was a sacred cause, the circumstances were the same, and Sicily with its customary generosity – apart from those who were already busy feasting at the table we had prepared in 1860 – answered our call at Marsala, 'Rome or death', with its customary enthusiasm.

It's worth repeating what I've said on other occasions: if Italy had two such cities like Palermo we would have reached Rome without any problems.

Pallavicino, the venerable martyr of the Spielberg prison and an old friend of mine, was the governor in Palermo. I disliked doing anything which could cause him any bother. But it was all the fault of the attitude of 'Leave it up to others': only those men who were not prepared to remain useless, who wanted to make a difference, would have the drive to make the attempt. So I gave the rallying call at Marsala: 'Rome or death', and in response an elite band of young men from Palermo and later from the provinces gathered at Ficuzza, a wooded estate a few miles outside the capital city.

Corrao and other comrades obtained supplies of weapons. Bagnasco, Capello and other patriots founded an organising committee. As well as old comrades from the mainland campaigns – Nullo, Missori, Cairoli, Manci, Piccinini, and others – there was a new Thousand ready to take the field and fight the tyranny of the Church, so much more harmful than that of the Bourbons. But in the eyes of the monarchy we had committed the offence of winning ten victories and added insult to injury by increasing its dominions – things which kings cannot forgive. Many of the men who had given their enthusiastic support to unification in 1860 were now well established and well satisfied; they criticised our undertaking or stayed aloof, scared of catching an infection if they associated with a restless and discontented revolutionary rabble. Nevertheless, thanks to Palermo's proud response and the involvement of the entire island, we were able to march as far as Catania without any serious obstacle being placed in our way. The inhabitants of Catania were equally enthusiastic; those who wanted to stop us going held back and did nothing when they saw the people's reaction.

We crossed over to the mainland on two steamers, a French vessel and one belonging to the Florio company, which happened to be in Catania. There were several frigates from the Italian navy just outside the entrance to the harbour and they could have prevented our embarkation and departure; they certainly had orders to do so. It is to the honour of their commanders – whom I applaud – that no attempt was made to oppose us. In such circumstances men of honour are duty bound to sheathe their swords.

Our passage across the Straits of Messina was highly dangerous since the steamers were too full. Many men had had to be turned away for lack of space on board. In my seagoing days I have seen many overcrowded ships, but never like these. The majority of the soldiers were new arrivals; they hadn't been counted and organised into companies and they were unknown to the officers; they poured onto the ships threatening to submerge them. It was pointless asking them to disembark – they wouldn't think of turning back – but it was dangerous, perhaps fatal, to go on. I stood undecided for a while, conscious of the responsibility I was taking on, weighing up whether to leave or not in these conditions. It would be impossible to issue orders as there was no room on board to move a step let alone walk about. The future of my country might depend on my decision.

It was getting dark. Either we set out or we stayed as we were, crammed together like sardines, in an impossible situation, waiting for an unavoidable fiasco to happen.

We left and once more fortune favoured the cause of justice. The wind and the sea were just right: there was a moderate wind at the Faro, just as there had been in 1860, and the sea was comparatively calm. After an uneventful crossing we reached the beach at Melito at dawn on the following day where all the men were able to disembark.

As in 1860 we took the coast road past Capo dell'Armi towards Reggio. Then the Bourbons were our enemies and we were seeking them out to fight them. Now the Italian army lay ahead: we wanted to avoid them at all costs, but they were equally determined to find us and destroy us.

It was an Italian battleship which first attacked us. It was moving along the coast in parallel with our march and fired some muskets in our direction so that we had to move the men inland to protect them. Some units sent out from Reggio with orders to attack us made an assault on our vanguard. We tried to let them know that we had no wish to fight them, but in vain: they ordered us to surrender. Obviously we didn't want to so we had to escape their fratricidal bullets.

Faced with such a state of affairs and wanting to avoid unnecessary bloodshed I ordered the troops to turn off to the right and take the road to Aspromonte. The Italian army's hostility towards us had naturally created alarm among the local people and made it very difficult for us to obtain provisions. My poor volunteers lacked everything, including the most vital necessity, food; whenever by some miracle we came across a shepherd with his flock he refused to help us as though we were brigands or worse. The priests and the reactionaries had had no trouble convincing these good but simple folk that we should be regarded as excommunicates and outlaws. Yet we were the same men we had been in 1860 and our purpose was as noble as the one we pursued then. Fortune was less kind to us, it is true; it is not the first time I have seen the local populace inert and indifferent towards those who wished to give them their freedom. This was not true of the Sicilians, I will readily admit: they were as generous and as enthusiastic in 1862 as they had been two years before. Their finest young men joined us; among the more experienced there was the aged Baron Avizzani of Castrogiovanni, who endured the privations and discomforts of the campaign like a youth. And there were many discomforts and privations! I was hungry, but many of my companions must have suffered from worse hunger.

After immensely difficult marches along paths which were practically impassable, we reached the high plateau of Aspromonte at dawn on the twenty-ninth of August 1862, tired and famished. We gathered some green potatoes to eat – raw at first, and then when the first hunger pangs had subsided, roasted. Here I must pay tribute to the good folk who live in that mountainous region of Calabria. They didn't appear immediately – the paths are poor and communications difficult – but in the afternoon they arrived carrying plentiful supplies of fruit and bread and other food. But the oncoming catastrophe gave us little time to enjoy their benevolence.

At three in the afternoon we sighted to the west, some miles off, the head of the column led by Pallavicini, on its way to attack us. The level where we had spent the whole day resting was too exposed and we could easily have been surrounded so I ordered us to move camp further up the mountain. We reached the edges of the beautiful pine forest which crowns Aspromonte; here we set up camp facing our attackers and with the forest behind us.

It is true that in 1860 the Sardinian army had threatened to attack us and it was only the great love we bore our own country which prevented us from starting a fratricidal war. In 1862, however, the Italian army was stronger and we were much weaker; they were vowed to destroy us and ran upon us as if we had been a band of brigands, or with even greater keenness. No warnings of any kind were given. They arrived and they charged us with astonishing casualness. They were obeying orders, obviously: it was a question of wiping us out, and since brothers born from the same mother might be expected to hesitate before trying to kill each other, those orders were to charge on us when they found us without stopping to think. When the column was within firing range, Pallavicini drew up his lines which started resolutely to advance on us, firing all the time – a tactic which the Bourbon troops also used and which in my opinion is ineffective.

We did not return their fire. For me the moment was truly terrible. We could either throw down our arms and submit like sheep, or shed the blood of our brothers. But no such scruples affected the monarchy's soldiers, or rather, their leaders. Were they counting on my hatred of civil war? This seems likely and would explain why they marched on us with such imperturbable confidence.

I ordered my men not to fire and they obeyed, except for a few excitable youths on our right wing, under the command of my son Menotti, who, when they were charged, countercharged, a little ostentatiously, and drove them back.

High up on the slope with the forest behind us, we had a good defensible position which ten men could have held against a hundred. But there was no point: since we were putting up no resistance our attackers would soon reach us. As often happens in such situations, the attackers grow bolder when they see their enemy is not resisting; the bersaglieri who were advancing on us increased their fire. I was standing between the two front lines to stop the massacre and so received two bullets from a rifle, in my left thigh and in my right foot.

Menotti was also wounded. When the order not to return fire was given most of the men had withdrawn into the forest. My officers, including our surgeons Ripari, Basile, and Albanese, remained with me and I owe my life to their care.

It is a repellent business to have to relate such squalid incidents. The episode was so full of them that even sewage workers would feel sick. There were those who rubbed their hands in delight when they heard the news that I'd been wounded, fatally as they at first thought and hoped. Some denied they had ever been friends with me and others confessed they had been deceived in praising my merits. But, in honour to mankind, I must also admit that there were good individuals who looked after me like a mother and nursed me with loving care, above all my dear friend Cencio Cattabene, who died before his time and was lost to the service of his country.

So the Savoys had caught their prey and in just the condition they wanted him in, fit for nothing. The usual meaningless civilities were extended to me – like the courtesy with which the most notorious criminals are led to the scaffold – but instead of leaving me to recover in a hospital in Reggio or Messina I was put on board a frigate and taken all the way up the Tyrrhenian coast to Varignano, all the while suffering from the wound in my foot, which may not have been fatal but was excruciatingly painful. But they wanted their prey securely within reach. I repeat: recounting such squalid matters disgusts me. I will not bore my reader with tales of wounds, hospitals, prisons, and the courteousness of the vultures who had me in their power. So I was taken to Varignano, La Spezia, Pisa and then to Caprera. My sufferings were many, but so were the caring attentions my friends lavished on me. The doyen of Italian surgeons, Professor Zanetti, had the honour of extracting the bullet. After thirteen months the wound in my foot finally healed; until 1866 I led a useless, inert existence.

The Campaign in the Tyrol

Nearly four years had passed since the day I was shot in Aspromonte. I soon forget such injuries, as the opportunists – those men who are guided by the utility rather than the morality of the methods they employ – were counting on.

Rumours had been circulating for days that we had entered into an alliance with Prussia against Austria; on the tenth of June 1866 my friend General Fabrizi came to Caprera to ask me, on behalf of the Government and our own followers, if I would lead the volunteers who were gathering from every part of Italy. I left for the mainland the very same day and immediately marched to Como where the largest numbers of volunteers had assembled. They were indeed many: young men full of energy and fire, always ready to fight for their country with no thought of reward. And to lead them there were the courageous veterans of a hundred former battles.

This said, no cannon were supplied since the volunteers could lose them; there were the usual defective rifles rather than the good ones which were given to the regular troops; a stinted supply of uniforms so that many volunteers faced the enemy dressed in civilian clothes. In a word, the usual mean tricks which the supporters of the monarchy have always played on the volunteers.

All the omens for the military campaign in 1866 and for Italy's prospects were promising, but the actual outcome was shameful. For a time we had ceased to be the ignominious proctectorate of France and, since we were incapable of acting alone, entered into a new alliance with Prussia, which was less unpalatable, and proved to be useful to us far beyond our deserts. Though its government had drained it dry, the nation was full of enthusiasm and ready to make sacrifices. Our fleet was large and faced a weaker and dispirited enemy. Our army was almost double the size of the Austrian forces and for the first time included in its ranks young men from the whole of Italy, from Sicily to the Alps, all of them keen to fight our old enemy; only the arrogant ignorance and incapacity of its leaders could have brought such an army to such a disastrous pass as Custoza proved to be.

There could have been a hundred thousand volunteers, but our uninspired Government, beset by the usual fears, limited the force to a third of that number. There were the usual problems with the supply of arms, clothing, etc. When the battle at Custoza took place, a few thousand men were at Salò, Lonato and Lake Garda, while the rear regiments were still in southern Italy waiting for shoes, weapons, etc.

Yet despite these setbacks it promised to be a brilliant campaign, one which would enable Italy to take its place among the leading European nations, which would rejuvenate the old matron and let her live again as in the early days of Roman glory. Yet, in the hands of Jesuitical army leaders, it all ended in a cesspit of humiliation.

The Government was under pressure from public opinion to establish the volunteer force, but its distrust and fear of these men who were fighting for the rights and liberties of their country remained: they supplied arms to some, but the way in which they were supplied and the force was organised and their various needs met betrayed the Government's dislike and malevolence. They were rushed to the border where hostilities threatened to break out in two days' time. The haste with which the army was moved and the unfortunate events which immediately followed were reasons for massing all the volunteers together in one force, but the powers-that-be in their wisdom – or rather with the usual blunders and cover-ups – did not want so many volunteers together at the same time and so, with some trumped-up excuses to hide their own shortcomings, sent half of them down south.

Here in all fairness I must mention that the King from the outset, when he told me he was going to put forward my name as commander of the volunteer forces, had also discussed the possibility of a campaign on the Dalmatian coast which would be led by me and Admiral Persano. It was said that the King's idea was resolutely opposed by his generals, Lamarmora in particular. The idea of operating in the Adriatic was immensely attractive and I complimented the King for suggesting such a bold and potentially beneficial strategic plan. In fact it was too good an idea for some of the brains in our esteemed Government; I soon realised that keeping five volunteer regiments down in the south was simply a way of making sure they wouldn't be under my command, just as they had done with the regiment of the Apennines in 1859. Extending the action of the war to the east was a truly magnificent prospect. A force of thirty thousand men on the Dalmatian coast could really have shaken the Austrian monarchy. So many supporters and friends from Greece to Hungary would have rallied to us – all the peoples at enmity with Austria and Turkey, who were ready to rise up and fight their oppressors if we had given the signal. The Austrians would have been forced to send out a large army against us and so have fewer troops to spare for the campaigns in the west; and if they didn't do this, then we could have gone on into their heartlands and lit the fuse which would lead to the liberation of the ten nations which make up that monstrous and miscellaneous empire.

So the campaign took place around the shores of Lake Garda, although when I'd been first approached I was told that I would be free to choose where to operate. Since it was to be Lake Garda, I asked for the flotilla stationed at Salò to be placed under my command, a request which was granted straight away. As it turned out, the wretched condition of the ships simply caused me problems; I had to rescue the fleet from a larger and much better organised enemy navy. The volunteers had to be drafted to man the ships and the defensive garrisons along the shore, especially after our defeat at Custoza and the retreat of our army.

An entire regiment had to stay behind in Salò for the sole purpose of guarding the harbour and the nearby stretch of shoreline and the forts which were being built along it for defence. General Avezzana and his officers, including a large detachment of volunteer marines from Ancona, Livorno and other Italian ports, also had to remain in Salò for the same reason.

The Austrian flotilla on Lake Garda comprised eight war steamers, carrying forty-eight cannon, properly manned and provided for. On my arrival I found just one gunboat carrying a single cannon ready for action in the Italian flotilla; the other five, like this, were steam-powered and also carried one cannon, but one was grounded and unfit for use and the other four had defective engines. We immediately set to work repairing these, but it was nevertheless only towards the end of the campaign that we had five working gunboats, each with a 24-calibre cannon, whereas the enemy had forty-eight cannon, 80-calibre and smaller. We also started to build rafts and arm them: these could have been extremely useful, but the lack of material and the slow progress of the work meant that not one was ever finished and ready to use.

Battles, Fights

All our regiments were called to the western shore of Lake Garda; according to our orders we were to operate in the Tyrol so I led the second regiment and the second bersaglieri towards the Caffaro bridge so that we could take control of it and the strong position of Monte Suello. We accomplished this quickly and skilfully, driving the Austrians back. The initiative had succeeded: with the rest of the available regiments I got ready to follow our vanguard into the Tyrol, when the fatal battle of the twenty-fourth took place.[34]

I received a communication from Lamarmora informing me of the unhappy outcome, ordering me to defend Brescia and advising me not to rely on the Italian army who were in retreat to a position behind the Oglio river: I called the vanguard back from the Tyrol and decided to assemble as many forces as I could at Lonato, where we could defend both Brescia and Salò as well as gather together the men who had got lost and material which had been left behind by the army. The volunteers, who were abundantly supplied with patriotism and enthusiasm but nothing else, advanced with forced marches towards Lonato, but it was unlikely they could reach their destination quickly: their rifles were defective and they were lacking important items of equipment, which they had to pick up while on the march. But a few days after the events of the twenty-fourth we entered Lonato and Desenzano. Having occupied these and established outposts at Rivoltella, and with our right wing extending as far as Pozzolengo, we were able to defend Brescia as we had been ordered to, as well as Salò with its arsenal, depots and flotilla; and, much to our satisfaction, we were also able to gather up soldiers and vehicles left behind by our army in retreat.

I do not like to criticise the defeated and I should not want my comments on the way the army was commanded to be interpreted as my revenge for the many wrongs I had to submit to from its commanders. Yet it has to be said: we were all expecting a brilliant outcome from a brilliant army, double the size of the enemy's forces, with vast means at its disposal, the best artillery force in the world, its well-trained troops fired up with enthusiasm; it was a bitter disappointment to us when this same army retreated in confusion behind a river thirty miles off even though the enemy was not in pursuit, leaving almost the whole of Lombardy undefended.

After it was beaten the main army retreated from the Mincio to the

Oglio. But why did the right wing of our forces on the Po have to retreat too? Ninety thousand men on the banks of the mighty Po were in retreat, but from whom? The enemy had eighty thousand men on the Mincio; it is true that they had just won a battle over an army which outnumbered them, but their men must have been jaded and battle-weary. Why retreat from the Po as far as the Apennines? The reasoning entirely escapes me. I do not know the identity of the Austrian general[35] who was in command in 1866, but he must have been a genius since he defeated an army more than twice the size of his, made up of soldiers who were certainly the equals of his men.

The Prussian victory at Sadowa in the north must have helped to stop the Austrian advance. Yet if this general had shown a little more determination he could have come and crushed my eighty thousand men with no artillery to defend them and then sauntered on into Lombardy and Piedmont with every chance of obtaining an advantageous peace.

Yet the volunteers showed not a trace of confusion or fear or dismay. The disaster weighed heavily on them, but their confidence in their country's destiny never faltered nor was the enthusiasm which had led them to leave their homes on the wane – if anything our dangerous and uncertain situation served to increase it. 'Let's fight on!' was the universal cry. And if they had had a month in which to organise and train, and had been properly armed they would have worked miracles. When one reflects in hindsight and with impartiality on the reasons for our army's defeat, leaving aside such factors as the incapacity of certain commanders and the local peasantry's unwillingness to support the national cause, it can be asserted, without mincing words, that the campaign strategy was mistaken from the outset. As usual we wanted to defeat the entire enemy with just one half of our army, whereas the Austrian general defeated half our army with the whole of his. As history testifies, the latter system has usually been found to give the better results.

The Italian army was divided in two: there were 120,000 men on the Mincio and 90,000 on the Po, and each division was larger than the enemy forces which comprised 80,000 men well-protected in their line of strongholds. In my opinion the main error committed by our commander-in-chief was to start by threatening the enemy lines at various points with separate divisions and then trying to give the decisive blow to the main body of the enemy army with a collective force of 180,000 men.

The Po estuary, where we could have had as many steamers and other types of boat as we needed, would have been in my opinion the best place for the passage of our army. Once we were in control of both sides of the river the rest of our forces together with all our equipment could have been brought over in a very short space of time. In coming out to fight us the enemy would have had to abandon the redoubtable Quadrilateral, the area defended by the four fortresses of Mantua, Peschiera, Verona and Legnago, which afforded them such protection.

The Austrian general took advantage of our mistakes and wisely concentrated all his available forces in the area round Verona, from where he attacked that half of our army which was on the Mincio river and which had led the offensive.

It is not so many years ago that Napoleon I employed the same strategy: he raised the siege of Mantua in order to defeat, one after the other, the two separate halves of the Austrian army positioned on either side of Lake Garda. They had made the mistake of dividing up on either side of the lake in order to attack the French, but the great general anticipated them and destroyed them.

After the Battle of Custoza we remained at Lonato and Desenzano until we were ordered to go back to the Tyrol, as the army was ready to return to the offensive. We left the second regiment under the command of Avezzana to defend Salò, the flotilla and the other key positions on the lake as far as Gargnano, and once we had completed the defence batteries on the western shore, we left for the Caffaro bridge with the first and third regiments and the second battalion of bersaglieri.

After we had abandoned the bridge the first time, the enemy, buoyed up by its victory at Custoza, had established a strong garrison here and at Monte Suello. I decided to make a sudden attack in order to chase the enemy off and so open the road to the Tyrol.

On the third of July we left Salò at dawn and reached Rocca d'Anfo by midday; there I found Colonel Corte, then in command of the vanguard, made up of the three divisions I have named; he was already preparing to dislodge the enemy from the frontier. He had sent Major Mosto at the head of five hundred men towards Bagolino along the mountain road and through the valleys to the west of Rocca d'Anfo, with the aim of carrying out a diversion on the enemy's right wing and rear. An Austrian outpost had been sighted from Rocca d'Anfo, at Sant'Antonio, so we sought to bypass it by sending a detachment from the first bersaglieri battalion under the command of Captain Bezzi through the mountains. But neither of the diversions succeeded because of torrential rain and impassable roads.

Perhaps I placed too much reliance on the volunteers' enthusiasm and would have done better to postpone the attack until the following day; the soldiers were tired and wet through and their weapons and ammunition were in very poor condition. But I thought a sudden and unexpected assault would be effective and I was counting on my men's enthusiasm and keenness so decided to go ahead and launch an attack. At about three in the afternoon, after Bezzi on the mountain to the left had reached the agreed spot and signalled, I ordered the column of attack which had until then been protected by the fortress to advance swiftly ahead against the enemy. Corte, accompanied by his aides, marched at the head of the column and with his usual sangfroid directed a characteristically vigorous attack while keeping good order. For a while it went well and the enemy fell back, but then reinforcements arrived from the summit of Monte Suello where they had been waiting; our men found themselves fighting against strong positions and eventually could advance no further. A large number of wounded carried by their comrades started to come back along the road and caused alarm in the rest of the column. But the day finished without a decisive outcome and we remained in our positions on the lower slopes of Monte Suello. I had been wounded in the left thigh and had been obliged to withdraw; I handed over command to Corte who with the help of Colonel Bruzzesi managed to hold on to the positions we had gained for the rest of the day. At dawn on the next day (the fourth) we found the enemy had withdrawn from Monte Suello so Cairoli's battalion from the ninth regiment occupied it. We also went on to take control of Bagolino and Caffaro.

The remainder of the volunteer troops, still unequipped, were advancing towards the Tyrol, but their progress was slow since they were obliged to look for food as they went along.

Little resistance was put up at Lodrone and Darzo; finally we took hold of the Dazio bridge and of Storo, where I set up my headquarters. Storo is a small village at the point where the Giudicaria and Ampola valleys meet and was a key position for us to gain – or would be if we could secure the mountains surrounding it, especially the Rocca Pagana, a lofty peak which towered almost vertically above the village. If we were to go on into the Giudicaria valley we also had to take control of the fortress at Ampola which dominated it and guarded the pass into the Ledro valley, from which the enemy could advance and seize Storo and the Dazio bridge and cut us off from our operational base at Brescia.

After we had covered our left by occupying Condino and the hills to the west, we turned all our attention to securing and surrounding the fort at Ampola. During this time the famous 18th brigade commanded by Major Dogliotti arrived bringing with it eighteen magnificent 12-calibre pieces. I was able to see what Italian gunners were capable of when they had such fine artillery: they are second to none. On the sixteenth of July the enemy tried to chase us out of Condino. Contrary to my orders, our men had pushed on ahead from Condino as far as Cimego and taken the bridge there over the Chiese river, but they hadn't bothered to garrison the hills around, an essential precaution in that mountainous region if the forces in the valleys are to be protected. The enemy, with its superior numbers of infantry, cavalry, and artillery, beat our troops back from Cimego; if it hadn't been for the artillery which had arrived a few days before things could have gone badly for us. Luckily our losses were limited, but still more than the enemy's; the principal cause, as usual, was the poor quality of the rifles which had been supplied to us.

We took the fort at Ampola and occupied the line of mountains which stretch from Rocca Pagana to the Burelli, Giovio and Cadre peaks; these overlook the two valleys of the Ledro and Giudicaria and so we were able to enter the Ledro valley and advance the head of our right column as far as Tiarno and Bezzecca. Our move to the right through the Ledro valley was doubly important because we needed to defend the arrival of the second regiment who were approaching in that direction having taken the road for Monte Nota towards Pieve Molina and Lake Garda, despite my orders for them to come to Ampola through the Lorina valley to help us in the siege of the fortress. They had strayed too far to the right and risked being wiped out by the enemy, although individual companies had fought bravely against larger forces.

I have mentioned that I had left the second regiment at Salò to protect the flotilla, arsenal and fortresses. They had now been replaced by the tenth regiment and ordered to march through the Vestino valley on our right, to climb that peak and then descend though the Lorina valley to Ampola. The march had been difficult and uncomfortable and many mistakes had been made. If the fortress at Ampola had surrendered to us only a day later or if our occupation of Bezzecca had been delayed, the regiment would have been lost, as we shall see.

I was concerned to occupy the Ledro valley in order to ensure the safe arrival of the second regiment so I had ordered General Haug to leave the siege of Ampola in the hands of Dogliotti and to move with as many troops as he could spare from the siege into the Ledro valley. But it was too bold a move before the fort had surrendered and couldn't be carried out. The fate of the second regiment continued to worry me and as soon as the fort was ours I sent the fifth regiment, the only one to have stayed in reserve, to the Ledro valley, together with the companies of various regiments which had assisted in the siege of Ampola, and two battalions from the ninth regiment which were occupying the upper slopes of Monte Giovio and other mountains. They arrived in the Ledro valley just in time; the enemy had mustered its forces at the top of the Conzei valley and was coming down along it with the aim of attacking the second regiment and preventing them from reaching us. The Conzei valley comes down from the north and continues into the Ledro valley at Bezzecca.

On the twentieth the road from Ampola was free after the fort there had surrendered to us and the head of our right column had occupied the village. During the night a battalion from the fifth regiment commanded by Martinelli was sent to reconnoitre on the eastern hills. When dawn broke they found themselves, either because they had made a mistake or through bad luck, surrounded by large enemy forces and were forced to retreat with many losses. Pursued by the enemy the survivors fell back on the main column occupying Bezzecca and the neighbouring villages to the north; a major engagement followed.

The Battle of Bezzecca

The enemy was buoyed up by its initial success and advanced on us boldly, driving us out of the Conzei valley. An artillery battery had been placed in front of Bezzecca and fired on them, but without effect; our officers at the head of the volunteers risked their lives and threw themselves forward in a charge to block the oncoming forces, but again in vain. The enemy seized all our positions up to and including the village of Bezzecca, then continued to advance, sending a detachment south of the Ledro valley to attack us on our right flank.

I had left Storo at dawn in a carriage as the wound I had received on the third of June was still painful; from the information I had received I did not expect to find my men engaged in such a fierce battle. On leaving Storo, therefore, I had sent orders that the seventh regiment and the first bersaglieri should begin marching in my direction at three in the afternoon. When I came near to Bezzecca the sound of artillery fire alerted me to the battle. I called Haug to me and asked him for an account of the situation; what he told me convinced me that it was a serious confrontation.

We both agreed that the battalions of the ninth regiment which had started to arrive should occupy the hills to the left. The taking of these positions by the regiment which was captained, I am proud to say, by my son Menotti, turned out to be a very good decision, and helped to begin to turn the situation round in our favour.

The volunteers in our centre and on our right wing were in retreat together with the battery, firing as they went. An enemy cannon had managed to kill all the horses and wound or kill all the gunners in this battery, except for one. After he'd shot the last cannon ball he sat astride the cannon as calmly as if he'd been on the drill ground.

While this was happening Dogliotti told me he had a new battery in reserve. I now ordered them to advance: they raced up, turned to the right and set up their artillery on slightly raised ground and started firing on the enemy at such a rate it seemed more like musket- than cannon-fire.

I ordered all the officers of my staff and as many of those who were within earshot to gather the men together and urge them forward. Canzio, Ricciotti, Cariolatti, Damiani, Ravini and others rushed forward at the head of a small group and, aided by the intrepid ninth regiment on the left, pushed the enemy, already badly shaken by the artillery fire, to flight, back beyond Bezzecca and the nearby villages. Their forces made a complete retreat, abandoning all the positions they had previously gained, up the Conzei valley and through the mountains to the east.

I will not describe here the other conflicts which took place away from the main battle in the mountains, in which glorious acts of bravery occurred which I did not witness. On the twenty-first the enemy had moved with a large force on Condino in order to divert attention away from its main movement on Bezzecca and were repulsed by General Fabrizi, chief of staff, with the Nicotera and Corte brigades and several artillery weapons.

After the twenty-first the enemy made no further appearance: I sent Missori with his guides to reconnoitre beyond Condino and he reported back that the valley was completely empty as far as the Lardaro fortresses. The purpose of moving and operating towards our left along the Giudicaria valley was to join up with the column led by Cadolini which had left Val Camonica and was marching towards us, through the Fumo and Daone valleys.

Now that the Giudicaria valley was clear there was no problem in meeting up with Cadolini. When we had reconnoitred the Lardaro fortresses, I decided to move to the right towards Riva and Arco. Reinforcements were already being prepared for Haug who was in command of this operation when, on the twenty-fifth of August, an order came to cease all hostilities and stopped it before it had begun. The 1866 campaign was so marked by disasters that it's impossible to know whether to blame fate or those who were in charge of strategy. The fact remains that after all our efforts and all the blood we had shed in reaching the Tyrolean valleys we were ordered to halt our victorious march just as we were about to achieve our goal. This is not an exaggeration: on the very day hostilities were suspended, the twenty-fifth, the way to Trento was entirely clear of enemy troops; we knew they were abandoning Riva, throwing the cannon from the fortress into the lake as they left; unsuccessful attempts were made for two whole days to trace their general, in order to inform him of the decision to suspend fighting; our ninth regiment was already descending entirely unopposed from the mountains behind the Lardaro fortresses, since they'd found that the garrison there consisted of less than a single company; and finally General Khun, Commander-in-Chief of the Austrian troops in the Tyrol, announced officially that since he was unable to defend the Italian Tyrol he was concentrating his forces on the defence of the German side.

Also on the twenty-fifth Medici, after his brilliant military exploits in the Val Sugana, was within a few miles of Trento, with Cosenz's division following behind: in a couple of days' time we could have joined forces in the capital of the Tyrol, mustering fifty thousand men. All the advantages were on our side; a large number of smaller units being formed in Cadore, Friuli and elsewhere would have joined us and swelled our numbers; we would have been ready for any bold undertaking! Yet here I am recording our misfortunes for posterity to read. I received a dispatch from our supreme command ordering us to begin our withdrawal from the Tyrol: I sent a telegram in reply: 'I obey', which provoked the usual peevish complaints from the Mazzinians, who, as always, wanted me to proclaim a republic and march on Vienna, or Florence.

The Roman Campagna

I planned the brief campaign of 1867 in the Roman Campagna while on a trip to the Italian mainland and to Switzerland where I had gone to participate in the congress for the League for Peace and Freedom. The responsibility for what occurred is therefore mine.

In 1849 I had been the General of the Roman Republic with extraordinary powers granted by the most legitimate government there has ever been in Italy; now I was living in idleness, which I regarded as blameworthy when so much remained to be done for my country. I thought – with reason – that the time had come to shake the crumbling edifice of papal power to the ground and give Italy back her illustrious capital.

Hell would freeze over before I got the go-ahead from those in power. Napoleon III's soldiers had left Rome; a few thousand mercenaries, the lowest of the low, kept a great nation at bay and prevented it from claiming its sacred rights.

I prepared for the crusade, first in the Veneto, and then in other Italian provinces which bordered on Rome. The French Government as well as our own in Florence and their followers kept an eye on me, as was to be expected. There were many worthy people who came to my aid, and not a few who opposed the undertaking, especially the Mazzinians who proudly but mistakenly proclaim themselves to be a party of action, but who in reality cannot tolerate any initiative for freedom. After travelling round Italy and on my return from Switzerland I was of the opinion that further delay was undesirable and decided to act in September.

At the same time as preparations for the campaign in the north of the country were under way I asked friends in southern Italy to undertake a simultaneous military operation on Rome from the south. But I was counting my chickens before they were hatched: one fine night in Sinalunga where I'd arrived to a cordial welcome I was arrested on the orders of the Italian Government and taken to the small town of Alessandria. I was left here for several days and then taken to Genoa and from there to Caprera. The island was encircled with warships: I was a prisoner in my own home, with frigates, battleships, steamers and several merchant vessels, which the Government had hired for the purpose, all keeping a close watch on me. My detention did not discourage my friends on the mainland, however, and they continued to prepare for the campaign which I was no longer able to lead. General Fabrizi, my chief of staff, together with other generous-spirited men, formed an organising committee in Florence. Acerbi led a volunteer column into the countryside round Viterbo and Menotti led another into the area around the Corese Pass[36] – both within the Papal States – while the heroic Enrico Cairoli with his brother Giovanni and seventy other men took a boat up the Tiber to supply much-needed arms to the inhabitants of Rome. Major Cucchi and a small group of brave men had run many risks in entering the city and organising an internal uprising which combined with the attack from outside forces would finally shake the monstruous power of the Papacy off its throne and remove its baleful influence at the very heart of our nation. Imprisoned on Caprera I did not receive detailed information about everything that was being done: I assumed that the plans I had had to abandon were being put into execution. Something too could be gleaned from newspapers and general public talk; I knew enough to be certain that my sons and my friends were on Roman territory, fighting the mercenary troops whom the priests had hired to defend them.

Could I remain idle while these dear comrades at my instigation were fighting for the liberation of Rome, the ideal to which my whole life had been dedicated? The Government's vigilance was intense and they had many means at their disposal for their surveillance; but my desire to carry out my duty and fight for freedom alongside my comrades was greater. On the fourteenth of October 1867 at six in the evening I left my house and set off for the northern shore of the island. I reached the beach and found the small rowing boat which had been bought on the Arno, waiting for me. It had been left a few yards from the beach next to a small boatshed. It was almost entirely hidden by a lentiscus bush so that my official guardians could not discover it. Giovanni, a young Sardinian who looked after the schooner which had been given to me by English friends and was kept in the harbour at Stagnalello, was waiting for me and with his help I pushed the boat out and got into it. Giovanni then left in the ship's boat from the schooner singing under his breath. I rowed the boat as noiselessly as a duck along the shore of the island to the left and emerged into open sea at the Punta dell'Arcaccio, which two other loyal friends of mine, Frosciante and the engineer Barberini, had checked beforehand to make sure it was clear with no danger of ambush.

The guards were numerous. They had taken possession of all the islets in the harbour at Stagnalello where they had a warship and other smaller vessels and from where they sent out patrols all through the night in every direction – apart from the one I was taking in order to escape their clutches.

It was the night of the full moon, which made my escape much more difficult. I had calculated that it would rise from behind the Teggialone, the mountain which dominates Caprera, an hour after sunset. So I had just one hour to try to get across to La Maddalena: for fear of being spotted I couldn't cross before the sun had set or after the moon had risen. But something unforeseen occurred which gave me an advantage. My assistent Maurizio had been over to La Maddalena that day and was now returning to Caprera. Perhaps he had been drinking a bit, but he paid no attention to the shouts of 'Who goes there?' from the warships which thronged the stretch of water known as La Moneta between La Maddalena and Caprera, so they started to fire on him, though luckily he was not hit. By chance all this was happening while I was attempting to cross over. By another stroke of good fortune, the sirocco was blowing and ruffling the water, which helped to hide the boat which rose only a few inches above the surface. I found I had not forgotten how to row with a single oar since I'd been in Indian canoes on the rivers of South America. The oar or the blade of it was about a yard along and I moved as soundlessly as any seabird through the water. While Maurizio had attracted the attention of most of my guards I was able to cross undisturbed on to Isolella which is separated from La Maddalena by a narrow and shallow channel which can be crossed on foot. I reached Isolella on the north-east steering the boat through the surrounding rocks; just as the moon was rising behind the Teggialone mountain I pulled the boat on shore and hid it in the scrub; then I set off south to cross the channel and reach Mrs Collins' house on La Maddalena. Two friends, Basso and Cuneo, had been waiting for me by the stretch of water since they had assumed I would make my crossing there, but they thought that all the gunfire they had heard had been directed at me rather than Maurizio and so had gone back to La Maddalena, having concluded that the attempt was over and that I'd either been killed or recaptured. I was old and ill and found it difficult to get across the rocks and shrubs on the island of La Maddalena, added to which I had had to cross the stretch of water with my boots on to protect my feet from the sharp stones, and the water in my boots made them squelch annoyingly at every step. But the moonlight which I'd feared on the water now helped me find my way across land. Having taken every precaution I finally reached the house where Mrs Collins made me very welcome.

Sardinia – Sea Crossing – Mainland

Here I stayed until seven in the evening of the fifteenth of October, when my friend Pietro Susini arrived with his horse. I mounted the horse and under Susini's expert guidance crossed the island of La Maddalena as far as Cala Francese on the western shore, where Basso and Cuneo were waiting for me with a skiff and a sailor. I got in and the six of us crossed the strait which divides La Maddalena from Sardinia. Once on Sardinia we sent the boat back and spent the rest of the night in a cave by the shore, near to the sheep pen belonging to Domenico Nicola; at six in the evening on the sixteenth, we set off on three horses we had rounded up and crossed the Gallura mountains and the Bay of Terranova until we found ourselves at dawn on the following day on the hills surrounding the port of San Paolo.

The boat which Canzio and Vigani had been supposed to arrange for us here was not to be found so we spent the morning in Nicola's sheep pen while Cuneo, despite the fifteen-hour horse ride, went on south to the port of Prandinga, where he found our friends had arrived safely after many mishaps en route and were waiting for us on the *San Francesco*, a fishing boat.

At three in the afternoon of the seventeenth we set sail with a fairly strong sirocco wind; at about noon on the following day we caught sight of Monte Cristo; in the evening we entered the straits of Piombino. The next day dawned stormy with a strong south wind and rain. The conditions were favourable to coming into land at Vado between the straits and Livorno. I spent the rest of the day in the boat in Vado before disembarking when night fell. At about seven in the evening five of us – Canzio, Vigiani, Basso, Maurizio and myself – made our way along the seaweed-covered beach to the south of Vado. The shore was marshy and we spent some time finding a way across it – my companions helped me when I had problems – eventually reaching the village of Vado. Here Canzio and Vigiani luckily found two cabriolets straight away so we left for Livorno. Once in Livorno we went to the house belonging to Sgarellino; only the women in the family were in, but they were extremely kind to us. Lemmi, who had been waiting for us for several days, turned up with a carriage to take us to Florence. We got in and arrived in the city in the morning, where Lemmi's family very kindly put us up in their house.

My arrival in the city could not be kept secret and on the twentieth my friends and the inhabitants turned out to give me a rousing welcome despite the fact that I was on a mission to make Rome the country's capital and so remove that privilege from the great city of Galileo and Michelangelo.[37] Yet they rejoiced as true patriots – Italy should take note.

My greatest wish was to rejoin my comrades and my sons on the field where battle would be joined so my stay in Florence was brief. On the twenty-second of October on a specially arranged train I left for Terni on the border with Roman territory; there I took a carriage to join Menotti at the Corese Pass, where I arrived on the twenty-third.

The position here would have been difficult to defend, especially for troops in as poor a condition as ours were, so we marched to Monte Maggiore; from here, on the night of the twenty-third, we set off in various columns for Monterotondo, where we knew that about four hundred of the enemy were stationed with two artillery pieces.

The columns commanded by Caldesi and Valsania were due to set out at eight in the evening on the twenty-third and arrive at Monterotondo towards midnight. They would then attempt to enter the town with an attack from the west, on the side where we thought the walls were most vulnerable, as indeed they were, since ruined stretches had been replaced by houses with external doors which were therefore easy to access. But the chance for a night assault was missed: with all the inconveniences they had to face – disorganisation, lack of supplies, tiredness, and the impossibility of finding reliable guides – this rightwing column, made up for the most part of brave young men from the Romagna, only arrived at Monterotondo during the day.

The leftwing column led by Frigezy arrived outside Monterotondo from the east and took over the Capuchin monastery and adjacent positions at ten in the morning; several units were sent out on the left to make contact with our troops on the right, although this proved impossible to carry out throughout the whole of the twenty-fourth since the enemy fire was very heavy on that side. The central column was led by Menotti – I had joined them directly from Monte Maggiore – and they had found the march along the difficult Moletta road heavy-going in parts; however, they were still the first to arrive, at dawn, and had taken up their positions in the hills to the north of Monterotondo.

I had ordered this column to occupy these positions, but not to launch an attack until the other columns had arrived when a combined assault could be made. But their eagerness was impossible to restrain; they threw themselves into an attack on the Porta San Rocco in the face of lethal gunfire from all the windows on that side of the town. I had gone off on the left for a moment to see if I could spot Frigezy's column arriving and was amazed and aggrieved to find out what the excessive courage of these Genoese bersaglieri had led them to attempt. We suffered many dead and wounded, but the attack did manage to establish a body of several hundred volunteers in the houses next to the San Rocco gate, who, with the help of fresh troops, were later able to burn down the gate and enable us to enter and occupy the town.

We spent the whole of the twenty-fourth of October then surrounding Monterotondo with our troops while the garrison manned by papal Zouave troops, most of whom were armed with excellent rifles, and their two cannon fired on us. We were unable to return their fire, partly for the usual reason that our own weapons were inadequate, and partly because their defences were so good it was impossible to spot one of them to target.

The town of Monterotondo is dominated by the palace belonging to the princes of Piombino, a young scion of which family was fighting with us. The palace or rather castle is very large and well fortified; the enemy had transformed it into a fortress with loopholes all round and a parapet on the eastern platform where their two cannon were placed.

We spent the twenty-fourth preparing for the attack: encircling the town, preparing fascines and sulphur to set the Porta San Rocco on fire, and making all the necessary arranagements for the assault. The three columns commanded by Salomone, Caldesi, Valsania and Menotti were combined for the decisive attack on the San Rocco gate; some soldiers were sent to keep the road to Rome under observation in case enemy reinforcements came from that direction. At the same time we launched our assault, Frigezy was to attack from the east, if possible setting fire to the castle gate.

We fixed the time for the attack at four in the afternoon of the twenty-fifth. The volunteers were ragged and hungry and wet through; they lay stretched out with exhaustion by the side of the roads which the heavy rain of the previous few days had turned into impassable bogs. I almost despaired of being able to rouse them in time for the attack on the next day and stayed with them to share their misery until three in the morning, when the friends who accompanied me advised me to go and sit in the dry inside the nearby monastery of Santa Maria. When we reached the church, the only seat available was in a confessional and I rested there a few minutes. Hardly had I sat down and rested my back, which was painful after being on my feet so long, when I heard a thunderous noise like a solemn roar rising from our troops who were rushing through the breach opened up by the burning gate; I stood up immediately, yelling out 'Charge!', and rushed as fast as I could towards the action. The whole gate had been burnt down and nothing remained but a heap of smouldering ruins; it had been hit by two of our cannon which were so small they resembled telescopes. As they waited for the fire to extinguish itself, the enemy were trying to barricade it again by bringing carts, tables and other large objects to create an obstruction. This didn't go down too well with our men who had put a lot of effort and run many risks in setting the gate on fire. The Zouaves had just begun by pushing a cart into the gap where the gate had been when an electric spark of heroic daring flashed through our ranks: in a fury they rushed on the burning gate like demons. No signs of tiredness or exhaustion or hunger then! Had I not seen the young men of Italy perform such miracles on previous occasions? My misgivings – the misgivings of a decrepit old man – had wronged them.

Neither the cart nor the burning ruins of the gate nor the hail of bullets which rained down on them from all directions could stop their headlong rush. It was like a river flood in full spate, breaking its banks and inundating the fields around. In a few minutes our men were all over the town and the garrison shut up inside the castle. By six in the evening we had taken and barricaded all the streets leading to the castle and started our assault on it by setting fire to the stables with fascines, bundles of straw, carts and whatever other combustible material we found to hand.

At ten in the morning on the following day we managed with only a few bursts of gunfire to drive back two thousand men who were coming from Rome to assist the besieged forces. An hour later the garrison, smoked out and fearing the castle would explode if all the gunpowder stored in the cellars underneath it caught fire, raised the white flag and surrendered. A short while before they surrendered the valiant Testori had broken cover and shown them a white flag to signal to them to give up; violating every rule of combat those mercenaries shot at him repeatedly and killed him. After such acts of barbarism – and there were many – on the part of these lackeys of the Inquisition, it was only with the greatest difficulty that I managed to save their lives when they surrendered, as our men were enraged with them. I was obliged to accompany them myself out of Monterotondo and then give them an escort of forty men under the command of Major Marrani to the Corese Pass.

What happened then in Monterotondo was typical of what occurs in towns taken by assault and where the victorious troops meet with silence and indifference, almost aversion, from the inhabitants. I must admit that there were disturbances and that they also prevented us from organising our forces as well as we should have done during the few days we spent in the place.

In the hope that our forces might prove more amenable to discipline outside the town and on the march, and in order to start our approach to Rome, we left Monterotondo on the twenty-eighth of October and occupied the hills round Santa Colomba. Frigezy was in charge of the vanguard and occupied Marcigliana, sending his men as far as Castel Giubileo and Villa Spada.

On the evening of the twenty-ninth I was at Castel Giubileo when a messenger from Rome arrived. He had relatives among the volunteers and was therefore known to us. He assured me that the Romans were ready to rise up in rebellion that very night. This news put me in some difficulty since I had very few men available; nonetheless I decided to advance at dawn the next day with two battalions of Genoese bersaglieri as far as Casino dei Pazzi, a stone's throw from the Nomentano bridge.

One of our guides, accompanied by an officer, arrived first at the Casino and found an enemy picket there. They fired their revolvers: the guide was slightly wounded in the chest and, as they were outnumbered, he and the officer decided to withdraw, letting off more shots as they went to warn me of the presence of papal troops. We retreated to meet the two oncoming battalions; once these had come up we were able to seize the Casino dei Pazzi together with La Cecchina, a dairy within shooting distance to the north, and the walled road which ran between them. We stayed there throughout the thirtieth waiting for the news of an insurrection in Rome or some other information from our friends within the city, but nothing came. At about ten in the morning two enemy columns came out to reconnoitre, one from the Nomentano bridge and the other, some time later, from the Mammolo bridge. The marksmen from the Pope's soldiers on our right advanced within firing distance and then fired on us all day; my order not to return fire was obeyed – it would have been pointless with our inadequate rifles – except when some Zouaves emboldened or annoyed by our lack of response advanced even closer to the Casino from where our men were able to shoot four of them dead and wound several more.

Our position so near to the city and the entire papal army was dangerous; when I saw the two columns coming out I asked Menotti who was a little way back to bring up some battalions to support us, which he immediately did. I was now convinced that nothing was happening in Rome and there was no chance that anything would take place with the arrival of the French forces, so I prepared to withdraw back to Monterotondo, lighting fires as we left in all the positions we had occupied in order to deceive the enemy.

The Mazzinians took advantage of our situation to spread discontent among the volunteers by suggesting that if they weren't going to Rome they might as well return home. And it's true: at home there's plenty to eat and drink, you sleep in the warm – and there's a much better chance of saving your own skin…

All the positions we had occupied – Castel de' Pazzi, Cecchina, Castel Giubileo, etc. – were too near to Rome and couldn't be defended against a larger enemy: we needed to fall back on stronger positions further away from the city. Monterotondo fitted the bill – and we could live more easily there too.

Mentana – 3rd November 1867

On the thirty-first of October the whole volunteer force re-entered Monterotondo and remained there until the third of November. We spent the whole time getting clothes and shoes for the soldiers who were most in need of them, and in arming and organising the men as far as we could. Three battalions under the command of Colonel Paggi were sent to occupy the strong positions of Sant'Angelo, Monticelli and Palombara. Tivoli was occupied by Colonel Pianciani with another battalion while General Acerbi at the head of a thousand men went to Viterbo. General Nicotera took a thousand men with him to take control of Velletri while Major Andreuzzi patrolled the right bank of the Tiber with a unit of two hundred men.

Up to the thirty-first of October many volunteers were lining up to join Menotti's troops so that they now numbered more than six thousand men.

Our situation was not of the best, but nor was it completely discouraging. It would have been better if we had had the support of the local people to arm and clothe and generally provide for the needs of the volunteers. The papal army was demoralised: we had beaten part of them at Monterotondo after which they stayed inside Rome not daring to come out and face our challenge. The attempted insurrection of the inhabitants in the city had been brutally crushed; now the Romans wanted revenge and led by Cucchi and others were preparing with renewed energy to work together with their liberators outside the city to topple once and for all the regime of priests and mercenaries. Their end seemed in sight. Yet the spirit of evil still watched over its principal support: the Pope and his realm of lies. From its throne on the banks of the Seine – to the shame of France and of the world – it threatened those scared rabbits who ruled us from the Arno, accusing them of cowardice. On hearing their master's voice the unworthy rulers of Italy assumed once more the mask of patriotism to deceive the nation and invade Roman territory: 'We are coming. We have kept our word. As the first shots ring out in Rome, we hasten to help our brothers.'

It was a lie – a lie! Yes, your troops moved quickly, but to kill your brothers in case they won the final victory – and you came in haste only when you knew that the Roman patriots had been massacred. All lies! You and your magnanimous ally occupied Rome and its territory only to enable the Pope's mercenaries – restored after their defeats, united and free once more to act – to move with all its troops and all the arms and means at its disposal against a band of volunteers, wretchedly armed and provided for, and to see them succumb. And if the Pope's army was not sufficient for the job – as turned out to be the case – then all Bonaparte's soldiers were there to lend a hand, as well as – it horrifies me even to think of this – the wretches in your own army who have to obey you. In 1860 did you not march against us? Why should you not do the same in 1867? Like the plains of Capua seven years before, the hills around Mentana were covered with the corpses of Italy's noble sons and foreign mercenaries. And the cause for which the soldiers I had the honour to command were fighting then was as sacred as the one which had led us on now to the walls of the world's ancient capital.

It is a painful duty to recall also another reason for the disaster at Mentana. I have already mentioned the Mazzinians' corrosive and entirely false propaganda which started as soon as we had retreated from the Casino dei Pazzi. Anyone with any sense will see that our position under the walls of Rome was untenable: the French troops were arriving and the men under my command lacked everything, had no artillery, no cavalry, and would have been incapable of putting up resistance to a serious sortie, even if it only involved the papal forces.

Even if there'd been no attack they still didn't have the means to survive for more than two days. In Monterotondo on the other hand, we were within sight of the city, we had what limited means were at our disposal all round us, we occupied strong positions, and at a great enough distance to get ready to face the enemy when it advanced against us.

But for the Mazzinians these were all just excuses. As if our own Government's treacherous and unremitting opposition and the power of the clergy backed by France were not enough to contend with! The Mazzinians too had to start sniping at those whose only aspiration was to liberate their own brothers from enslavement. 'We can do better than that,' so I was told in Lugano back in 1848 by Mazzini's supporters – who are now the monarchy's men. That's how far back Mazzini's war on me – a war of pinpricks – goes.

'Let's return home to proclaim the republic and build the barricades' – so my soldiers were saying in the Roman Campagna in 1867. And indeed the prospect of going home was much more inviting than staying on with me in November, with no clothing and no provisions and with a battle looming against the assembled forces of the Italian army, the Papists, and the French. As a result of the underhand tricks played on us by the Mazzinians, over three thousand men deserted in the period between our retreat from the Casino dei Pazzi and Mentana. I leave the reader to imagine what the effect is on those who remain when half their comrades announce quite openly their decision to desert – on their morale and on their confidence in what they were doing. The damage was untold. I could forget it if the criticisms had been directed against me personally. But they were aimed at undermining the national cause. How can I forget them, how can I not bring them to the attention of the elite body of young men who heeded them and were led astray.

Mazzini was certainly a better man than his followers. On the events which occurred at Mentana he wrote to me in a letter dated the eleventh of February 1870: 'You know that I didn't think your plan would succeed. I was convinced that it would be better to concentrate all the means at our disposal on supporting a powerful insurrection within Rome rather than carrying out operations in the surrounding territory. Once the campaign had started, however, I gave it all the support

I could.' I do not question Mazzini's sincerity here: yet the fact remains that the damage was done: either he didn't manage to tell his supporters in time, or, despite his advice, they continued to spread their harmful propaganda.

From the top of the tower of the Palazzo Piombino in Monterotondo, where I spent most of the day watching Rome, our troop at their exercises in the plain, and every movement in the surrounding countryside, I could also see the procession of our men as they headed for the Corese Pass and home. Their remaining comrades noticed this too and when they mentioned it to me I would reply, 'Oh no, those aren't our men – they're countryfolk coming and going from their work.' As people always do in desperate circumstances, I attempted to disguise or make light of the rancour I felt.

In view of my men's low morale, and because the border to the north was blocked by the Italian army which prevented supplies reaching us, we were forced to move our operations elsewhere and find another base where we could find the wherewithal to survive, keep ourselves going, and wait on the events which would finally decide the fate of Rome. So I decided to march towards Tivoli on our left, from where we could leave the Apennines behind us and head nearer the south. We were supposed to set out on the morning of the third of November, but there was a delay as we waited for shoes to be supplied and distributed and we didn't get going until midday. We left Monterotondo on the road to Tivoli. The order of march was the following: the columns under the command of Menotti were to march in good order preceded at about one to two thousand paces by a vanguard of bersaglieri. Ahead of the vanguard there was to be a party of scouts on foot preceded by mounted guides. On all the roads coming from Rome on our right there were to be flankers on foot and on horseback, keeping as close to the city as possible and always on the right. On the hills around, observation posts were to be set up which would alert us in time to any enemy movement. A rearguard was to follow the main column to move on any men who were straggling and to make sure no one was left behind. The artillery was to march in the middle of the columns. Each column was to be followed by its respective baggage train.

This was more or less the order of march from Monterotondo to

Tivoli. Things started to go wrong, however, when it appeared that the mounted guides at the front – and there were only a handful of them – were captured by the enemy, so that the papal troops coming down the Nomentana road almost succeeded in taking our vanguard by surprise before engaging with them. As we passed the village of Mentana, the sound of gunfire told me the enemy had arrived. To start marching back in such circumstances when some of our troops were already fighting would be equivalent to flight: we had to stay and fight, by occupying the strong positions nearby. I sent an order to Menotti, who was with the vanguard, to occupy these positions and to resist. I then got the rest of the columns to follow, directing them to the left and right to support the advance columns, while some companies remained in a column to the right as reserves.

Our line of battle that day was the road between Mentana and Monterotondo, which is in good condition but low-lying and sunken. So we had to find a good position for the two cannon we had captured from the enemy on the twenty-fifth of October. It proved very difficult to move them: there were no skilled men or horses and the terrain was very uneven and broken up with hedgerows and vines.

In the meantime a fierce battle was raging all along the line. Our positions equalled those taken by the enemy; in fact they were better since they were unable to use their artillery at all during the day and for a while we succeeded in holding our positions against more numerous and better-armed forces. Yet it has to be admitted: the volunteers were demoralised, for the reasons already described, and their performance fell far short of their reputation. Some distinguished officers together with a small group of brave soldiers gave up their lives rather than cede an inch of ground to the enemy, but the majority showed no such bravery. They relinquished excellent positions without putting up the resistance I would have expected.

The battle began at about one in the afternoon; two hours later the enemy had managed to push us back about a thousand metres, position by position, towards the village of Mentana. By three o'clock we'd got our artillery into an advantageous position and began to bombard the enemy successfully. Our whole line made a bayonet charge and we let off a hail of gunfire from the windows of the houses in Mentana: the field was strewn with enemy corpses. We had won and the enemy was fleeing; we retook the positions we had lost and until four o'clock we were in control of the battlefield.

But, once again, discouragement started to spread among our ranks. We were victorious yet we failed to follow up our victory by routing the enemy forces as they abandoned the field. Rumours that French troops were approaching began to circulate; there was no time to find out how they'd started, although they obviously came from the enemy. We already knew that the Italian army was against us, arresting our men as they came to the border and blocking all supplies and communications getting through to us. So the Italian Government, the priests and the Mazzinians had succeeded in unsettling our men. And not every man is capable of brushing off such anxieties and doing his duty by continuing to march ahead.

At about four in the afternoon the rumour that a column of two thousand French soldiers was about to attack our rear proved the final blow to the volunteers' constancy. It was false: what was true was that an expeditionary unit led by Failly, sent in support of the papal troops, was just reaching the battlefield. All the positions we had regained with such valour were abandoned once again. Masses of our men started to flee down the road, heedless of my attempts and those of many officers to bring them to order. All to no avail. We lost our voices shouting and scolding, but it was all in vain. All of them fled back to Monterotondo, leaving artillery behind them, which only fell into the enemy's hands on the following day, as well as a small band of courageous men who continued to fire on the enemy from the houses in Mentana.

It's easy to be brave when your enemy is in retreat: the papal troops which had been in retreat in the face of our attack now returned to the fight emboldened by the arrival of the French. They pressed home as we retreated: we lost many men, killed and wounded, to their superior rifles. The French, whom we at first took to be the papal soldiers, advanced while sending out a continuous hail of bullets from their terrible 'chassepots' which caused more fear than physical harm. If only my young volunteers had obeyed me and held onto the positions we had reconquered at Mentana – this could have been done without much risk – and simply defended them, the third of November might have gone down as one of the great days in the struggle for Italian democracy, even in the conditions we were in, grossly outnumbered and short of equipment and men.

In many of our previous battles we had been on the losing side until the end of the day when a favourable wind blew us back on course for victory. In Mentana on the third of November, if we had managed to hold on for one more hour after four o'clock, it would have been dark and our enemies might have thought it advisable to retreat towards Rome rather than remaining in their exposed position where we could have harassed them continually throughout the night.

As it was, by five o'clock all the columns, apart from the few defenders left in Mentana, were fleeing in disorder down the road towards Monterotondo. We just about managed to occupy the Capuchin monastery with a few hundred men. We had no ammunition left. The general opinion was that we should retreat over the Corese Pass.

From the tower in Monterotondo I was able to see for myself how unfounded the information was that two thousand French troops were approaching along the Roman road, although I myself had heard it from many on the battlefield. It seems incredible that such things can happen, yet they do. Even several of my officers, whose loyalty was unquestioned, told me they had heard it. In the vicissitudes of battle, hearsay is all. When you're in the midst of them it's no good trying to find the source of such a rumour – the blackest treachery lies behind it. In the meantime it spread dismay among the men with the speed of lightning. It can be attributed to human wickedness. There is still too much such wickedness to purge in our country's corrupt society, under the influence of priests and their friends!

The presence of military police on the battlefield is essential in any army, but such was the hatred of the volunteers for police of any kind that it was difficult if not impossible to introduce them.

As night fell on the third of November we retreated to the Corese Pass and spent the rest of the night still on Roman territory, inside the local inn or nearby. Several commanders told me that some of the men wanted to fight on and try again, but in the morning I realised that they'd either never existed or had changed their minds in the meantime.

On the morning of the fourth of November we surrendered our weapons on the bridge and the unarmed soldiers were allowed to cross over out of papal territory. I must praise General Fabrizi, my chief of staff, for taking charge of the other arrangements for disarmament. This valiant veteran of the struggle for Italian independence had fought with his usual courage at Mentana, urging on his men to do their duty and setting them a personal example; worn out with tiredness and old age he had been accompanied by some soldiers back to Monterotondo.

Colonel Caravà, who was in charge of one of the Italian regiments and had been one of the officers under my command in previous campaigns, treated us with unfailing and praiseworthy correctness. He greeted me with great friendliness, did everything within his power for me and for the volunteers, and put a train at my disposal to take me to Florence.

But the Government took a different view of the matter. Crispi, now in the Italian Parliament, sat with me in the train and told me that in his opinion there was no reason to place me under arrest. I thought otherwise since I knew from past experience the kind of men I was dealing with. But I allowed myself to be persuaded by my friend – besides, there was nothing else I could have done – and continued on my journey to the capital.

What followed was the familiar story of pettifogging treatment, from the Government, the carabinieri and the bersaglieri, the attendant fears and anxieties, and all the rest of it. We travelled in haste until I was eventually deposited in the familiar surroundings of the fortress in Varignano from where I was allowed to return to my home on Caprera.

NOTES

1. A river whose estuary lies between Uruguay and Argentina. Garibaldi spent the years between 1835 and 1848 in South America, fighting for various republics which had broken away from Brazilian imperial power in Brazil and Uruguay.

2. Giuseppe Mazzini (1805-72), revolutionary and republican who was the ideological leader of the struggle for Italian unification.

3. Carlo Alberto (1798-1849), King of Sardinia 1831-49. His Government outlawed Garibaldi as a radical republican in 1834 for attempting to foment a mutiny in the Sardinian navy against the Savoy monarchy.

4. The five days from 18th to 22nd March 1848 when, in the wake of the February revolution in Paris, the Milanese rose up against the occupying Austrians and drove their troops out of the city.

5. The armistice followed the defeat of the Piedmontese army by the Austrians at the Battle of Novara in March 1849. Carlo Alberto, who subsequently abdicated in favour of his son Victor Emmanuel (1820-70), agreed to leave Lombardy under Austrian power in return for the Austrians leaving Piedmontese territory intact.

6. The Varesotto region is the largely mountainous area round Varese in Lombardy.

7. A specially trained infantry regiment established in 1836, famed for their bravery.

8. In 1815, after the congress of Vienna, central Italy was divided into a number of duchies, largely restoring the pre-Napoleonic status quo: Modena, Parma, Lucca and the Grand Duchy of Tuscany.

9. Pellegrino Rossi (1787-1848), lawyer and politician, liberal Prime Minister in the Papal Government under Pius IX. On 15th November 1848, an assassin stabbed Rossi in the neck with a dagger. The assassination sparked the revolution which drove Pius IX into exile and established the Roman Republic.

10. Vittorio Alfieri (1749-1803), poet and dramatist. His political convictions made him an emblematic figure in the Risorgimento. The line comes from his play *Virginia* (1777).

11. In referring to the priesthood Garibaldi plays on the Italian word 'negromanti' to allude both to what he regarded as their superstitious practices and to their black clothes.

12. In the Roman constitution the *comitia* were the ordinary and legal meetings or assemblies of the people.

13. The Zouaves, a special troop of Algerian soldiers which, from 1830 onwards, formed part of the French army. In 1866 a Zouave troop fought in the papal forces.

14. Tomás de Torquemada (1420-98), founder and head of the Spanish Inquisition.

15. Eleuterio Foresti (1789-1858), an Italian patriot who belonged to the secret society of the Carbonari. He was imprisoned by the Austrians in the Spielberg prison from 1818 to 1836.

16. Camillo Benso, Count di Cavour (1810-61), statesman in the Piedmontese Government under Victor Emmanuel I; his political and diplomatic goal was to see a unified Italy under the constitutional rule of the House of Savoy.

17. The volunteer legion commanded by Garibaldi in the 1859 Lombardy campaign.

18. It was in fact the twenty-third of May 1859.

19. The armistice following the Battle of Novara in March 1849 left the Austrians in control of Lombardy while Piedmontese territory remained intact.

20. The administrative head of a town.

21. The Franco-Sardinian allied forces under the command of Napoleon III defeated the Austrian army at the Battle of Magenta near Milan on 4th June 1859.

22. Marcus Furius Camillus (d.365 BC) was renowned for his defeat of the Gauls after they had sacked Rome in 390 BC.

23. The armistice of Villafranca in 1859 between the Austrians and the French, in which Victor Emmanuel and Cavour were not consulted, arranged for the restoration of the *ancien régime* in the central Italian states of Tuscany, Parma and Modena, whose rulers had fled to be replaced by provisional governments annexed to the Sardinian Government in Piedmont. Victor Emmanuel and Cavour resisted such a measure.

24. In the states belonging to the Papacy, papal troops had reoccupied Perugia after the city had rebelled and massacred its inhabitants.

25. The 'Mille', the traditional name given to the volunteers who followed Garibaldi in the 1860 campaign in southern Italy against the Bourbon dynasty.

26. The uprising of the inhabitants of Palermo against French rule on Easter Sunday in 1282.

27. 'It is said that at the time of their first occupation of the island the Romans were defeated by the natives at a great battle on this site' (Garibaldi's note). It is more probable that 'Pianto' is from the Sicilian word for 'vineyards' *chiantu* and that 'Romani' was the name of the family which owned them.

28. 'At the Battle of Copenhagen, Parker, the chief Admiral, indicated to Nelson who was engaged in the conflict that he should retreat. The conqueror of the Nile was told by one of his officers of the signal to retreat: he put a telescope to his blind eye and said: "I see nothing!" He went on to win the battle.' (Garibaldi's note).

29. From a dialect Sicilian word meaning youth or boy, often one in service (e.g. as an apprentice). In this specific context, it refers to the local insurgents on the island who had started the rebellion against the Bourbon rulers and who subsequently joined Garibaldi's volunteer forces in 1860.

30. Francis II (1836–94), the last Bourbon king to rule over the Kingdom of the Two Sicilies.

31. The Greek and later Roman name for Sicily.

32. Agostino Bertani (1812–66), a physician, patriot and politician who was among the organisers of the 'Cinque Giornate' of Milan (see note 4).

33. Ferdinand II of Naples (1810–59) was notorious for his repression of political dissent within the Bourbon Kingdom of the Two Sicilies.

34. The Italian army was defeated and forced to retreat by the Austrians at the Battle of Custoza on 24th June 1866.

35. It was the Archduke Albrecht of Habsburg (1817–95).

36. 'At that time the Corese bridge marked the frontier between Roman and Italian territory' (Garibaldi's note).

37. After Turin, Florence was the second capital of Italy from 1865 to 1870, after which the government was finally transferred to Rome.

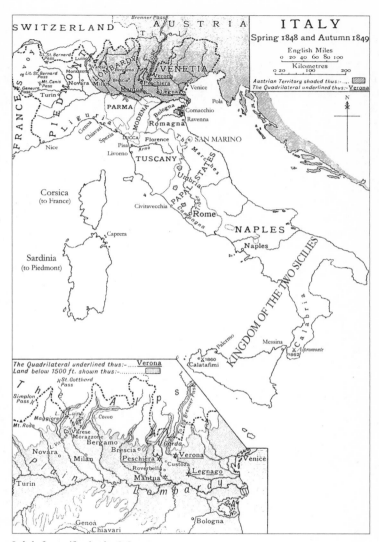

Italy before unification in 1848.

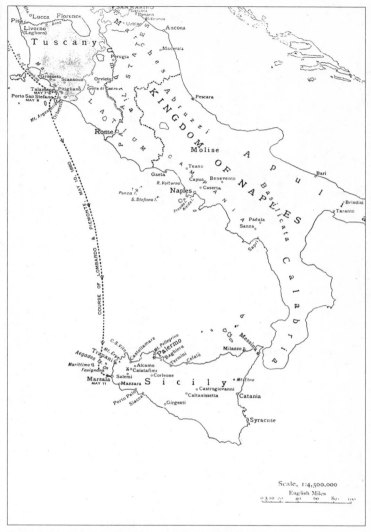

Southern Italy in 1848: the Papal States and the Kingdom of the Two Sicilies.

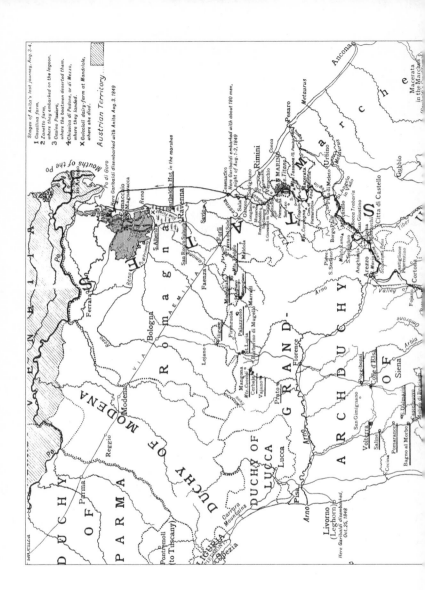

Stages of Anita's last journey, Aug. 3-4.

1 Cavallina farm.
2 Zanetto farm,
   where they embarked on the lagoon.
3 Ossino Pastori,
   where the boatmen deserted them.
4 Chiavica di Pastore, or di Mezzo,
   where they landed.
X Guiccioli dairy-farm at Mandriole,
   where she died.

Austrian Territory.......

Mouths of the Po

Here Garibaldi disembarked with Anita Aug. 3, 1849

Here Garibaldi embarked with about 180 men,
night of Aug. 1-2, 1849

Here Garibaldi disembarked
Oct. 25, 1848

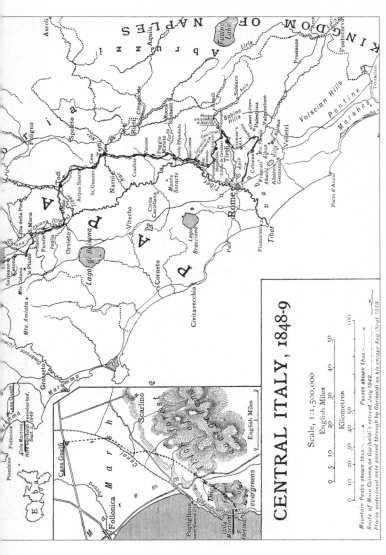

Central Italy and the route of Garibaldi's retreat from Rome in 1849.

CENTRAL ITALY, 1848-9

Scale, 1:1,500,000

English Miles
0   5   10   20   30   40   50

Kilometres
0   10   20   30   40   50   100

Mountain Peaks shown thus ⌃
Passes shown thus ⤳
Route of Main Column on Garibaldi's retreat July 1849 ⤳
Places underlined were passed through by Garibaldi on his escape Aug.–Sept. 1849

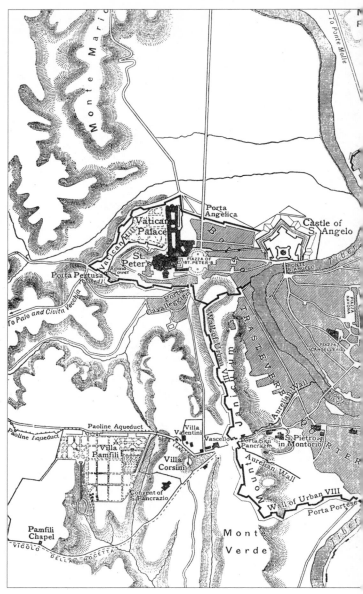

Rome at the period of the French siege of the city in 1849.

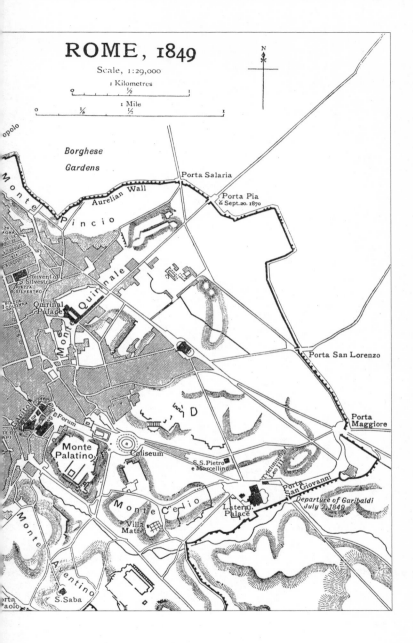

ROME, 1849

Scale, 1:29,000

1 Kilometres
½

1 Mile
⅛   ½

...opolo

Borghese

Gardens

Monte

Pincio

Aurelian Wall

Porta Salaria

Porta Pia
& Sept. 20. 1870

Convent of
Silvestro

Quirinal
Palace

Monte Quirinale

Porta San Lorenzo

D

Porta
Maggiore

Cam...

Forum

Monte
Palatino

Coliseum

S.S. Pietro
e Marcellino

Trofeo...

Porta
San Giovanni

*Departure of Garibaldi
July 2, 1849*

Monte Celio

Latern.
Palace

Villa
Matte...

Monte

Aventino

Porta
Paolo

S. Saba

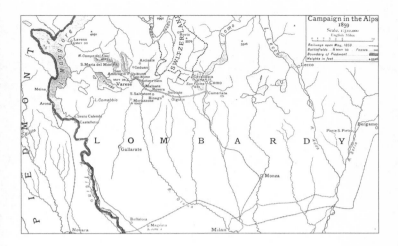

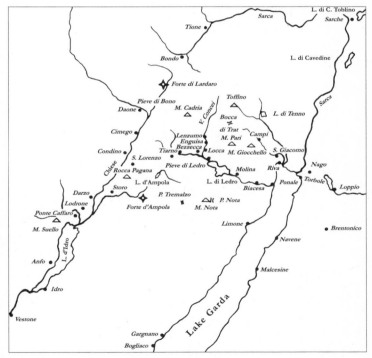

Top: the area of the Lombardy campaign in 1859.
Bottom: the area of the Tyrol campaign in 1866.

Giuseppe Garibaldi was born in Nice in 1807 and joined the Sardinian navy as a young man. In 1835, under the influence of the Italian patriot and revolutionist Giuseppe Mazzini, he became involved in an unsuccessful republican plot and fled to South America. It was in Brazil, where he fought in the Uruguayan Civil War, that he met Anita Ribeiro da Silva, whom he married in 1842. When revolution swept through Europe in 1848, Garibaldi joined the forces of King Charles Albert of Sardinia in the war against Austria. After the Sardinian defeat he went to Rome and fought against the French forces for Mazzini's short-lived Republic. During his long retreat across central Italy, his wife Anita died. He was refused asylum by the King of Sardinia and went to the United States. Garibaldi resumed his life at sea, but in 1851 he returned to Italy and bought part of the island of Caprera, north of Sardinia. By this time he had renounced the dream of an Italian republic and given his support to Camillo Benso, Count di Cavour. Garibaldi's popularity converted many of Mazzini's republican followers to the monarchist cause. However, following the war of 1859 against Austria, Garibaldi attacked Cavour, denouncing the cession of Savoy and his native Nice to France. In 1860, he embarked upon the conquest of the Kingdom of the Two Sicilies, and with around one thousand volunteers he landed in Sicily, and conquered the island. He then crossed to the mainland to take Naples. After meeting the King at Teano, he relinquished his conquests to Sardinia and returned to Caprera. Shortly afterwards, in 1861, Victor Emmanuel was proclaimed King of a united Italy. In 1862, Garibaldi led a volunteer corps against Rome, which remained outside the new kingdom, but was defeated. He commanded a volunteer unit in the Austro-Prussian War of 1866, and in 1867 he was defeated by French and papal forces while attempting once again to capture Rome. In the Franco-Prussian War of 1870–1 he commanded a group of French and Italian volunteers and won a battle near Dijon. Garibaldi was elected to the Italian Parliament in 1874, but his political career was undistinguished. He died in 1882.

Stephen Parkin is the curator responsible for the early printed Italian collections in the British Library in London.

SELECTED TITLES FROM HESPERUS PRESS

Author	Title	Foreword writer
Jane Austen	*Love and Friendship*	Fay Weldon
Honoré de Balzac	*Colonel Chabert*	A.N. Wilson
Charles Baudelaire	*On Wine and Hashish*	Margaret Drabble
Aphra Behn	*The Lover's Watch*	
Charlotte Brontë	*The Green Dwarf*	Libby Purves
Mikhail Bulgakov	*The Fatal Eggs*	Doris Lessing
Giacomo Casanova	*The Duel*	Tim Parks
Anton Chekhov	*Three Years*	William Fiennes
William Congreve	*Incognita*	Peter Ackroyd
F. Scott Fitzgerald	*The Rich Boy*	John Updike
Gustave Flaubert	*Memoirs of a Madman*	Germaine Greer
E.M. Forster	*Arctic Summer*	Anita Desai
Elizabeth Gaskell	*Lois the Witch*	Jenny Uglow
Théophile Gautier	*The Jinx*	Gilbert Adair
André Gide	*Theseus*	
Nathaniel Hawthorne	*Rappaccini's Daughter*	Simon Schama
E.T.A. Hoffmann	*Mademoiselle de Scudéri*	Gilbert Adair
Joris-Karl Huysmans	*With the Flow*	Simon Callow
Franz Kafka	*Metamorphosis*	Martin Jarvis
Katherine Mansfield	*In a German Pension*	Linda Grant
Guy de Maupassant	*Butterball*	Germaine Greer
Antoine François Prévost	*Manon Lescaut*	Germaine Greer
Marcel Proust	Pleasures and Days	A.N. Wilson
François Rabelais	*Gargantua*	Paul Bailey
François Rabelais	*Pantagruel*	Paul Bailey
Stendhal	*Memoirs of an Egotist*	Doris Lessing
Virginia Woolf	*Carlyle's House and Other Sketches*	Doris Lessing
Emile Zola	*For a Night of Love*	A.N. Wilson